PENGUIN

HARMONY HEIGHTS

After graduating from the London School of Economics with a law degree and later called to the Bar in both the United Kingdom and Malaysia, Ong Chin Huat studied History of Art at the British Institute of Florence in Italy. Deciding to pursue a career in journalism, he became the first Chinese person to work in the editorial department at *Hong Kong Tatler* as the Social Editor. After a stint as a columnist at the *South China Morning Post*, he started his own PR Consultancy specializing in fashion and luxury goods. He has been a judge for the Miss Asia Pageant in Hong Kong, Miss Charm de Chine in Shanghai and Mrs. International Global Grand Final in Kuala Lumpur. Currently, he is a freelance writer, fashion stylist and TV Host and has contributed to *The Star*, *Life Inspired*, *Luxurious Magazine*, *Harper's Bazaar*, *Design Anthology*, *Elle* and *Conde Nast Traveller* amongst others. He hosted a TV Show called 'Hong Kong High Life' on ATV Hong Kong as well as a talk show named 'Driven' on TheStarTV.com. Voted as one of Hong Kong's Best Dressed Personalities by the Hong Kong Fashion Designer's Association, he has met and interviewed everyone from movie stars and business tycoons to politicians and world-class athletes.

You can follow him on Instagram at @chinhuat_ong

Harmony Heights

Ong Chin Huat

PENGUIN BOOKS

An imprint of Penguin Random House

PENGUIN BOOKS

USA | Canada | UK | Ireland | Australia
New Zealand | India | South Africa | China | Southeast Asia

Penguin Books is part of the Penguin Random House group of companies
whose addresses can be found at global.penguinrandomhouse.com

Published by Penguin Random House SEA Pte Ltd
9, Changi South Street 3, Level 08-01,
Singapore 486361

Penguin
Random House
SEA

First published in Penguin Books by Penguin Random House SEA 2024

Copyright © Ong Chin Huat 2024

ISBN 9789815144512

Typeset in Garamond by MAP Systems, Bengaluru, India

www.penguin.sg

For my dearest mum, Mabel Ong,
who taught me that kindness matters and
Ginger, my beloved toy poodle
who was my constant companion
while writing this book

Chapter 1

Googling properties in the centre of town, Jan Tee noted down the different areas and the amenities which were available in each one. She had been doing this for the past three weeks and almost knew the entire city and its surrounding neighbourhoods by heart. She had already shortlisted several potential homes and had sounded them out with Erika, who had ultimately decided to leave it to her. After writing down a couple of names—specifically those of two guarded and gated semi-Ds and a condominium—she heard Sonya call out for her and left her desk, along with the hastily scribbled list, to check on her.

Later that afternoon, when things were quiet again and Jan had some free time on her hands, she resumed her work on the list. She abandoned the pen and paper and decided instead to type out the list of properties that she wanted to show Erika. Jan had made the list not in accordance to size, type, or area but—and this was typical of Jan—by price. She and Erika had decided on a budget, and she was determined to stick to it.

The first property on the list was a condominium called Harmony Heights.

* * *

Padma Ramakrishna hurriedly pushed the bag of clothes under the dining room table as her husband walked out of their bedroom. *Thank goodness the tablecloth is large enough,* she thought to herself while taking a sip of her masala chai.

This week had been one of her most triumphant. She had done it not once, not twice, but thrice! And what was better was that she had gotten away with it every single time. Well, almost. Her third time she was stopped by the security guard as she was leaving the store. But it wasn't because the detector went off. No, it was to let her know that her handbag was wide open, and her purse was within reach of a pickpocket. When the security guard initially approached her, she broken out in a cold sweat. Her heart was racing a mile a minute. However, when she heard what he had to say—made difficult by the blood pounding in her ears and his broken English—she felt a rush of relief. She smiled at him, zipped up her bag and walked off.

The rush of adrenaline coursing through her veins always made her feel invincible and powerful. It was like sex but on a different scale.

When she had got home, the phone had been ringing. She rushed to answer, annoyed that she had to delay the task of storing her 'trophies'—as she secretly called them. Then came dinner and another fifty things to do, causing her to forget about the bag. She might have completely forgotten to hide it if she hadn't happened to see it this morning.

'Good morning, dear,' she said to her husband, Gopi, who mumbled something about his unironed trousers. She didn't catch what he said and didn't really have the energy to enquire further. Most days and nights, it was like this. She just switched off. Life was more pleasant that way. It made her wonder about people who needed a hearing aid. *Did they really bother to wear them?* If she had to use one, she would definitely turn the volume to zero each time she came home.

While Padma pondered over the pros and cons of being able to shut out the noise of the world, her train of thought—and swinging feet—were brought to a halt when her foot hit something solid. She'd accidentally kicked the bag of clothes that she'd hidden under the dining table. This brought her back to the present moment. She wondered if she could collect more trophies today. She was on a roll, and it made her high. She began planning, trying to work out the logistics that would allow her to succeed. She was so lost in thought that she didn't even notice her husband leave. When she came back to herself, she realized her husband was no longer puttering about. His coffee mug sat on the table, cold and untouched.

* * *

Dr Desmond Choo woke with a sharp pain on the left side of his head. It couldn't have been a hangover since he hadn't had anything to drink the previous night. It must be the stress. Stress at work, stress at home, stress everywhere. Stress was something he couldn't seem to escape. It hounded him at every corner.

He dragged himself to the bathroom and took some Xanax. He thought about how lucky he was to be a physician. It allowed him to get his hands on all these meds that weren't legally available to the average person. The drug was just about to take effect after his shower, and he was at the verge of feeling good, when he saw his wife walk into their bedroom. The mere sight of her irritated the hell out of him. She was a nervous and fidgety woman who did her best to constantly upset him. She caught sight of him, averted her eyes and scurried away like a mouse. Dr Choo shook his head in irritation, walked to the door, and slammed it shut. He'd yelled at her at the top of his voice the night before, and she still hadn't learnt a damn thing.

* * *

Lillian Gan cleared the breakfast table as fast as she could. She dumped the plates, cups, and saucers in the overflowing kitchen sink. The sight of unwashed dishes made her sick. But there was no time to do them just now. She had to get to the management office to find out about what had happened to the Chans. She had seen the bailiffs turn up yesterday and seal off their apartment. This burning desire of hers, to know what had happened, consumed her entire being.

Grabbing her wicker basket, she glanced quickly at her father who was slumped on his chair with the newspaper. 'I'm going to the market,' she told him. She had to buy him lunch and then cook their dinner. She thought about what she could cook and what she needed to buy for it. It was Wednesday so it had to be pork. That was what was usually on special offer at the market on Wednesday. Her mind was cataloguing the ingredients required and their cost as she prepared to leave. She was closing the door when she heard a faint snore. Uncle Gan had fallen asleep.

* * *

Dato' Sri Terence Fong revved up his yellow Lamborghini Huracan and stepped on the accelerator a couple of times to warm up the engine and inject fuel into the throttle valve. The low octane sound of this made him feel good and hyped him up. He was ready for the day and starting it with this monster of a car helped boost his confidence. With agility, he manoeuvred his prized possession around the driveway and out onto the main road. He felt like he was a movie star whenever he was behind the wheels of the Huracan. People gawked, motorists looked, and even the traffic police saluted him when he passed them. *How amazing that a car can get you so much respect*, he thought to himself.

* * *

Zainal Daud decided to take a different route to work this morning. As the boom gates lifted, he heard the roar of Terence Fong's Lamborghini behind him. The sound of the car ruffled his nerves and unsettled him.

He took a deep breath to calm himself and began to think about all the work he had to do. This put him in a foul mood. He recalled his wife's caustic remarks from earlier that morning about him not getting anywhere in his company. This irritated him further. Thinking about his wife made him think of her credit card bill. He could feel the beginning of a stress-headache come on. *How could anyone spend so much in a month?* Their life together had come down to them constantly bickering about her spending. He would ask her to stop spending and she would ask him to earn more money. This was their usual routine. Was this all his marriage boiled down to? Fights about money and her constant dissatisfaction about his career trajectory? *Surely there must be more to it than this*, he thought to himself.

Chapter 2

Driving along the highway, Jan glanced at her Apple watch to check the time. She had just about enough time to view the two apartments during her lunch break. She had a ton of work to submit before Friday and she really wanted to be in the good books of her new boss. Having just relocated from Sydney, she wanted to prove her worth at her new workplace and missing a deadline wasn't how she planned to do it.

The animated voice from Waze instructed her to turn right in 500 metres. Leaving the highway and entering a slip road, Jan's gaze was immediately caught by the tree-lined avenue she found herself driving along. She spotted a row of shop-houses with a provision store, laundrette, and 7-Eleven before driving further in.

'You have reached your destination,' Waze announced to her as she approached Harmony Heights. Jan looked around the verdant surroundings and felt a sense of ease come over her. As she swerved into the driveway, she was stopped by a uniformed security guard. In her barely-there, Malay-tinged-with-Aussie accent, she told the Nepalese guard that she was meeting an estate agent to view an apartment. He muttered something into his walkie-talkie and signalled his colleague sitting inside the guard house to lift the boom gate.

Another guard stationed at the condo motioned to Jan in the direction of the guest car park located on the right-hand side of the condo. It was quite empty at this time of the day, so Jan didn't have any problems finding somewhere to park. Getting out of her car, she spotted Ms Ng sitting in the driver's seat of her Honda, her gaze glued to her phone as her fingers furiously worked over the screen. Jen checked Ms Ng's car plate number to make sure it was her. Confirming that this was indeed Ms Ng, Jan knocked on her car window, causing the other woman to startle and look up.

'Ms Ng? I'm Jan,' she greeted the real estate agent with a smile while the motorized car window slid down. 'Nice to meet you. Hope you didn't wait too long.'

'Not at all! Nice meeting you finally! Come, let's go and see the apartment.' Chirpy and energetic, Ms Ng exuded a positive vibe, which Jan liked. Ms Ng fumbled around her bag for the entry card as the two women made their way from the visitors' car park to the entrance of the building.

Upon entering the building, Jan quickly scanned the lobby. The first thing she noticed was the utilitarian nature of the design. There were no frills or ornamentation of any sort, just a rattan sofa with two armchairs and a coffee table occupying a corner. Two elevators and a security counter with a guard manning it filled up the remaining space.

Ms Ng waved to the guard—she was obviously a regular visitor to Harmony Heights, as the guard clearly recognized her and nodded back.

'What floor is the apartment again?' Jan asked.

'Twenty-fifth floor and it's a corner unit. It's the largest one on the floor with two balconies.'

Just then, the ping of the lift sounded, and the doors opened. The fluorescent lighting inside the lift contrasted sharply with the dim, candescent lights in the lobby. No one ever looked good under harsh lighting and both Jan and Ms Ng were no exceptions. The late-night Jan spent finishing off her report was showing clearly under her eyes.

Walking out of the lift, Jan noticed the airy and light-filled corridor leading up to the apartment. Turning a corner, she noticed that unlike the other units on the floor, the apartment she was about to view didn't face the other flats and seemed to have a little privacy.

A gust of wind greeted Jan as Ms Ng opened the wooden door to the apartment. Light and breezy, the whitewashed flat was completely devoid of any furniture—just the way Jan liked it.

'It has three bedrooms and three bathrooms,' Ms Ng said, studying Jan's facial expression. The few years of experience she had as a realtor had taught her that looking at a client's face was always a good indicator of whether they were interested in the place or not. 'You do know this is a quick sale *ya*?' Ms Ng added, referring to the fact that the current owner had defaulted their mortgage payment and thus had to sell the property before foreclosure.

Jan nodded while taking photos of the living room with her phone. After inspecting the last bedroom, Jan checked her watch again and realized it was time to go. She had a meeting at 2.30 p.m. for which she couldn't be late.

'Do you want to bring your husband to take a look?' Ms Ng enquired innocently.

'It's not my husband, it's my partner.'

* * *

Harmony Heights was located in a genteel and fairly well-to-do neighbourhood in an all but forgotten part of town. Appearing somewhat worse for wear—partly due to a much-needed exterior paint job—this pre-millennium apartment block had been built in the early nineties with a Bauhaus-inspired sensibility, embellished with neoclassical design elements such as Grecian columns that flanked the *porte-cochère* entrance and the pointed pediments above its windows. Much of its inhabitants belonged to a middle to upper-middle class demographic.

This condominium had been highly sought after when it was first launched in the market, thanks in part to the savvy marketing strategy that promoted Harmony Heights as a low-density residential retreat nestled in the fringe of the city but not too far from the centre. Many who came to the launch loved the fact that it catered to the young executive or modern family who wished to live an elevated lifestyle amidst lush greenery.

As with most residential high-rise projects built around that time, the architectural style of Harmony Heights was a mishmash of different architectural influences, a collision of modern and traditional styles all incorporated into a rectangular block. Architectural purists would probably cringe at such design choices but this hodgepodge of styles gave it its own unique character and a certain cachet amongst those whose appreciation of the arts was limited to the Mona Lisa.

Functionality intact, the well-ventilated and open-air common areas and spaces reflected the architect's consideration of practical factors such as the climate of Malaysia—a tropical country. Painted white with azure blue trimmings, Harmony Heights consisted of thirty-seven floors. A triplex penthouse occupied the top three storeys and the apartments came in four different sizes and layouts. The smallest one was 1,800 square feet and the largest unit was 3,500 square feet. The triplex penthouse was not for sale, as it had been built for the developer who gave it to his daughter Candy as a wedding present.

Harmony Heights also had two tennis courts and a thirty-eight-metre-long swimming pool. Along with such facilities, the residence also had adequate parking space with two car parks allotted to each unit in a generously sized, multi-storey car park located adjacent to the building. As one of the first condos in the city built in the early nineties, Harmony Heights may have seen better days, but it was still highly sought-after in the secondary market for its sweeping, uninterrupted views, and tranquil surroundings.

* * *

Lola Li glanced at her phone with squinted eyes while still curled up in her comfy bed in her apartment in Mont Kiara. Even though the curtains were drawn, the morning sun still managed to shine through them, and it hurt her eyes.

11.46 a.m. and she was still tired. A few things ran through her sleepy head but the most pressing issue was that of deciding what to wear when her boyfriend—as she would like to call him—visited her that evening.

Stretching her lithe body like a cat, Lola yawned as she reached for the phone. She wanted to see what her friends were up to on Instagram and if there was anywhere worth going to that day. The fear of missing out—FOMO in Instagram-speak—was a debilitating concern for her.

Growing up in a mid-sized family where she was the middle child made her painfully aware that being left out and ignored was the second worst thing to experience. The first was the feeling of being unloved.

As Lola was scrolling through her feed, something caught her eye. Janice—an acquaintance from when she had been a flight attendant—had posted a photo of her new Kelly bag. Lola expanded the photo with her well-manicured fingers to study the details. The stitching on the bag and palladium hardware looked authentic enough but the gain of the leather seemed just a tad too coarse.

'It's a fake,' she muttered under her breath as she made her way to her en-suite bathroom to begin her day.

* * *

After breakfast, Azizah Rozali called out to her Indonesian helper, Widya, to clear the table. Even though Widya had been working with Zainal and his wife for almost two years, she knew deep down that this was just a temporary hiatus. They had been very kind to her and she had nothing to complain about. Neither did they have any little children to babysit nor did they have elderly parents she had to care for.

'Can you iron the dress that I have hung on the rack?' Azizah asked, although it was really an order. 'Turn down the heat on the iron, *ya*? It's silk and I don't want it scorched.'

Widya obeyed. There were some days when all that ironing and cleaning and scrubbing and chopping and slicing and frying and whatever else she did for the Rozalis would drive her up the wall. On such days she would placate herself by thinking of the money that she could squirrel away in her bank account. She needed just a couple more months of her salary to break free.

Later that morning, while sipping her coffee, Azizah felt that pang of emptiness inside of her. She did everything she thought a good wife could do yet nothing left her feeling fulfilled. With her daughter now studying in Australia, she had plenty of time on her hands. Once upon a time, many moons ago, before she had met Zainal, she had a promising career as a singer. She even released two albums, one in Malay and the other in English. Her record company hailed her as the new Sharifah Aini. Everything seemed to be in place for her to achieve stardom.

But fate had dealt her a bad hand. Her father fell into great debts in his import and export business and shortly after, her mother was diagnosed with the big C. It was all too much for the twenty-four-year-old songstress to bear. As the only child, the weight of these catastrophes fell heavily and solely on her shoulders. She fell into a deep, black hole of depression and lost her voice. She couldn't speak, she couldn't talk and worst of all, she couldn't sing.

Her record company gave up on her and she gave up on herself. As ephemeral as the short-lived fame Azizah experienced had been, she knew she had to survive. 'A woman is like a teabag, you never know how strong she is until she gets into hot water,' her counsellor at the Woman's Aid Organization used to tell her during those dark days.

An old classmate had suggested working at an insurance company that just happened to have an open position and she decided to give it a go. She was glad that her new chosen career didn't require her to rely on her looks. Although her looks were certainly above average, Azizah knew it was the tricks up her sleeves she employed that added to her allure. The make-up, false eyelashes, highlighted hair, high heels, and body-skimming clothes created a whole that was greater than the sum of its parts. Glamour, they say, is an illusion, and Azizah was a master illusionist.

Azizah liked to recount the tale of how she had met the then dashing twenty-nine-year-old Zainal. 'He fell for me in front of the photocopy machine!' She would announce to rapturous laughter at her dinner parties. 'I didn't even notice him but approached me to ask me if I knew how to photocopy a document on both sides!'

Her husband Zainal, of course, would smile and keep mum. He knew it wasn't the complete truth and Azizah was a great embellisher of facts. But being the magnanimous man he was, he indulged her. As an assistant manager then, he was able to help Azizah out financially and pay a portion of her father's debts. He, of course, had a vested interest. Nine months after they met, Azizah and Zainal tied the knot.

She didn't particularly mind working but she chose to resign a few years into their marriage.

Chapter 3

Glancing out at her balcony, Padma saw it was going to be a scorching day ahead. The pungent aroma of her chickpea curry had permeated the living room where she was seated and she felt pleased with herself for teaching Nita, her helper from India, a repertoire of dishes her own mother had taught her.

Both her and her husband were Hindu and vegetarian, which meant she had to be more inventive when she planned her daily menu. Her daily trips to the farmer's market and provision store were something she looked forward to. She usually brought her maid Nita along, but of late, she preferred to go alone.

It was at the wet markets that it all started. It was innocent at first. Haggling with the Bangladeshi stall owner, she would ask him for an item or two as a gift. He obliged her, as she was a regular customer who bought quite a lot from him. This would soon progress to Padma slipping a tomato or two in her basket when no one was looking. She became bolder as time went by and graduated to stealing brinjals and kaffir limes. Hiding them behind the plastic bag of spinach and cauliflower, she experienced a rush, knowing that their existence was a secret only she knew of.

* * *

Datin Sri Candy Fong put on her ruby and diamond earrings from DeGem while studying her perfectly made-up face in front of the mirror. Her complexion was flawless save for a few wrinkles around her eyes when she smiled. At thirty-six years of age, she could easily pass for someone in her mid-twenties. But this youthful appearance didn't come for free. Her thrice-weekly Pilates sessions as well as HIIT sessions with her personal trainer ensured she maintained a slim figure despite having twins.

That's not mentioning her monthly visits to her dermatologists for touch-ups with botox and fillers as well as her facials and other non-invasive beauty treatments such as the Pico laser—all of which added up to a hefty bill at the end of the month. But bills were the last thing on Candy's mind. Her hubby took care of all her expenses.

Candy had met her husband Dato' Sri Terence Fong when a mutual friend set them up. She had just returned from her studies in England, and he begun working in his father's company. Coming from similar backgrounds—his father was a construction contractor while her father was a property developer—they hit it off almost immediately.

Although the Chinese saying of two front doors matching applied to them, Candy also knew deep down, she was marrying slightly below her. While both of them were equally well-educated at overseas universities, when it came to actual wealth and assets, Candy's family was miles ahead.

She wasn't on the rebound or anything when she accepted Terence's marriage proposal, which came swiftly after a nine-month courtship, for want of a better word. But, being the dutiful daughter she was, she knew it would make her parents happy, especially after her last relationship.

While studying in England she had met an English boy who really swept her off her feet. Tall and blonde, Trevor Sutton was in the same course as Candy. She'd had a few boyfriends before, but it was Trevor who really wiggled his way into her heart and made her experience a feeling she had never felt before.

Their relationship lasted for the duration of their three-year Psychology and Counselling degree course. Of course, her parents got wind of her English boyfriend and made it known to her, in no uncertain terms, that they did not approve. Torn between her filial obligations and what she considered her first true love, Candy let her head prevail over her heart. She convinced herself her relationship with Trevor would never work and she would always be considered an outsider to his family and friends. Being practical and realistic, she ended their relationship after she graduated and left the UK for home. It broke her heart and she broke his, but that's life.

As a reward for terminating her relationship with a *qweilo* and returning home, Candy's parents bought her a brand-new Porsche 911 Carrera. Zipping around town in this dashing sports car made Candy the new it girl. *Tatler* even did a feature article on her and a group of other returnees titled 'Young,

Gifted, and Back'. Photographed getting out of her Porche and wearing black leggings and a cropped Chanel bolero tweed jacket, Candy was the best looking of the six people they featured. Three guys and three girls, armed with prestigious degrees from blue-chip universities and hailing from wealthy and established families.

That was then. Almost fourteen years ago. Today, two kids later, Candy's days were filled with fashion shows and CoolSculpting treatments, manicures, and afternoon tea with her girlfriends. Where did all her ambition go? Her yearning for achieving great things and making her mark in the world evaporated as quickly as the Frederic Malle Parfum Spray she just spritzed around her shoulders. Life got so cozy and comfortable with Terence that she got complacent and didn't even bother anymore.

* * *

Erika Saunders walked into her office—her gait determined—with a sense of purpose. Wearing a black pinstripe suit and white shirt, her short, auburn hair and direct gaze gave everyone in the bank the impression that she meant business. As one of the few *mat sallehs* in the office, she automatically commanded respect, an attitude of diffidence amongst locals, which was a remnant of Malaysia's colonial past.

Although new, having just transferred from Australia, she quickly established herself in her position as senior vice president with aplomb. Fair and straightforward, Erika's style of management was no-frills, no politics (as much as possible), and no brown-nosing. Throughout her high-flying career, she had got by on the virtue of her merit and competence—delivering on her promises and walking her talk. She, however, was not quite familiar with the inner workings of this Southeast Asian country where it was possible to not get ahead based on competence and merit alone and possessing noble qualities didn't guarantee to get you far.

Coming to Malaysia with her partner Jan had been a big step for her, both personally and professionally. Despite the slight reduction in pay, moving from the headquarters in Sydney meant an upheaval in many aspects of her life, her professional one by no means the most significant. She had to put her ageing father in an assisted living home for the elderly to ensure he was well cared for and safe while the home both she and Jan had purchased together in the suburbs was rented out. Furthermore, their adopted daughter, Sonya, was uprooted from her preschool; an experience that was undoubtedly traumatic for a five-year-old.

As an expatriate, Erika was differentiated from foreign workers not just by the colour of her skin or her country of origin, but by her salary plus the benefits she received in kind. Often referred to as an 'expat package', this included relocation expenses, hardship allowance, education allowance for Sonya, car and home travel allowance as well as health insurance. As a liberal, Erika would be the first to question what made her different from Widya, Azizah's live-in Indonesian domestic helper, and more deserving of these necessities. But the answer was glaringly obvious. The word 'expat' itself held connotations of education, wealth, and privilege while the term 'migrant worker' carried with it the assumption of low-paid manual labour.

No matter how much academics and politicians tried to spin and reconcile the difference in meanings between these two labels, no one would deny that the working conditions of an American investment banker in Hong Kong was a universe

apart from that of a Bangladeshi construction worker in Dubai
or an Indonesian maid working in Harmony Heights.

Being acutely aware of her expat privilege, Erika never
wanted to be seen as a Karen and made a concerted attempt
to appear agreeable and amiable in her dealings with anyone
at the bank. As the head of her division, she made sure to
listen to all opinions during group discussions with her team
members. With her superiors, she was humble and respectful
so as not to come across as the arrogant *mat salleh*. As a
senior vice president leading a team that consisted of all local
Malaysians who were younger in age and less experienced
professionally, it was her job to guide them with the goal of
them eventually being able to lead their own teams. It was a
task Erika relished and took great pride in doing.

But that's not to say everything at her workplace was
hunky-dory. Naturally, there were a few issues that Erika,
with her liberal tendencies, found unsettling. Like when a
colleague of hers, Kim Leng, who led another team, clinched
a mega deal but it was Malek who was promoted to senior VP
instead. She didn't call it out as she would have done back in
Australia. As an expat and a demographic minority, Erika was
very conscious about how she came across. In her effort to
be culturally sensitive, she toned down her usually outspoken
nature. She was a *pendatang asing* in the true sense of the word,
albeit a highly qualified and well-educated Caucasian one. But
as she didn't know how long she would be living or working
in Malaysia, she didn't want to rock the boat. Instead, she just
toed the line.

Chapter 4

As her white Vellfire pulled into the driveway of the Four Seasons Hotel, Candy slipped on her Chanel sunglasses and adjusted her blue and white Majolica-print charmeuse Dolce & Gabbana dress. She readied herself for all the small talk she excelled at. While she was excited to catch up with some of her girlfriends that she hadn't seen in a long time, she also had to brave all the air-kissing and ass-licking that would come her way. She knew this was all part and parcel of being a socialite, but it didn't make it easier.

The spring/summer collection of Malaysian designer Amir Amaluddin usually brought out the *crème de la crème* of Malaysian society. As one of the top fashion designers in the country, Amir was versatile enough to cater to the three main races in the country. For Hari Raya, he would design a line of Muslim outfits for Eid, complete with headscarves. During Chinese New Year, *cheongsam*-inspired outfits were rolled out and for Deepavali, a collection of modern saris were displayed by models who sashayed down the runway in his thrice-yearly festival collection.

Today however, was for Amir's latest spring and summer collection—one of his most popular and commercially successful collections. As Candy strode into the foyer area of the ballroom, PR supremo Raja Adam broke off the conversation he was having with a group of people and rushed over to Candy.

'Dah-link! I'm soooooo glad you could make it today!' He gushed, looking uber-trendy in a vintage Martin Margiela deconstructed shirt and Rick Owens dropped-crotch baggy pants. 'I've seated you on the front row, between Puan Sri Heather Liow and Tengku Fauziah, I know they would love to catch up with you,' he said, his eyes darting over Candy's shoulder to see who else was entering the room. As a minor royal, Raja Adam—simply known as Adam to close friends, who numbered in the high hundreds—knew the *beau monde* of KL society like the back of his hand.

'Thanks so much my dear,' Candy replied. 'Have you seen Renee and Pamela?' She asked Adam, referring to her two close social allies and partners in party crimes.

'They are over at the bar, getting a drink! I'll let Amir know you are here. He'll be delighted to catch up with you. Oh, also! Remember you can order any outfit you see on the runway to your measurements, okay?' And with that, Adam, who had spied another VIP entering the foyer, left in a flurry of air kisses and expensive perfume.

Making her way to the far end of the foyer, Candy saw the usual suspects who wouldn't miss this event for the world. There was Frances Tay, the private banker who used events like this to meet high-net-worth individuals and hopefully make them her clients. As the top private banker in town, she wasn't going to let any upstart shove her from her hard-earned perch. Pushing her way into the VIP section, she was the type who didn't take 'no' for an answer and didn't care who she mowed down on her way to success.

Then there was Juliana Rahmat, a free agent after her second divorce. Willowy and elegant, this former model definitely turned heads wherever she went. With an Instagram following of almost 500k, it was a full-time job for her to plan, pose, and photograph her OOTDs every single day, and as far as Candy knew, she hadn't even repeated any outfits yet. Wearing a mishmash of labels—a Saint Laurent leopard print silk top paired with Balenciaga culottes and knee-high Rick Owens black boots—this fashionista gave a new meaning to the word spendthrift.

The media was, of course, also in attendance. Candy recognized Shirley Goh, the editor-in-chief of *Mode Magazine* who fancied herself as a sort of Malaysian version of Anna Wintour. With a tad too many accessories (mostly gifts from fashion houses) and kabuki-thick foundation, she was an example of how staying till midnight in the office and never challenging your publisher would eventually lead you to the top, even if you were bereft of any taste, imagination, or personality. She refused to consort with her peers, believing that she was superior to them. Using the magazine to get acquainted with, then insert herself in upper echelons of KL society was the modus operandi she had employed in her social mountaineering pursuits. However, she would have a rude awakening when the friendships she so artfully cultivated quickly evaporated when she was eventually let go due to the dwindling circulation and waning readership of the glossy magazine as a result of the shifting media landscape.

Holding court amongst a group of ladies was Dinesh Lakliani. Hailing from a prominent Sindhi family in KL. This mid-forties man-about-town was considered one of the most eligible bachelors amongst the Indian community. He had never been married but was constantly seen with a string of beautiful women on his arm. Many people suspected that he was gay, but it could just be green-eyed monster, and rumour-mongers, working overtime. Presently, he was casually dating Shivana, the only daughter of Datin Padma Ramakrishna who lived in Harmony Heights.

'Wow! You look AH-MA-ZING!' Pam exclaimed to Candy as she approached her two BFFs. Having known them since her Garden School days, there was nothing she couldn't tell them. After graciously returning the compliment to Pam, it was Renee's turn now to gush. Lifting Candy's Bottega Veneta's Chain Pouch Shoulder Bag in blue, her eyes widened in admiration.

'I LOVE this! I wanted it in lime green, but they didn't have it. I'll have to see if I can find it online,' Renee said. 'Oh God! I just remembered I'm over my budget this month . . . it'll have to wait till next month!' She said, looking crestfallen.

Bonded firstly by boys, then make-up and fashion, and now husbands and children, Candy, Renee, and Pamela, all mirrored each other in a cookie-cutter way. While their husbands got together to play golf during the weekends or sing karaoke, the three wives spent their days lunching, shopping, and beautifying. Of course, they also supervised their kids' homework and schooling but these mum-duties, if truth were told, were chores secondary to their personal agendas.

Just as the champagne Candy was sipping was beginning to give her a nice buzz, the double-doors of the ballroom were pushed open, and the specially invited guests started to filter in. As seating was assigned, it was glaringly obvious who was where in the pecking order. The front row had been reserved for Amir's biggest clients, but his *biggest* client wasn't anywhere to be found at the Four Seasons, as she was ensconced in a palace somewhere.

The second row was reserved for the less extravagant or irregular customers as well as the media. The third row saw vendors and suppliers as well as friends of Amir who had come to support him and didn't pay much mind to where they sat. As for the fourth row, well, those sitting there were either completely oblivious of any social recognition or just couldn't give two hoots.

Greeting her fellow front-rowers with air kisses, Candy indulged in small talk with them until the lights dimmed and the music boomed. Models paraded down the catwalk in billowing kaftans and slinky dresses. Colour and print were the theme for this collection and being a master of cut, Amir wowed his eager audience who applauded and whistled at Amir when he came out and took his obligatory bow at the finale.

Chapter 5

Lowering the flame of the cooker where a clay pot of beef rending was brewing, Widya covered the pot with a lid and walked out of the kitchen and to the dining room. She had to clean the master bedroom and bathroom, which would take her up till lunch time. Then, after an hour's break for lunch, she would have to do the laundry and start ironing the three baskets of clothes. Once she was done with that, it would already be around 5 p.m.—time to prepare dinner for Zainal and Azizah.

It seemed to her that housework was a never-ending chore and there were days when she wished everything would grind to a complete stop so she could break free. But, of course, that was just wishful thinking on her part. She accepted her lot in life and knew that she was luckier than most from her village back in East Java. What she earned in Malaysia being a domestic helper was far more than any job she could find back home. Yes, it was tedious and yes, it was mundane, but what was the alternative?

With six siblings, Widya was the third daughter born to a farmer and his homemaker wife in the village of Ngadas in East Java. Situated in the regency of Malang, the village stands 2,100 metres above sea level on the slopes of Mount Bromo and is one of the highest villages on the island of Java. The only thing Widya missed about her home was the cool and refreshing climate during certain months of the year but apart from that, she led an austere and isolated life.

With minimal schooling—she just had her high school diploma—Widya's hunger for knowledge had never been satiated in the village classroom. She dreamed of leaving for the city to meet urbanites who could teach her more and show her the real world. But that never happened. Helping her father with his small plot of land—ploughing, growing and harvesting various vegetables, fruits and rice—didn't quite fulfil her. Widya saw her mother cook and clean for her father, herself, and her siblings, and thought, *I don't want to do this too.*

So, when an agent from another province had come calling to recruit young girls to work overseas, Widya jumped at the chance. They gave a small presentation in the village town hall and explained what sort of work signing up would entail. They promised training and counselling. Widya listened carefully and made notes in her head. Everything they described were things she was capable of doing. And when the recruitment officer reached the end of the presentation and told them the basic salary, Widya couldn't believe her ears.

The starting salary was more than her father earned in six months! How could she let such an opportunity slip by? Without even asking her parents, she approached the agent and said she would like to sign up. It was a two-year contract and was renewable thereafter. What's the worst that could happen? If she didn't like it, she would just leave. Simple.

'Widya, please come to my bedroom,' Azizah hollered. Widya quickly went to her employer to see what she wanted. When she entered the bedroom, she saw Azizah standing in front of her dresser, fumbling for something.

'Have you seen my pearl necklace? I'm sure I left it here last night.' Azizah motioned to the top of her dresser, where a melange of accessories and jewellery was scattered.

'No ma'am,' Widya replied.

'Have you ironed my dress yet? I need it soon.'

'I'll do it now.' Widya replied quickly and left the room. She didn't want her employer to bark anymore orders at her and her hands were full already. She was also planning to steal a few minutes off in the afternoon to see Iqbal.

She had met Iqbal one afternoon when she'd gone to collect the letters from the mail room. He was watering the plants in the foyer, and she could see him looking at her from the corner of her eye. When she turned to meet his gaze, he instinctively smiled at her, and she smiled back. It didn't take long for him to start talking to her, especially since she made it a point to go to the mail room at the same time each afternoon.

When they began to talk, Widya found out that Iqbal was different from any other man she'd known. Shy and timid, he struggled to think of words and form sentences. When she looked into his eyes, he always seemed to have a distant, faraway look. But the effort he made and the innocence and pureness she saw in his eyes endeared him to her. She didn't know it then, but Iqbal had Asperger's Syndrome. It wasn't severe but was enough to make him drop out of school because of his learning disabilities.

Coming from a small village and a single parent family, Iqbal's chances for getting care and accessibility that accommodated his disorder had been practically nil. Being born poor meant that Iqbal was destined for a hard life.

His mother, Fatima, had prayed and prayed for him after Iqbal's father passed away and left her a widow. 'Why did Allah bestow this fate on me?' She would often ask. 'Who will look after my dear Iqbal when I am gone?' She would ask. But the answers never came. When he couldn't catch up at school and failed all his exams, Fatima cried the whole night. It broke her heart when he dropped out of school. The other villagers tried consoling her but none of their comforting words could erase the hurt and pain she felt in her heart.

As there had been no work for Iqbal in the village, he decided to move to the capital city to look for work. He could stay with an uncle who had moved there a decade ago. His uncle helped find him a few odd jobs, but Iqbal didn't really enjoy doing them. He delivered pizza for a while but when this job as a gardener popped up, Iqbal didn't hesitate to take it. It reminded him of being back in his *kampong*, tending to the plants and scrubs.

This had disillusioned Fatima about life. She was not one for comparisons, but she sometimes wondered what it was that decided who was born with a silver spoon and who was cast away. Was it all just down to fate and Allah's decision?

* * *

When Zainal reached Tawfik Insurance located on the forty-sixth floor of a sparkling new glass and steel tower in the heart of town, the receptionist greeted him with a smile. He then walked to his own office located in the far corner with a commanding view of Kuala Lumpur. Never in his wildest dreams had he thought he would rise up the ranks of this Shariah-compliant insurance company, which had grown to become the third largest in Malaysia.

At school, Zainal had by no means been a straight-A student. Average intellect, average abilities, and average looks. Nothing about him stood out. His teachers overlooked him because he was neither a star pupil nor a bad hat. Just like sandwich classes, he was ignored and disregarded. He didn't shine and didn't cause any problems. In an education system based on grades and merit, it seemed to him that only the two extremes got the attention and support they needed.

He had studied hard and had barely managed to scrape by and get admitted to a local university. He chose a finance and business course, a decision he was initially unsure of. He didn't know if that was the right course for him to pursue. His parents left the choice to him and didn't offer much guidance. Looking back today, Zainal understood that this was a blessing, as it made him think for himself and not rely on others for his career goals and aspirations.

He had continued to remain under the radar all through his years at university. He wasn't spectacular and didn't win any scholarships or academic accolades. He was coasting along with barely there pass marks and finally graduated with a lower second-class honours degree. Nevertheless, he was proud of himself for making it this far. Most of his schoolmates had dropped out and hadn't even gotten past Sijil Pelajaran Malaysia (SPM). This was a national examination taken by fifth-form students to obtain the Malaysian certificate of education or SPM.

But what Zainal possessed, which was even more important than any paper qualification, was a golden personality. His amiable and easy-going demeanour meant everyone who met him took an immediate liking to him. He fitted in anywhere and everywhere. In school and later at university, he made friends with everybody and as he was sincere and genuine, all cliques—large or small, popular or disliked, cool or nerdy—took to him and accepted him as their own.

His sense of humour made him even more likeable. He made light when things got dark and was comforting when others were hurting. His ability to get along with all sorts of people was probably his most redeeming quality. And that was what Azizah noticed about him when she first met him. Unassuming and dependable, he was the kind of man she had been looking for.

Turning on his laptop, Zainal looked at the stack of paperwork piled high on his desk. He had plenty to accomplish today. He already had several WhatsApp messages from his clients and staff that urgently required attention. As he was scrolling through his email, something caught his eye. A letter of notice from his credit card company. He flinched when he thought of what it would contain. He knew what it was going to be about. It wasn't about his credit card at all, but rather about his supplementary card holder—his wife.

Clicking it open, he saw the letters in bold and red.

OVER THE LIMIT.

He had just settled last month's payment in full and boom! Here it was again. How did one month go by so quickly? What did Azizah buy that made her breach the credit limit? He wanted to have a talk with her about it but somehow it always slipped his mind. Sometimes, it was better to just pay up without bringing up the issue. With Azizah's moods, it would surely end in an argument and at the end of a hectic day, fighting with her was the last thing he needed.

Maybe it was her age and the changes her body was going through, but of late, Azizah had been especially prone to meltdowns and outbursts. The slightest thing could set her off. Most of the time, he would walk on eggshells at home and so would their maid Widya.

She hadn't been like this before. When they first met, Zainal thought that Azizah was the most beautiful woman he had ever laid his eyes on. Her sparkling eyes always seemed to be slightly flirtatious, and her hour-glass figure caught the eyes of every man in the office. He didn't quite believe it when she smiled at him the very first time. *Why would she smile at me?* That was the first thought that raced into his mind. There were better looking men in the office, and some were in higher positions and earning a great deal more than him.

His self-deprecating attitude was something that made Zainal appealing in Azizah's eyes. She'd had a fair share of suitors when she was a songstress, but they all seemed very full of themselves. It became clear to her, when she dated those men, that she was only second fiddle to them. They thought they played the lead roles, and she was merely a supporting act. That was not what she wanted in any relationship.

Initially, she had neither noticed nor minded. It was the early stages of a relationship, when she was head over heels in love and only capable of seeing their good qualities. Those days were the most magical, when her head was in the clouds and her feet, off the ground. But as the relationships progressed, clarity seeped into her rose-tinted lenses. All their faults and warts were exposed and visibly clear. That's when she started getting irritated with them over the slightest things and stopped adulating them. These relationships happened back when she was in her early-twenties, and they left her disillusioned with love. But with this realization, came an epiphany and she knew, from such an early age, that there was no Mr Right.

Chapter 6

With a scowl on his face, Dr Desmond Choo veered right after entering Harmony Heights. It had been a bad day at his clinic, and he had a lot of angst bottled up inside him. He revved up his BMW as he entered the multi-storey car park located on the west side of the condominium. His nurses had been giving him attitude, as he asked them to work overtime due to a patient throwing up all over his desk. The constant calls from his suppliers were getting on his nerves while the barrage of bills and invoices made his stomach churn. However, being swaddled inside his X5, with its massaging seat, customized ambient lighting, and music blaring through its state-of-the-art audio system, brought him a degree of comfort and consoled him. Purchased recently, this luxury SUV was the trophy he had awarded himself from the earnings of not his daytime practise but his night-time one.

Taking the lift to his apartment that was on the seventeenth floor, he grimaced as soon as he set foot in his flat. It was a complete mess with newspapers piled up high at the entrance and every visible surface cluttered. Hway Ping, his wife, scuttled in and out of the kitchen bringing dishes to the dining table.

'Why don't you clear the pile of newspapers sitting at the doorway?' Desmond asked his wife, the tone of his voice edged with irritation. 'It's been there for ages! What are you doing every day?'

Startled, as she hadn't heard him come in, Hway Ping froze for a few seconds before her husband's presence brought her out of her automated ritual.

'I'll clear it tomorrow,' she replied timidly. Pleasing her husband was what she had learnt to do early on in her marriage. He brought home the bacon, so he called the shots. Everything he said was followed and his word was final. No one questioned or challenged him on his decisions and even Yi Wei, their seventeen-year-old daughter, followed the rules in the Choo household. Autocrats didn't just exist in history books, they were alive and well and, in this home, they were manifest in the form of Dr Desmond Choo.

'Not salted veggies again! Don't you have any imagination?' Desmond complained to Hway Ping as he pulled out his chair at the head of the rectangular dining table. His wife's cooking wasn't the best but the least she should do is vary her repertoire of dishes. A meek woman devoid of any personality, it certainly wasn't a surprise that Desmond would marry someone like her. His autocratic and imperious nature demanded he sought a life partner who would be submissive and compliant. A yin to his yang.

'They are leftovers from last night. I'll cook something different tomorrow. What would you like?' Hway Ping asked, trying to please her husband the best way she could.

'I'll let you know in a while. It's been a hectic day, and I cannot think now.'

Glancing at the clock on the wall, Desmond discovered that it was almost nine o'clock. It was a bit late for dinner and he was famished but he had to take care of some business in the clinic. Working late had become the norm for the 'good doctor' in the last six months or so. After closing at 6 p.m., Desmond let his staff go home save for one, nurse Lim, who helped him for a few hours. As a gynaecologist, Desmond's clinic was usually full of women coming in for check-ups. Most were below fifty years of age, although he did see a few who were older.

Carrying our pelvic examinations, pap smears, cancer screenings as well as treatments of vaginal infections were all a normal day's work for Desmond. He hadn't planned on becoming a gynaecologist when he studied medicine but somehow this was how things turned out. He had a good friend at medical school whose father was a gynaecologist and seeing the car he drove in and his address, Desmond knew that it was an area of medicine he'd specialize in.

Coming from a family where his parents had lived hand to mouth, Desmond knew the pangs of being poor. His father couldn't afford a car and travelled to work by bus everyday while his mother took in laundry from neighbours to wash and iron to make ends meet. As the only son with two sisters, his parents scrimped and saved just enough to send Desmond to med school, an opportunity that both his sisters were deprived of.

At university, where his social net had been cast in a wider circle, it became blatantly clear who the haves and the have-nots were. Students from wealthy families drove their Audis and BMWs to attend lectures and they all invariably stuck together during break time. All Desmond could do was watch them from afar. 'I'll drive a BMW one day,' he told himself as he watched some of his course mates zoom off after lectures. No one could get everything in life, but Desmond was determined to get what he wanted. No matter the cost.

'Where's Yi Wei?' He asked his wife as he gobbled down a spoonful of rice with braised pork belly. The tasty dish somewhat reduced the irritation he was feeling towards his wife.

'She's had dinner earlier already and is in her room studying now.' Hway Ping had waited to have dinner with her hubby, as she knew that was what he liked. His more relaxed tone and loosened body language made her less stressed too. Their marriage might not be ideal but the best she could do was put in effort on her part. As a stay-at-home wife and mother, she had no choice.

Just like her mother and her mother's mother, who had never questioned their lot in life. It was accepted and tolerated. With little skills and no career of her own, Hway Ping didn't feel like she had anything to contribute. She was a pale shadow of her husband, playing second fiddle in their relationship and taking a back seat when it came to making any important decisions for the family. She existed only to prop him up and that suited Desmond fine because he didn't want an equal in his marriage. He did not want his wife to work either. Working would mean that Hway Ping would have a level of independence that he wasn't comfortable with. Anyway, what he earned as a gynaecologist was enough for them.

In her pink-walled bedroom, Yi Wei firstly made sure the door was securely locked. Her parents were in the habit of suddenly barging in and she certainly didn't want that to happen. Tidying up her bed and drawing her curtains shut, she turned on her large selfie LED ring light. Adjusting the brightness, she walked over to the full-length mirror on the opposite wall to check her make-up and lipstick.

* * *

As a young boy, Terence Fong had enjoyed trading Matchbox cars with his peers. He amassed quite a big collection of these miniature toy cars, and he would trade or sell the ones he had duplicates of to his classmates. He later graduated to collecting and trading comic books like Archie and Spider Man. He would rent them out making at least RM 3 to RM 4 per comic book. This meant that during lunchtime, he was able to buy his lunch plus a treat like an ice cream cone.

Later, at university, he had dabbled in selling vintage T-shirts he bought online from overseas stores, as well as fragrances that were not available in the official outlets. Whether these goods were genuine or not remained dubious, but he made a tidy profit from this side businesses. They were enough for him to be financially independent and not rely on his parents for any pocket money.

His parents had by no means been impoverished—his father was a small-time building contractor who eventually moved on to bigger projects; the entrepreneurial spirit apparently coursed through his veins. While the jury is still out on whether the claim that entrepreneurs are born is true, in Terence's case it couldn't be truer. His drive and aggressive streak coupled with his daredevil, risk-taking nature made him a natural in the world of wheeling and dealing.

Graduating with a business degree, it was only natural for Terence to eventually start his own company. He looked for tenure at a bank after he left university. It was an option, somewhere to park himself, while he looked for greener pastures. Opportunities came knocking at his door and more often than not, he took them. Connecting a businessman looking for spare parts with a supplier in China or acting as a broker to flip over a condo or two might be seen as making a quick buck, but to Terence, it was money in his pocket at the end of the day.

After his internship at the bank had ended, he joined his father's construction company for a while, as it was expanding and his father needed help. From building shoplots in outlying areas to planning bigger and more lucrative projects nearer to the city centre, Fong Senior took his time to build his business, never biting off more than he could chew. Fong Tong Chew's crowning achievement came one day when he bid for the contract to build a thirty-five-storey condo in a leafy suburb and won. He had never attempted a building project on such a scale before and was initially apprehensive about his own abilities.

He'd endured sleepless nights, worrying about whether he had the wherewithal to pull it off. Yes, he had experience as a contractor but building five two-storey shoplots could hardly compare to building a thirty-five-storey high-rise complete with amenities such as a swimming pool, an adjoining multi-storey car park, and a tennis court. The success of this project could be his big break to bring his business to another, more rarefied level. The pressure he felt was both intoxicating and draining.

Asking Terence to help out with this project was only natural. It would have happened so in any Chinese family. As the eldest son, Terence was expected to eventually return to the fold and help with the family business.

'Terence, when does your training programme end at the bank?' His father had asked his not-quite-prodigal son one night at dinner. Mr Fong wasn't a man of many words so when he spoke, others paid heed.

'In two months time, dad,' came Terence's reply.

Picking up a garlic prawn with his slender chopsticks, his father enquired without looking at Terence: 'Have you learnt anything useful during your internship?'

'Many things. I've been there for almost two years. There's lots to learn during that time,' Terence replied, knowing full well he craved a more exciting career with a faster tempo.

'That's good. Tell me one thing you have learnt?'

'That banking is not the business I want to be in.'

Chapter 7

Driving back to her office, Jan was heady from the apartment-viewing. The size was perfect for three of them. 3,500 square feet with three bedrooms and three bathrooms was exactly what she and Erika had in mind. It was much bigger than their home in Sydney and of course the rent was much lower. Moving back to her hometown wasn't that bad after all.

When Jan walked into her office, she could hear and sense the buzz of busyness permeating the air. A few of her colleagues were rushing off to meetings while her subordinates were all transfixed with the screens of their laptops. She sometimes wondered if they were really working that intensely or if it was just for show when she was around. She dismissed the thought when one of her staff came over to her to ask about a project she was working on.

Glancing at the proposal that Hanna had prepared, Jan immediately noticed how sketchy and devoid of details it was. 'I think you need to put in more information in this proposal. The client will not accept it as it is.'

'That was what I wanted to ask you. Apart from the theme and venue of the launch, what else can we submit?'

'Leave it with me and I'll go through it. We can have a brainstorming session later to see if we can come up with any more ideas on how to make it more exciting and enjoyable for the guests and media.'

Hanna put the file on top of a growing pile of papers that Jan had to work through by the end of the week. There was a lot of work to finish and with her impending move, Jan felt overwhelmed. She didn't have any more time or patience to go flat hunting and was relieved that the very first flat she had seen fit all the criteria that she and Erika agreed upon. Jan put it down to beginner's luck.

Just as she turned on her laptop, her phone rang. It was her boss who was asking her for the weekly report. Jan scrambled to look for it and it was then that she realized that she had completely forgotten to do it. A searing sensation of hot and cold engulfed her. She quickly rushed to the ladies and locked herself up in a cubicle. With her heart palpitating so hard that she broke out in a cold sweat, she felt like she was unable to breathe. Jan started hyperventilating. The cubicle she was in felt like it was spinning, and Jan closed her eyes and rested her head on the side of the cubicle. She started the 4-7-8 breathing technique her therapist had taught her. Breathing in to the count of four, holding her breath to the count of seven and finally breathing out slowly to the count of eight. This was supposed to calm her body and activate her parasympathetic nervous system.

After a few minutes of deep diaphragmatic breathing, Jan opened her eyes and felt much better. She exited the cubicle and splashed cold water on her face. Steadying herself, she managed to walk back to her office without anyone noticing anything. A thousand thoughts raced through her head but the one that she chose to pay attention to was that of telling Erika about the apartment she had viewed that day in Harmony Heights.

* * *

The management committee of Harmony Heights consisted of six members who were made up of a cross section of residents of the condominium. Tasked with managing and maintaining the common areas of the condo and ensuring the service charges collected from all the residents were properly utilized and accounted for, this motley crew couldn't have been more disparate than if you had walked blindfolded into a *pasar malam* and randomly selected six people.

There was Lillian Gan, a retired civil servant who made everyone's business her own. Approaching her mid-sixties, this spinster loved snooping around other people's units just to get a bit of juicy gossip about them. She lived in Harmony Heights with her father who suffered from Alzheimer's disease. She was only in the committee because her overriding desire to know anything and everything about anyone superseded her overall feeling of boredom and her desire to extract herself, albeit only for a few hours, from the all-consuming task of being her father's caregiver.

Tan Wing Shing, also retired, was voted in by another resident and owned three apartments in Harmony Heights. With the amount of service charges he was paying, it was self-interest more than anything else which made him agree to becoming a committee member.

Sukhminder Kaur was a housewife who spent her days tending to her potted plants and mending her children's clothes. She thought it would be fun to be on the committee but didn't realize what a thankless job it was going to be.

Karim Abdullah was a former state assemblyman who had harboured greater political ambitions in his younger years but unfortunately had never progressed beyond his role in the state assembly. He spent most of his days volunteering at his local state constituency.

Nisha Vaswani was a homemaker who ran a part-time business baking cakes and cookies. With three kids in school, her time was tied up chauffeuring them around. It had been her husband's idea for her to join the management committee and she had agreed to do so on a lark.

And finally, heading the management committee was none other than Dato' Sri Terence Fong, husband of the resident glamour puss Candy and son-in-law of the developer of Harmony Heights. Being involved in the building and construction of Harmony Heights certainly made him more than qualified for this role but more than that, it gave him a certain gravitas.

Managing this mishmash group of people, some of whom may have had—but most did not—corporate experience and some had never even sat on a committee before, was challenging for Terence, to say the least. Meeting once a month to discuss any ongoing improvement work and answering complaints from disgruntled residents was usually what topped the agenda.

Like any group of people, Terence found a few members he bonded with and others that he just tolerated. He took it all in his stride and was not overly affected by committee dealings. Not taking things personally and viewing interactions with his committee members objectively had worked for him so far.

Terence, unlike his father, had the advantage and benefit of being educated abroad in England and was thus broad-minded and liberal. But, funnily enough, he found the women on the committee petty and more concerned with shallow, inconsequential things. They slowed down any progress or action he wanted to take.

The management committee members met once a month to discuss matters pertaining to the condominium—discussing matters as large as repainting the entire building to something as mundane as repairing the fencing. Any suggestion of improvement to Harmony Heights—for instance that of paving the driveway—was met with a thousand questions from Lillian. Questions about the type of asphalt or tar which they would use, the timeline of the project, the budget it would take up, the contractors who they could approach to tender for the job. Replacement of the water pipes was met with a barrage of objections and questions from Nisha about why they had to be replaced instead of just being repaired due to the exorbitant costs, while buying a new set of sofas and armchairs for the lobby had got all the ladies in a tizzy as to the type (leather or rattan) and the store where they could obtain the best discounts. Deciding on the colour of the sofa took a two-hour discussion.

The two men on the committee, being much older and as a result more mellow, just looked on with bemusement at these grown women who would discuss at first, disagree next, and finally begin arguments that would only cease on outsider intervention. *Surely their lives can't be that empty,*

Karim Abdullah thought to himself, *that they would occupy their minds with such inconsequential details?*

But occupy they did and asserting their authority, no matter how little it was, sometimes became more important than the issue at hand. *Power struggles and politics knew no bounds when it came to humankind*, Terence reminded himself, as he tried to calm a potentially explosive encounter between Sukhminder and Nisha over the security guard's shifts. The level of pettiness displayed by these women was astounding to say the least.

Mr Tan and Karim Abdullah knew better than to take sides when the three women argued and just kept mum and remained non-committal. From their own personal experiences with their wives, they knew women had minds like weathervanes and it was best not to meddle with their quarrels. They might seem like arch-nemeses today but, who knows, they might become best friends tomorrow. In a way, this peculiar trait was good in that they didn't bear any grudges, and nothing was personal. But it was bad for a bystander who couldn't gauge what the weather was like— stormy or sunny.

Mr Tan and Karim Abdullah were more interested in properly managing the money they collected each month from the residents' payment of service charges and contribution to the sinking fund—a pool of money set aside to cover capital expenditure such as refurbishment, repainting, and the general improvement of the condominium. Sure, as a corporate body, the management corporation had to prepare and submit audited financial statements annually and the management committee members were the ones responsible for the accuracy of these financial statements.

Although the cashflow required for the day-to-day running of Harmony Heights was particularly of interest to members of the management committee, it was the sinking fund which was of interest to Terence. It was basically a gold mine if one thought about it. A constant stream of income flowing into a bank account each and every month from every resident, barring the defaulters. At RM 1 per share unit (as opposed to per square foot because it was a fairer and more equitable way of calculating the service charges and sinking fund charges), it worked out to be a substantial amount each month and anyone with a modicum of mathematical ability would tell you it was golden goose.

The accumulated amount in the sinking fund was placed in a fixed deposit to generate a higher return and was a contentious issue as the amount could be easily accessed by the chairman and the building manager. Nevertheless, not many residents asked to see the monthly bank statements of the sinking fund, and just took it as gospel that the financial statements they were given each year before the annual general meeting were accurate and correct.

Chapter 8

With a powerful backhand volley, Shivana loped the tennis ball straight toward her instructor. Before he could have a chance to move, it hit him straight in his crotch and he let out a yelp.

'I'm so sorry! I didn't mean to! Did it hurt?' She called out from her side of the court.

'Bloody hell!' Rohan uttered under his breath. Did she do it on purpose? But despite the agonizing pain, Rohan just brushed it off. He just about managed to stifle a grimace and paint a grin on his face. 'I'm fine . . . no worries!' He yelled across the tennis court even though it hurt like hell. His male ego, however, prevented him from showing any signs of pain so he just grinned like an idiot and bore it.

It was just past twelve noon, and her weekly Friday tennis lesson was over. Shivana helped her instructor pick up the balls and waved him goodbye as she rushed away. She had a lunch appointment at 1.30 p.m. and she certainly didn't want to be late for it.

She ran up the stairs from the tennis court past the pool and entered the condo through the rear gate. Her mind was racing, worried about her lunch date with Dinesh and she couldn't help thinking of their last meeting together. It had been bittersweet, as he had seemed so distant. She wondered what had been on his mind and what was so important that he wasn't paying any attention to her.

As she got into her apartment, Padma, her mother was just finishing performing puja for Lakshmi, the goddess of fortune, beauty, and prosperity.

'Quick Shivana, you have to meet Dinesh, go shower now!' Padma instructed her daughter. 'I told you not to play tennis at this time, the sun is so strong.' Of course, what Padma really meant was that her only daughter shouldn't go out—unlike mad dogs and Englishmen—in the noonday sun. Although Shivana was fairer in complexion than most of her Tamil friends, Padma wanted Shivana to remain fair, at least until the day after her wedding, whenever that might be.

Feeling irritated and wanting to snap back her mum, Shivana bit her tongue and told herself getting into an argument with her mother right now was not worth it. Jumping into the shower, she turned on the cold water full blast. It felt so nice and refreshing after playing tennis in the heat and humidity for an hour. Just to appease her mother, Shivana made an effort to look her best when she had lunch with Dinesh.

At twenty-three years old, Shivana needed very little make-up to look good. Just a coating of mascara, a smudge of eye liner and a dusting of translucent powder, and oh yes, a little tinted lip gloss and she was ready to go. Her complexion was flawless and didn't need any foundation. She didn't care how fair or light-skinned she was so why did her mother? She put it down to her mother belonging to a different generation, one with a disparate set of values. Tying her luxuriant black hair in a ponytail, she mentally rehearsed what she wanted to talk to Dinesh about later.

Wearing a leopard print chiffon top and jeans, Shivana exposed just the right amount of cleavage, which she knew would excite Dinesh. It was one of her ploys but after their last meeting, she wanted to make sure she had 100 per cent of his attention.

The elevator descended from the sixteenth floor, stopping on the third floor, where Shivana was waiting. The doors opened, revealing another person. When Shivana saw Lillian Gan inside the lift, she hesitated but as she was in a hurry, she relented and stepped in. She really didn't want to be in the same lift as Lillian.

'Going somewhere nice?' Lillian broke the ice and smiled at Shivana.

Caught by surprise, as she had been fixing her earrings, Shivana smiled back at Lillian. 'Yes, I am. And how are you Madam Gan?'

'I'm fine. Just going to the supermarket. Its half-price Friday today and everything is sooooo cheap!' Lillian said. 'You smell nice, what perfume are you using?'

As usual, Lillian would bombard anyone except those she didn't talk to or didn't like with a thousand questions whenever she saw them in the elevator. Her nosey nature preceded her and much to the chagrin of most residents at Harmony Heights, she never took the hint when somebody answered her curtly or even ignored her questions completely.

'It's Jo Malone English Pear and Freesia,' Shivana replied and was relieved when the ping of the lift sounded as it stopped on the ground floor. 'Good luck with your shopping!' She said as she quickly walked out of the lift. Lillian was about to enquire about how Shivana's tennis lessons were going but didn't get a chance to.

As Shivana got into her Grab car, which was already waiting for her in the porch of the driveway, she was glad that she hadn't eaten much at breakfast. Half an apple with some hot tea was all she had. Of course, being a strict vegetarian, her food options were very limited already.

When she arrived at the restaurant on a little side street in Bangsar, Dinesh was already there waiting for her. He was chatting in a very animated manner with the waiter who was smartly dressed in a uniform complete with a long white apron. Shivana assumed Dinesh was enquiring about the specials of the day. As soon as Dinesh saw Shivana, he rocked forward from his chair and stood up. They didn't exchange air kisses anymore like they used to when they first met but, nonetheless, she was happy to see him.

'Traffic bad?' Dinesh enquired as soon as they settled. 'Let's order wine, it's a Friday,' he continued without even waiting for Shivana to answer his first question.

'Sure, I can't believe this week has flown by so quickly,' she said while perusing the menu. 'I'm still full from breakfast.'

'What did you have?' Dinesh asked, curious what his svelte girlfriend could have eaten five hours ago which still filled her tummy.

'A big bowl of oats with fruit,' Shivana lied.

Dinesh and Shivana had been dating for about six months before going steady about a year ago. She met him at a mutual friend's wedding held in Bali and beneath the full moon on a cool and breezy Balinese night, knew that she had found her match. She had been more aggressive than him in their courtship and had taken all the initiative. Of course, her mother was instrumental in guiding Shivana along in snaring Dinesh. As a well-educated, young Indian man from a wealthy Sindhi community, Dinesh was quite the catch and Padma couldn't have been happier when her daughter told her about meeting the 'perfect man' after she returned from Bali.

Of course, perfection never exists in anyone or anything, but Shivana was young and naïve, and even though Padma knew it, she didn't want to taint the rose-tinted glasses her only daughter was wearing.

* * *

Arriving home at night, Jan couldn't wait to tell Erika how her day had gone. Both of them were so busy as of late that they hadn't gotten a chance to catch up. She was excited about the spacious apartment she had viewed a couple of days ago at Harmony Heights and she was sure Erika would like it too. A 3,500 square foot apartment just outside the heart of town was a godsend, not mentioning the price. They would have never gotten such a large place back in Sydney for this amount.

This was one of the main reasons Jan had decided to return and she had somehow managed to convince Erika to come along. It wasn't surprising that Malaysia was often ranked as one of the best places to retire in. Not to say that either Jan or Erika were going to hang up their hats any time soon, but the affordability of housing and lower costs of living made it appealing for the modern-day family.

Just as Jan finished cooking dinner—a Kung Pao chicken stir-fry—and was checking on the rice, Erika walked in. Their daughter Sonya was glued to Cartoon Network on the TV and seemed oblivious to both her parents greeting each other in the entrance hall with a tender embrace.

'I saw the ideal apartment,' Jan told Erika excitedly. 'It's large and spacious and located on a high floor with great views.' Jan's powers of persuasion were second to none when she chose to use them. 'You would just love it. Here, let me show you the shots I took.' Grabbing her iPhone from the counter, Jan clicked it to life and proceeded to search for the images. Passing her partner her phone, Jan went behind the counter in their rented service apartment to dish out the rice.

'Looks good. How much is it?' Erika asked.

While picking up a piece of chicken with some rice for their three-year old daughter, Jan replied, 'Half a mill, you know it's a quick sale *ya*? The current owners have defaulted on their mortgage repayments and the bank is about to foreclose. It is way below the market value.'

'Is that in Aussie or Ringgit?' Erika asked.

'What do you think? Of course in Ringgit, it's a bargain.'

Later that night after dinner when Sonya was fast asleep and Erika was finishing off a report on her laptop, Jan retreated into the bedroom and took out her amethyst pendulum from a half unpacked cardboard box. She wasn't superstitious in the strict sense of the word, but it didn't hurt to get some confirmation. Jan had dabbled in numerous spiritual practices over the years—from Reiki healing to ancient Egyptian divination—all in the name of knowledge and self-awareness.

As she laid out the pendulum chart with the 'YES' and 'NO' on opposite ends and 'MAYBE' and 'DON'T WANT TO ANSWER' between them in a circle, Jan closed her eyes and took several deep, cleansing breaths to clear her mind. Holding the pendulum in her dominant hand, she asked aloud, 'Is the apartment I saw today at Harmony Heights the right one for us?'

To her surprise, the pendulum started swinging almost immediately, first vertically then in a circular fashion. Round and round it went and Jan's eyes followed the amethyst pendulum until it suddenly changed directions and swung anti-clockwise. This time it was skewed to the left and then after a few seconds it just swung continuously to YES.

Chapter 9

A week later, as Azizah prepared to go out, she opened her purse to check if she had sufficient cash. As she counted the 50 and 100 Ringgit notes, she suddenly noticed that the wad of cash she had, appeared thinner than the last time she'd looked at it. As her driver already WhatsApped her to say he was waiting in the driveway, she didn't have time to check her other handbag or the locked drawer, so she brushed it aside.

On the way out she saw Widya straightening the cushion on the sofa and told her what three dishes to prepare for dinner. From a distance, Widya reminded her of her daughter who was studying abroad. They were about the same age and had a similar build, although Sofie, her daughter, had a more confident mien and strutted about with a self-assured demeanour.

She pushed away any idle thought she had and focused on her day ahead. She was going to see her doctor for her menopausal symptoms. She had been having trouble sleeping and had been experiencing mood swings, the likes of which she'd never had before. Well, that might not be entirely true, but her low points were getting worse while feeling good only came when she was indulging herself, mainly while shopping.

As she walked out of the lobby of Harmony Heights, she saw a removal truck parked in the guest car park and several men carrying boxes. *Either someone is moving in or moving out,* Azizah thought to herself. When her driver caught sight of Azizah, he drove to the front of the porch and got out to open the door of the Mercedes Benz E300 sedan for her. It was only when she was comfortably ensconced in the back seat, racing off, that she caught a glimpse of a triracial family—made up of two women and a child—walking into Harmony Heights with their luggage in tow.

Arriving at her doctor's office, Azizah tried to recollect how her morning had gone. Her hubby seemed stressed and preoccupied, something she attributed to his work. Ever since he had risen up the ranks of the insurance company, Zainal had gotten further away from her emotionally. Late nights at the office and weekend corporate team-building events left very little private time for her and Zainal. She missed those newly married days when he would rush home from work just to be with her. They were so blissfully happy during those early years that everything after paled in comparison.

But, of course, Azizah never complained outright to Zainal that she was seeing less of him now. It was she who kept pushing him and strategizing all his moves. As she had also worked in the same company before resigning after having their first child, she knew the inner workings of Tawfik Insurance; like who Zainal should align himself with and which camp he should pledge allegiance to. Like any company, Tawfik Insurance was rife with politics and only those who knew how to play the game would emerge as winners. Never mind how good you were at your actual job, who you buttered up mattered more.

When the nurse called her name, Azizah snapped out of her deep reverie. She put down the magazine she was holding and walked into Dr Rahaina's consultation room. The doctor, a gynaecologist, welcomed her with a sympathetic and gentle manner that made Azizah feel very comfortable, allowing her to open up to the doctor easily. 'How can I help you today?' Dr Rahaina asked Azizah with a smile after she settled herself on a chair beside Dr Rahaina.

'I've been experiencing trouble sleeping and I've been having hot flashes as well,' she told Dr Rahaina.

'How's your mood been?' Dr Rahaina asked, glancing at the laptop as she retrieved Azizah's medical records.

'Good sometimes then not so good other times,' Azizah replied candidly, after all she had been her gynaecologist for over twenty years and there was literally nothing to hide. 'Just like anyone else I suppose.'

Dr Rahaina stifled a chuckle at that last statement. Blunt and direct, Azizah wasn't one to sugarcoat anything, least of all when it came to her well-being. It was refreshing at times, but it could also be cutting when her frankness hit too close to home or touched someone's frayed nerves.

'But I have to tell you there are some days when I wake up feeling hopeless and down and just don't feel like getting out of bed,' Azizah revealed.

'Tell me more,' Dr Rahaina dug deeper. 'Are there times you feel good?'

Without hesitation, Azizah replied emphatically, 'Yes, there are. But they have been few and far between.' Pausing for a second only because she didn't want to come across as trite, Azizah decided to continue. 'But then there are times when nothing bothers me . . . not even my husband's lame jokes!'

This was a red flag and it piqued Dr Rahaina's interest. 'Tell me how you behave on those good days?'

'Well, I feel like an energizer bunny. It's like when you have two double espressos and just want to do things.'

'How interesting. What sort of things do you do then?'

'I start getting quite restless and can't sit still. So, I tidy up around the apartment or bake cakes,' Azizah replied. Before adding a revelatory adjunct. 'I might also spend the day shopping.'

'Do you enjoy shopping?' Dr Rahaina asked, weighing her words carefully.

'100 per cent! For sure! It gives me such a thrill!'

* * *

Getting home from class, Yi Wei made a beeline to her room and locked the door shut. She unclipped her hair and sat down on her dresser, proceeding to quickly apply her make-up. Patting on her cushion foundation, she eyed the clock on her dresser. She had approximately an hour before dinner, and she wanted to record her video in time. With a deft flick of liquid eyeliner, Yi Wei drew a cat's eye extending the black line beyond the end of her almond-shaped eye, elongating it. She chuckled when she capped the eyeliner and saw that it was called 'Better Than Sex'. Dapping on bubble gum pink lip gloss Yi Wei puckered her lips before grabbing her hairbrush and bending forward to brush her luxuriant and glossy hair.

At eighteen years old, Yi Wei was probably at the peak of her beauty. She, of course, didn't know this and simply assumed that life would begin at forty or fifty or at whatever age the writer of the article of the beauty blog about growing old gracefully chose to use. Born with a fair complexion—which she had inherited from her mother—along with her long limbs, gave her a statuesque presence amongst her classmates. An early bloomer, Yi Wei looked more mature compared to her school friends but that didn't bother her in the slightest.

She had first started noticing boys and men looking at her when she would hang out with her girlfriends at the shopping mall. She had never experienced that kind of attention before, so she initially regarded it with a mixture of awe and curiosity. Then, when random men started striking up conservations with her at Starbucks or while queuing at bank ATMs, it dawned on her what they were really interested in.

Yi Wei had a calm demeanour, and she took it all in her stride. Slowly, she grew to like it, enjoying all the attention that was lavished on her with very little effort or participation on her part. She recalled an incident when she had been with three other girlfriends on a Saturday afternoon. They went to watch a movie and afterwards they decided to go somewhere to grab a bite to eat. While her friends went to order at the self-service counter—being students, they couldn't afford going to a restaurant where they would be served—Yi Wei sat at the table looking through her Instagram. Suddenly, a middle-aged man came up to her to ask if he could share the table with her.

As it was a table for four and thus fully occupied, he couldn't. But what made Yi Wei feel uncomfortable was the overly friendly demeanour of this man and the way he looked at her. She might not have had extensive experience with the opposite sex, but she knew enough to understand that his lecherous manner would have made anyone uneasy.

After brushing her hair, Yi Wei changed into black lace panties and a matching bra that she kept hidden in her bottom drawer. Glancing at the clock again, she drew her curtains closed and then walked across the room to turn on the LED ring light beside her bed. Adjusting her iPhone, which was placed on a tripod, she made sure the phone was recording and then walked to her bed and got on all fours.

Chapter 10

The management office of Harmony Heights was located at the basement of the building at the end of a long and rather dark corridor. The windowless and fluorescent-lit room was partitioned to accommodate the resident manager's own office as well as a spare room for documents and files.

Most residents at Harmony Heights avoided going there because of the dingy and unwelcoming placement of the office. It gave some people the creeps walking along the dark and narrow corridor with locked doors on either side that housed the back-up generator and also functioned as storerooms.

Mr Arumugam, the resident manager of Harmony Heights ran the office like a headmaster would run a school. Some would even go as far as to say he behaved like a prison warden and treated the residents as if they were prisoners. A short and stout man with a strict manner, his no-nonsense demeanour and unpleasant bearing was probably cultivated by him to stop residents from approaching him to complain or enquire about matters pertaining to the management of Harmony Heights.

As the nerve centre of the condominium, the management office was where all the administrative duties required to run Harmony Heights were performed. The monthly invoices to all the residents for the service charges and sinking fund contribution were issued from within its four white walls. Service providers and contract workers were dealt with by Arumugam and his efficient assistant, Ms Chew. They also dealt with all correspondences and notices with regard to the annual general meeting, which, as the name suggests, was held once a year.

Fielding several calls from residents daily, the administrative assistant Ms Chew was adept at handling most complaints and reports on her own. She screened most calls the management office got—unless it was from the chairman of the management committee or any other important issue from the subcontractors that required Arumugam's say-so. Both of them adopted a strict and no-nonsense approach when dealing with residents; some would even go as far to say they were aloof and standoffish. Such practised behaviour by Arumugam and Ms Chew was, of course, deliberate. They did not wish to entertain any frivolities and wanted to deter any resident from becoming too familiar with them, thus preventing any request for special favours.

It wasn't a very demanding job for Ms Chew, as she started work at nine in the morning and left at five sharp. It suited her fine, as she was married and had children to look after. As for Arumugam, being the resident manager meant that he was on call 24/7 so his duties were much more extensive and demanding than those of Ms Chew's. Whenever something went wrong, and it often did, it was Arumugam who had to fix it. Be it a power blackout in the middle of the night, a burst water pipe on a public holiday, an argument between a resident and the security guards, or a fire in a unit, it was Arumugan who always had to douse the flames and fix it.

* * *

It took Candy Fong approximately three minutes to ride the elevator from the ground floor to the penthouse of Harmony Heights, where she lived. Occupying the top three floors of the condominium block, the 8,000 square foot triplex had its entrance on the thirty-fifth floor. Her father was the developer of Harmony Heights and the triplex penthouse had been a wedding present from her father to her and Terence.

As she turned the key of the heavy wooden door, she was almost blinded by the sunlight streaming in from the double-volume, floor-to-ceiling glass windows which faced the entrance hallway. A curved marble staircase located just in front of the windows led to six bedrooms, all with en-suite bathrooms on the next two levels.

Candy removed her Chanel sunglasses as soon as she saw her white, miniature Pomeranian scuttle towards her.

'How's my precious little baby?' Candy said in baby talk as she bent down to scoop up Coco into her arms. 'Have you eaten yet my darling? I'll call the groomer over tomorrow so you can have your spa day.'

Right on cue, Coco licked Candy's face several times before she pulled her beloved pet away from her. She didn't want Coco to taste or ingest any of her make-up. Candy carried Coco and turned left towards the kitchen where two of her helpers were busy preparing lunch. They greeted her with a smile and nod and then continued chopping and stirring away.

Grabbing a bottle of kombucha from the fridge, Candy exited the kitchen and proceeded to the internal lift which took her to her bedroom on the next level up. Just as she removed her high heels, she heard her phone ring and fished it out from her Louis Vuitton Capucines handbag.

'Hi Candy! Did you look at your Instagram today?' A voice shrieked out from the other end of her iPhone.

'No, I haven't, I just got home . . . why? What's up?' Candy asked, her interest aroused by the breathless excitement of her friend.

'OMG! Adele just had the biggest falling out with Juliana! Can you believe it? And it was all played out for everyone to see on Instagram! She called her a big fat liar and a fake. Quick, take a look before one of them deletes it!'

Plopping Coco on her king-size bed, Candy told Pam to hold on and swiped her iPhone for the Instagram app. Scrolling down, she finally found Juliana's post and looked under the comments. There were twenty-six comments under Juliana's latest post and viewing them, Candy saw that it was all just made by the two dueling divas.

Reading through the barrage of insults the two hurled at each other on social media, Candy continued to speak to Pam on speaker. 'Jeez, couldn't they have WhatsApped each other instead of doing it on Instagram? Now everyone knows everything.'

'Maybe one of them just made a sarky comment and the other took offence and replied and it just escalated from there. Sometimes when you get mad, you are not aware of what you are doing.'

Pam then proceeded to tell Candy about the quarrel between Adele and Juliana. It involved inviting the current girlfriend of Juliana's ex-husband to her party and not including Juliana. Not exactly earth-shattering in the grand scheme of things but probably vital to someone who had been insecure about her social standing since her divorce.

'Well, someone should tell Juliana that once you get divorced from a prominent figure, you become a persona non grata. That's how the world works,' Candy proffered.

'Yes, but she didn't think Adele would do this to her. They were such good buddies before!'

'Good buddies when she was still a Datin and married to Hafiz. The operative word here is "before".'

Wanting to end the conversation, as she was getting bored, Candy told Pam she had to go and hung up. There was always some sort of drama with the social crowd and Candy usually distanced herself from any kind of conflict or drama. She didn't have the stamina to get personally involved and she preferred to stay away from that kind of negativity.

Candy walked out from her bedroom to the internal elevator and took it to the uppermost floor of her penthouse. As their triplex had been partitioned before they moved in—a corner of it was sealed off to create another flat, in this case, a sort of home office for Terence with a separate entrance—the top floor had thus been turned into Candy's own boudoir, a personal sanctuary which housed her almost 1,000 square foot walk-in wardrobe with a separate study. It was here that

Candy often retreated to when she needed to be alone and needed time to reflect.

Today, however, she wasn't in a pensive mood. She had to select an outfit for the dinner party she was hosting that night. Facing the rail of clothes which dominated the centre of the room, she picked up a device and clicked it. Immediately the motorized garment conveyor whirled to life, moving from right to left. And there, right in front of her was her pride and joy. From Alaia to Zimmermann and every other designer in between, this was Candy's carefully curated wardrobe. It wasn't just a collection of designer clothes, it was her prized possession, one that showcased her immense style.

As a dyed-in-the-wool fashionista, Candy just couldn't bring herself to discard anything from her wardrobe. From shoes and bags to jeans and belts and everything in between, she had kept everything ever since she was seventeen years old. Her wardrobe was the envy of many of her peers and the idea of installing an electronic wardrobe conveyor had first come to Candy after she saw it in the movie *Clueless*. Even though she was only a young teen then, she vowed that when she had her own home, that was the first thing she would install.

She might not have a 90210 zip code but Candy's designer-laden closet could rival any housewife, whether in KL, Singapore, or Beverly Hills. Arranged in a unique manner—not by colour as most women did or by type of garment. Candy's wardrobe was organized by designers and labels. So, for instance, under K there was Kate Spade and Karl Lagerfeld, under S there was Sandro and Saint Laurent, under V, Valentino and Versace, and C was probably the largest section as it contained all her Chanels, Carolina Herreras, Celines, and Christian Diors.

And don't ask why some designers were grouped by their first names while others by their last. That was how Candy's mind worked when it came to fashion. She had tried once to arrange her closet according to colour but it just confused her. When she couldn't find something she wanted to wear for an event once, she had decided to abandon the colour-based sorting system and had decided, instead, to group them according to the designer's name.

As she was hosting a dinner in her home, she wanted to wear something soft and floaty. She pressed P for her Pucci collection. Whirling into action, the electronic clothes rail moved slowly and when it stopped, Candy was faced with a sea of brightly-coloured prints and patterns. Flipping through her collection, she decided on a lime green and yellow, swirling, psychedelic print silk maxi dress with bell sleeves. She thought it would pair perfectly with the yellow Manolo Blahnik cross-strap sandals she had just ordered from Net-a-Porter.

Chapter 11

The minute she heard the front door close, Widya stopped cleaning and reached for her phone. She texted Iqbal to let him know she was free for about twenty minutes during her lunch hour and would be able to meet him. She hadn't seen him for a few days, and she missed him. She needed some sort of respite from all the cooking and cleaning and Iqbal provided this to her.

Her mind then drifted back to her employer *Puan* Azizah. Widya had been noticing her erratic behaviour of late. She was moody, forgetful, and kept repeating herself. She never raised her voice at Widya but there were times she did show her annoyance. Despite such instances, Widya knew that on the whole, her employers were good and decent people.

Turning off the boiling clay pot of chicken curry on the stove, Widya checked the time and just then a WhatsApp message pinged on her phone. She felt a rush of euphoria and excitement. 'In ten minutes. See you.'

In her haste to meet Iqbal, Widya forgot to take off her apron. She grabbed her key and phone and rushed out the back door located at the rear end of the kitchen. The service elevator brought her straight down to the back of the building and she was able to walk discreetly along a hedge-trimmed path to their rendezvous point. No one would see her or Iqbal, as it was lunchtime, and the other maintenance staff of the condo would not be around.

The two tennis courts were located down an incline on a lower level with a staircase leading down to them. Both she and Iqbal usually met at the end of the second tennis court where they sat on the lower steps shaded under a huge rain tree out of view of anyone. This time when she arrived, Iqbal was already there waiting for her. From a distance, she saw him smiling and waving at her and a warm and comforting feeling enveloped her. It was probably the release of serotonin in her brain but whatever it was, all the stress she was feeling melted away.

'I bought you a packet of *nasi lemak* and a drink,' Iqbal said to her as she bent down to sit next to him on the step. 'I just have half an hour to have lunch today, as I need to do a few more jobs around the pool.' Iqbal handed her a banana leaf wrapped package and a Milo carton. Widya couldn't help but feel touched by his kind gesture. She had never met a man who had shown her so much tenderness and looking at him now made tears well up in her eyes.

'Thank you so much, Iqbal,' she said, smiling back at him. 'How was your morning? Busy?'

Iqbal proceeded to tell Widya about all the work he had done that morning. He also told her about his desire to start sketching again. Before he dropped out of school, Iqbal had done relatively well at art, even though it was very elementary. His primary school only had colour pencils for him to use but it was enough to spur Iqbal's interest in art. When he sketched something and was fully concentrating, it was like he was transported into another realm where time stood still. He was completely at ease with portraying on paper what his eyes would see in that realm.

'Do you like working here?' He asked Widya all of a sudden, interrupting himself as he was in the midst of telling her about what he would like to sketch. It was a non sequitur and totally unrelated to what he had been saying previously but Widya was now used to Iqbal's style of communication and was not taken aback by the sudden and abrupt change of subject.

'It's fine for now,' Widya answered. 'Both my employers are good to me, and it isn't too much work, as it's just the both of them.'

'They don't have children?' Iqbal asked innocently. 'No family? No son? No daughter?'

'Yes, they have a daughter studying abroad, but she comes back only once a year. I have only met her once.'

After eating their *nasi lemak*, both Widya and Iqbal sat silently while looking in the distance. She wanted to tell him about her plans for the future but wasn't quite sure if he would understand. He slowly moved his hands and took a hold of hers and for an instant Widya felt that nothing on earth mattered more than this moment.

'I have to leave now. I'm doing double duty as the pool boy now. They are paying me RM 100 more for doing it. See you soon!' Iqbal said to her while he got up and paused for a moment to look at Widya. 'If you are free later after work, you can WhatsApp me.' He walked off and left her sitting alone. It was mundane but this short break brought Widya so much joy.

* * *

Dr Desmond Choo summoned his nurse to the office when there was a brief respite between his patient appointments. He had asked her to order several medical supplies like cotton swabs and rubber gloves, but she hadn't done it yet. His patience was running thin, as his staff had been very inefficient of late.

'Where are the things I asked you to order last week?' He barked at Nurse Ho the moment she stepped into his office.

'I ordered them yesterday. They should arrive tomorrow,' she replied.

'Yesterday? I told you a week ago!' He raised his voice. 'Did you forget?'

'I was busy following up about the test results. We had a lot of lab results to attend to,' she answered back.

'You are not new here, you know what is important and what to do first!' Desmond retorted.

'We are short staffed.' Nurse Ho answered.

At this point Dr Desmond's anger was triggered. How dare she answer him back? He had to put her back in her place and assert his authority.

'You have three fucking nurses to assist you here. What the hell do you mean by short staffed?' He shouted. 'Go chase the supplier now and get the hell out of my office!' At this point, his whole face turned red with anger and his external carotid artery popped out of his neck. It was a frightening sight to say the least. As Nurse Ho exited his office, he threw the stethoscope he was holding against the door and narrowly missed her.

Chapter 12

It would be very Lillian-like to catch the movers when they were in the midst of carting Jan and Erika's furniture and personal effects into the condo. She was in the car park and was just about to go out when she spied the large removal truck parked beside the lobby in the driveway, and she was overwhelmed by this itching desire to know who was moving in.

Locking her car, she made a beeline for the lifts inside Harmony Heights and impatiently pressed the button. Right on cue, the lifts opened, with two burly men carrying a bubble-wrapped coffee table standing inside.

'Can I squeeze in?' Lillian asked the two movers sweetly. When they nodded, she wiggled herself into the already packed elevator. 'Which floor are you going to?'

'Twenty-five,' came one of the mover's brief reply.

'Oh great! I'm going there too!' She answered, although her apartment was on a different floor. In local lingo, Lillian would be described as a *kaypoh* or nosy parker. She had always been like this, it seemed she inherited this quirky and most annoying trait from her mother, who had also been just as inquisitive.

When the elevator reached the twenty-fifth floor, the movers carried the coffee table slowly out of the lift while Lillian helped them hold the lift open. As soon as they got out, she followed them. She soon saw that they were headed toward apartment D, the larger corner unit.

Trailing the movers, Lillian waited till they entered the apartment before she peeked in to take a look. There were several cardboard boxes in the entrance hall as well as in the living room. Bubble-wrapped furniture as well as some covered in plastic wrap were placed around haphazardly. Without any curtains or blinds, Lillian was astounded by the amount of light which streamed into this high-floored flat as well as the unobstructed views she caught from the windows and balcony.

Seeing that the movers were in another room, she tiptoed into the kitchen to see how it was equipped. As she flicked on the lights, she saw the kitchen had been newly renovated, with pristine, glossy-white cabinets as well as a new, built-in Miele cooker and oven.

No wonder the Chan's couldn't afford to pay the mortgage, Lillian thought to herself, *the renovation must have cost them a bomb!* Just as she backed out of the kitchen, she stepped on someone and turned around to see Erika just behind her. Taken aback, Lillian was dazed for a moment or two before she regained her composure.

'Oh gosh! I'm so sorry!' She said as Erika took a step back, putting several inches between them.

Surprised to see someone other than the movers in their apartment, Erika raised her eyebrows and trained a quizzical look at the stranger as if to enquire what Lillian was doing in their newly purchased flat.

When no explanation was forthcoming from Lillian, Erika asked, 'Can I help you?'

'I was er . . . er . . . looking for ehm . . . the property agent,' Lillian stammered, hoping that the well-dressed, Mat Salleh woman standing in front of her would believe her. 'I was told she would be in this flat and I came to look for her as I wanted to enquire about it.'

Sharp as a whistle, Erika could spot a lie (and a liar) from a mile away, but she was feeling charitable that day. Furthermore, she didn't want to embarrass or confront anyone on the first day of moving in.

'The agent isn't here. We are the new owners. Hi! I'm Erika Saunders,' she said, extending a hand.

Just then, Jan walked in with Sonya. The look on her face was also one of curiosity. 'Who's this?' Jan asked, looking at Erika, then at Lillian who by now felt embarrassed at her intrusion.

'I'm not sure,' Erika replied, and then she turned to Lillian who was trying to move away. 'What's your name?'

'My apologies, I'm Lillian and I live in this condo too. I came up as I was told the property agent would be in this flat. I came in because I thought I heard her in the kitchen.'

'No worries,' Jan replied. 'She's not here though'. By now Sonya was getting impatient and wanted something to eat.

'Mamma, I'm hungry!' Sonya called out, tugging Jan's hand.

'In a while sweetie, we'll order pizza.' Jan replied in a maternal tone.

'I better get going, nice meeting both of you!' Lillian said and quickly made her way out of the kitchen and the apartment without even waiting for the new residents to reply.

* * *

A thousand questions reeled in Lillian's mind as she rode the lift down to her apartment. *Who were these people who had just moved in? Where did they come from? What did they do for a living?* And probably the most pertinent question of all which stuck to the forefront of her inquisitive mind was: *Were they a family?*

Needless to say, Lillian's mind was preoccupied for the rest of the day (and night!) ruminating about the new occupants of apartment 25-D. Swirling around her head were so many questions that she even forgot to go grocery shopping, which had been the reason for her being in the car park in the first place.

Getting back to her flat, she quickly called her friend Nisha, whom she had met in the management committee of Harmony Heights. 'Hello Nisha! This is Lillian, how are you? Good? Just wanted to ask you if you've received the minutes of our last committee meeting yet? No? Then I'll call Ms Chew and remind her to send them to us. I'm just curious about the way the tendering process will be conducted for the retiling of our pool.'

And on and on she went about the way the hedges around the swimming pool were not trimmed evenly enough and how the cleaners mopped the common areas in a less than satisfactory manner. Just as she was about to hang up, Lillian asked Nisha if she had heard of anyone moving into apartment 25-D.

'I saw some movers today carrying furniture into the apartment and met the new owners. It must have been a quick sale, as the Chan's moved out not too long ago. Who are they? Two women and a little child.'

Before Nisha could reply, Lillian heard her father call out from his bedroom. Abruptly ending the call, she told Nisha she had to go and hung up. Her father who was in his late eighties must have been hungry. 'What is it, Pa? Do you want something to eat?'

As she walked into his bedroom, piled with clothes, newspapers, and boxes, she saw her father sprawled out on his bed, his body shrivelled up. He was just wrinkled skin covering a skeletal frame. His head was propped up on a pillow and he bore a lifeless expression. Having been diagnosed with Alzheimer's, one of the most common forms of dementia, the burden of caregiving had now fallen squarely on Lillian.

On closer inspection, she saw a wet patch on the bed sheet around his crotch. 'Oh my God, Pa! You peed on the bed! Why didn't you control yourself! Now the room will stink, and I will have to wash the mattress and change your sheets! It's sooooooo much work for me!'

Growing up as the middle child, Lillian had been the least favoured of Uncle Gan's three children. The old man adored Lillian's youngest sister who was the baby of the family. He used to call her his 'little angel' and used to buy her a gift almost every week. From Barbies and Easy-Bake plastic ovens to Ladybird books and frilly princess dresses, Christine would get everything she wanted. He lavished just as much attention on Lillian's older brother, albeit in a more controlled manner. As the first-born, Uncle Gan wanted Richard to succeed in life and took time to help his eldest son with his homework every night and coached him before his exams.

Somehow, Lillian just fell through the cracks of her parent's affections. Her mother had passed away when Lillian was only twelve years old and her father, Uncle Gan, had been distant and aloof towards her for most of her formative years. If love was in finite supply in the Gan home then Lillian certainly hadn't got her quota.

But life has a funny way of twisting circumstances around and, as it turned out, Lillian's brother migrated to Australia for better prospects for his career and his children's education. He hardly ever returned home. Christine, on the other hand, had followed her husband to Singapore when he was transferred there and since then, little was heard from her. So, the least favoured middle child, Lillian, who had been emotionally neglected and ignored, put-down often times, ridiculed for not being able to find a husband and mocked for not having her own family, was now the sole caregiver for Uncle Gan. If the mother of all ironies could be exemplified in real life, then this must be a shining example.

Chapter 13

After parking her car, Padma grabbed her shopping and headed for the exit to the car park located next to Harmony Heights. She had just finished her twice-weekly food shopping and was headed home to prepare lunch. Entering the lift, she pressed the button for the third floor and just as the lift door was about to close, Nisha, who lived on the twenty-second floor, caught it just in time and managed to get in.

There was an awkward moment when she saw who was in the lift. There was history between the two women, but Nisha didn't care. Of course, Padma didn't speak to her or Sukhminder or any other Indians living in Harmony Heights whether they were Tamil, Punjabi, or even Sindhi, as Nisha was. As the wife of a judge, albeit a retired one, Padma considered herself a cut above them all and having the honorific title of a Datin made her feel even more superior.

When the lift got to the second floor, Lillian got in and being the busybody that she was, she looked at Padma with two huge bags of groceries then winked at Nisha. 'Just finished your shopping?' Lillian asked the obvious to break the ice. Padma gave an uppity nod without activating her vocal chords. 'Where's your driver? Shouldn't he be helping you with your groceries?' Lillian asked, knowing full well that once her husband had retired from the judiciary, they'd had to dispense with the services of their government-supplied chauffeur.

'He's not available today,' Padma replied reluctantly.

Pushing further, Lillian asked again. 'Not available? How come?'

'He only comes when we need him,' came the terse reply from Padma.

'He should be here every day, a Datin like you shouldn't be without one,' the sarcasm almost palpable.

Lillian was about to ask her one more question when Padma was saved by the ping of the lift as it stopped on the sixth floor.

As she walked out hurriedly, both Lillian and Nisha burst out laughing at Padma and the pretence she was putting up.

'That was a nice move, dear,' Nisha said, adding, 'someone should pull that stick out from her ass!' Both of them started giggling again. 'Who the hell does she think she is? Living on the third floor and her husband is just an ex-government servant.' Nisha's second comment revealed an unspoken social distinction through the pecking order of the residents living at Harmony Heights.

There was an invisible hierarchy of status, an unwritten code if you like, whereby it was understood that those who lived on the higher floors were somewhat superior to those who resided on the lower ones, in the case of Harmony Heights, the tenth floor being the watershed. It could be termed as a subtle form of segregation and harsh by any standards as well as superficial and nonsensical, but it was nonetheless embedded into the psyche of the old-timers and long-term residents. This mindset probably originated when the units were first offered for sale by the developer and were priced according to the floor they were situated on.

* * *

Desmond Choo was in a foul mood when he got home that evening. A difficult day at work was compounded by the fact that his nurse had been uncooperative and rude. He couldn't wait to pop a Xanax but he had to eat something first. He was glad he didn't have to stay late that night, as his nerves were frayed. For three nights each week, Desmond turned his clinic into an abortion centre. Of course, it was done on the sly, as it is illegal to perform abortions in Malaysia. But Desmond was making a mint out of it and the money was enough to justify his action.

His wife naturally didn't know anything about it and just thought that he came home late on Monday, Wednesday, and Friday nights because of his legitimate work at the clinic. Being a staunch Christian, she would have been mortified if she ever found out. God forbid.

Desmond used to be religious too, once upon a time. In fact, it was at church that Desmond had met his wife Hway Ping during his last year at medical school. She was seated across the aisle from him during a Sunday service and she caught his eye when she'd dropped the Bible. When he met her for the first time he was attracted to her because of her docile and compliant nature. He felt a new kind of strength and chivalry whenever he was with Hway Ping, something he had never felt before.

The fact that she was emotionally as well as economically dependent on him made him feel purposeful and heroic. It gave Desmond a kind of high. Who would have thought that this initial frisson would turn into a case of toxic co-dependency in its purest form?

As he emerged from the shower and was about to have his dinner, Hway Ping came into the bedroom and started asking him about his day. That was, however, the last thing Desmond wanted to talk about, so he just brushed it aside. But if there was one aspect of Hway Ping's personality which was in sharp contrast to her usual timid self, it was her persistence. She wanted to know about how the nurses in his clinic were doing and what he had for lunch that day and whether it was a fruitful day in terms of takings.

When Desmond expressed his dislike to her line of questioning by snapping back at her, Hway Ping retaliated by nervously launching into a lecture about how God sees and notes everything, which drew his ire even further.

It had first started with a small push and shove. But when Desmond's anger grew bigger and greater, he slapped her on her upper arm once or twice. Finally, when she summoned the courage to answer back after he yelled at her, he raised his hand and hit Hway Ping on her face. For a few seconds after he first hit her, there was a shocked expression on her face and a deafening silence. It was as if she couldn't believe that Desmond would ever hit her.

But hit her he did and since then, whenever she irritated him and got him angry with her occasional acts of bravado, he struck her. He noticed lately that she had been acting up more frequently. *Was someone influencing her?* He had already warned her not to speak of this to their neighbours or to anyone else for that matter. But what Desmond didn't realize was that a cornered dog is more likely to turn and bite, or in Hway Ping's case, bark.

Initially, she had been cowering and fearful of him. Afraid he might cut her off financially as he had done several times before. After any nasty fight, Desmond would usually exert his alpha-male status by depriving Hway Ping of her monthly allowance. This was a vindictive move on his part, but it was his way of showing her who was the boss. Cross me and you'll pay, was Desmond's modus operandi.

And to get reinstated in his good books Hway Ping had to go back to square one and become agreeable and obedient again—to acquiesce to his whims and wishes. That was what happened time and time again and the cycle kept repeating itself. Desmond did the same with Yi Wei. When she wanted to take fashion instead of pharmacology, Desmond threatened to not pay for her university fees. Using money as a weapon was the only way he could regain control over both of them.

Chapter 14

'How was your lunch?' Padma quizzed Shivana the minute she entered the flat, last Friday after her lunch date. 'I hope you weren't late. Did Dinesh enjoy himself?' Ever since her daughter had started dating Dinesh, Padma had been on high alert. Shivana's previous boyfriend did not meet Padma's standards and as such, she had withheld her approval. She secretly hoped during those times that Shivana would somehow come to her senses and see that she was merely wasting her time with him. What prospects did a personal trainer have?

Shivana had met Kevin in her gym when she had signed up for a personal training package and he had asked her out. *He is fit and handsome but that isn't enough to start a life with my daughter*, thought Padma. She refused to acknowledge Kevin and showed her disapproval blatantly. Even though he was Tamil, just like them, Padma wanted someone better for her only child.

Dinesh was another matter. Hailing from a well-to-do Sindhi family, he was quite the catch in Padma's eye. She always believed that one should marry up and not in the other direction. It had been the same thing with her own husband. When she met Gopi, he was a bright shining star in the legal profession. He had just joined the Attorney General's Chambers as an assistant district public prosecutor. While Padma didn't have a college degree, she had trained as a legal clerk. A chance meeting with Gopi in the courtroom sealed the deal for Padma.

She gave up her work soon after marriage to start a family. But she had multiple problems conceiving a child and gave birth to Shivana in her early forties, just as she was about to resign herself to the fate of being childless. It was a blessing from Lord Ganesh who she believed removed all the obstacles in her path and allowed her to have a child. She prayed to him twice every day for years. She also prayed endlessly to the holy trinity of Brahma, Vishnu, and Shiva, the divine creator, preserver, and destroyer. And then there was the goddess Lakshmi. As a woman, Padma connected most closely with this goddess who represented wealth, fortune, and beauty. Who didn't want all three?

Glancing at Shivana walking into her bedroom, Padma noticed how loosely her clothes hung on her body. Her jeans were loose even though they were supposed to be skinny jeans. Her chiffon leopard print blouse was billowing as Shivana strode past her. But Padma just brushed it off. Her daughter was always svelte. It was probably all that tennis she was playing.

What she didn't know was that as soon as Shivana got into her bedroom, she recounted in her head what she had eaten at lunch with Dinesh. A vegetarian lasagne covered with cheese tasted good but now she felt bloated and nauseous. Throwing her Gucci handbag on the floor, Shivana rushed to the toilet and knelt down before she shoved her index and middle fingers down her throat and threw up.

* * *

Looking into the rear-view mirror from the back seat, Candy was able to study Shamsul better. She noticed her driver's eye looked slightly puffy and bloodshot. But apart from that, there was a distant faraway look in his eyes, and this made her feel uneasy. Several times, she called or WhatsApped him to pick her up and he didn't pick up or answer for a good ten to fifteen minutes. This annoyed her but she put it down to his lackadaisical attitude.

Shamsul had been working for them for about nine months already but like everything else, there were some things she liked about him and some things she didn't. She knew there was no perfect employee. Heck, she herself wasn't a perfect employer. She was willing to overlook some of Shamsul's shortcomings but of late he had been slipping. Forgetting to pick up her twins at kindergarten a few weeks ago was one. She'd hit the roof when she had found out and had given him a stern warning.

That was why she had decided to go along to pick up Max and Melissa today. She thought that if she went along with him a few times, he would realize that she meant business.

As she approached the kindergarten, she saw someone familiar at the entrance. She had seen this woman before but just couldn't place her. A Chinese lady with an Indian child stood out wherever she went. When Max and Melissa got into her Vellfire, Candy was happy to see them. When Candy and Terence had first found out she was expecting twins, Candy didn't really know what to think. She hadn't known anyone who was a twin and none of her family members had twins.

But as it turned out, it was truly a blessing. Having fraternal twins in Chinese culture was seen as a blessing of good luck and fortune. For Candy, who didn't enjoy the experience of being pregnant, it meant she didn't have to go through it again. If it had been two girls, she would have definitely had to try for a son but, in this case, her duties as a wife were done and dusted. She had killed two birds, or produced two heirs, with one stone.

When Candy arrived back at Harmony Heights, her driver dropped her and her two children at the main entrance and then drove the MPV to the car park. It was his lunch hour, so he looked forward to having some time off. Most of his free time was spent in a spare apartment that had been converted into a utility and storeroom as well as in Terence's home office on the thirty-sixth floor, a floor above the main entrance to Candy's penthouse.

It was there that he would eat, rest, and do any minor repair work that needed to be done. Apart from being a chauffeur, Shamsul was also in charge of maintenance around the Fong's home. Replacing a light bulb in their chandelier, changing a fuse, or fixing the water heater, he could carry out minor repairs due to his past experience as an electrician.

Walking into her walk-in wardrobe, Candy did a quick scan of her evening outfits, as she had to choose something to wear that evening for a dinner Terence and her had been invited to. She hated wearing black, which explained why her extensive closet was a profusion of colours and prints. Candy clicked on the remote control and the motorized clothes rack started moving. She sat on her fringed velvet ottoman and waited till the conveyor reached the letter S, as she wanted to wear a Saint Laurent pink and yellow sequin embroidered shift dress in silk georgette.

Having selected her outfit for the night, she walked to the adjoining room where floor to ceiling glass cabinets that were lit with LED-lights from within housed her collection of handbags. The way she arranged her bags was markedly different from the way she organized her clothes. Instead of grouping them by designers, her precious handbags were grouped by colour because it somehow seemed easier for her to find a handbag by colour after she chose her outfit. Looking at her collection of pink handbags, she initially fancied the Delvaux Brillant Mini in Bloom Pink but then she switched her attention to the Bottega Veneta's Jodi mini knot Hobo bag. Suddenly she thought of her pink Rose Tyrien Birkin in Epsom leather but a quick search amongst the other pink bags yielded nothing. *How strange,* she thought. She hadn't used that bag for some time and hadn't seen it either. She tried to remember if she had given it to the bag spa for cleaning, but she was sure she hadn't.

Buzzing her maid on the intercom, she asked Lucia to come up immediately. 'Have you seen my pink Birkin bag?' She asked her Filipino maid as soon as she appeared.

Lucia, whose main responsibility was to take care of Candy's needs as well as her clothes and personal effects, quickly answered. 'No ma'am, I haven't.'

'When did you last clean this room?' Candy asked, trying to modulate the tone of her voice so as not to appear alarmed or angry.

Pausing for a few seconds to think, Lucia then remembered. 'About three days ago.'

'Was anyone with you in this room?' Candy continued her cross-examination of her maid.

'I was alone ma'am.'

'You took the key from the locked cabinet downstairs, ya?'

'Yes ma'am.'

'Okay. Can you help me look for it in the other room? I already looked all over in this room and it's not here. Can you remember if I gave it to the bag spa?'

'No, you didn't ma'am.'

Chapter 15

It all started with signing up to TikTok when someone in Yi Wei's college showed her a make-up tutorial on this hot new social media app where one could make and share fifteen-second video clips. She couldn't wait to try it when she got home and immediately set up her iPhone to record a how-to eye make-up video.

Like Instagram and Snapchat before, after a while Yi Wei got bored of it. She made about twenty make-up tutorials—from applying foundation and blusher to face contouring and creating pouty lips. There was only so much you could do with your face and Yi Wei did it all. She didn't get that many views, which also discouraged her.

One day, she chanced upon an OnlyFans while scrolling through Twitter. It intrigued her and after watching an episode of 60 Minutes Australia, which exposed how much money a content creator could make from OnlyFans, she decided to give it a go.

And from the get-go, it took off. She firstly created an alias and called herself Sherilyn. No one used their real names for an OnlyFans account due to the somewhat sensitive nature of the videos. Yi Wei thought about it for some time before she created her account. As a content subscription platform, OnlyFans had originally been used by fitness trainers, chefs, and musicians amongst others to monetize their content, whatever it was. It quickly evolved and became synonymous with its X-rated content whereby those brave enough to bare it all or engage in explicit sexual acts could make money from subscribers—or so-called fans, who'd either pay a monthly subscription or a one-off fee.

So far, so good, thought Yi Wei to herself. She wasn't going to tell anybody, not even her closest friend about what she was going to do. 'They can't trace me, it will be anonymous and I'm in control,' she said aloud to herself. And besides, what she was going to show wouldn't be categorized under a R18 rating, as she would be clothed through her recordings, even though it would be scanty.

Her first attempts at filming a video had been a disaster. Apart from the technical aspect of it—the lighting was way too harsh and the camera angles made her look stumpy— Yi Wei's movements were awkward to say the least. It certainly looked amateurish, and she knew no one was ever going to pay any money to look at it.

But Yi Wei, or Sherilyn as she was known on OnlyFans, persisted. She was determined to eke out victory and make some much-needed and hard-earned cash so she could do what she wanted. She practised after lectures and late into the night. She studied music videos of Cardi B, Nicki Minaj, and anyone else who had made twerking their trademark. Yi Wei's persistence and consistency became her calling card at this new part-time job which promised riches and financial independence. Or at least enough money not to be dependent on her father.

As part of her arsenal, Yi Wei bought sexy and revealing lingerie and sky-high stilettos. She amped up her make-up, adding bright red lipstick, smoky seductive eyes, and fluttering false eyelashes. She grew out her hair and then highlighted it so it fell seductively around her shoulders as she posed and preened at her iPhone.

But her efforts paid off. It took Yi Wei three months and numerous dry runs to finally get the courage to post a video— which she deemed passable—on OnlyFans. Confined to just her queen-sized bed, Yi Wei was dressed in a black lace bra and panties with black leather patent stilettos as she danced and hammed it up to Rihanna's 'Only Girl in the World'. She tried to obscure her face by letting her long, luscious locks cover half of it but with her heavy 'Lady Marmalade' bordello-inspired make-up, no one would be able to recognize her anyway.

Sure, it was NSFM-material and for a conservative country like Malaysia, it might be a tad too risqué. But it was something she would wear and do in private anyway. *So why not make some money out of it*, she thought. Of course, what her parents would think if they ever found out was a fear that did enter her mind. As a regular church-goer, her mum would freak out. But how could she find out unless someone told her? That was the risk Yi Wei was prepared to take.

As for her father, she was getting tired of him constantly using money to control and threaten her. A wrong word or a slight rebellion on her part, and he would threaten to cut her off financially. When she wanted to get a tattoo on her arm, he warned her he would stop paying for her college fee. After a particularly nasty fight, he also stopped giving her mother her monthly allowance.

If his wife became financially independent, that would mean a loss of control for him and he didn't want that. For his wife to be able to earn her own living and be financially independent would apparently emasculate him. It was probably his upbringing, where his father had been the sole breadwinner, or his type A personality that made him a control freak. Whatever it was, having both his wife and daughter dependent on him and under his control made him feel great and fed his ego.

* * *

Although their apartment was only partially furnished, Jan could already visualize how their home would look. They had already ordered the child-friendly linen sofa and their dining table was arriving the following week. Jan made sure their beds and mattresses were delivered before they moved in so they could at least sleep comfortably on their first night while their personal effects were slowly being unpacked.

On their first day in the new apartment and while Sonya was doing some colouring on the floor, Jan took out a white sage bundle and lit it slowly. She wanted to smudge the apartment before Erika got home. She believed that energy, whether good or bad, resided in any dwelling, especially if other people had lived there before, and burning sage would rid the apartment of all unwanted energy.

'What's that smell, mamma?' Sonya asked, looking at Jan walking around, moving her arms while holding a smoking bunch of dried leaves.

'I'm cleaning the place, darling. As we just moved in, our new home needs to be cleaned.'

'Don't you clean with a vacuum mamma?'

Jan just smiled at Sonya. 'Yes, we do but there are many different ways of cleaning.'

'Mummy, can we go swimming?' Sonya asked Jan after fifteen minutes of smudging.

'Sure, we can. Just let me finish up here and we can go now,' Jan replied softly while waving smoke from the burning sage to a corner of the living room.

'Can you find your swimsuit?' She asked Sonya. 'I think I packed it in your overnight bag.'

* * *

Candy was lying on a sun lounger in her vibrantly coloured Missoni zigzag print halter neck, one-piece swimsuit with a huge floppy straw hat when she saw a woman and child walking towards the swimming pool. She recognized them immediately as the mother and daughter she'd seen at her children's school earlier today. As Jan walked past, Candy lowered her sunglasses and smiled at her.

'Hi! I think I saw you at Mont Kiara International School today,' Candy said. 'I'm Candy.'

'Hey Candy, it must have been me, I was there picking up my daughter. I'm Jan by the way.'

'Nice to meet you Jan. How old is your daughter?' Candy asked, smiling at Sonya who was clutching a unicorn pool float and itching to jump in the pool.

'She's five, Candy. Can I sit next to you?' Jan gestured to the empty lounger next to Candy.

'For sure, but we are in the shade though. If you want to get some sun, the far end would be better.'

'It's good here, I can keep an eye on Sonya.'

After putting Sonya at the shallow end of the pool and settling down, the two women started chit-chatting. Candy found out that Jan had moved in recently and she and her partner Erika had moved to Malaysia from Sydney about a month ago. Jan was originally from KL but had gone to study in Australia and after graduating, she hadn't returned. Erika, though, had been born and bred in Sydney. Jan found Candy extremely simpatico and didn't pry into her personal affairs. But what was most endearing to Jan was that Candy didn't look at Jan as if she was some strange and exotic species living an unconventional life.

Candy, on the other hand, was disarmed by Jan's warm and open demeanour. She was honest and straightforward with nary a thing to hide. She didn't put on any airs, which Candy found very refreshing, as it was very different from the way people acted in the social circles she usually moved in.

After a few minutes of chatting, Candy had to go, as she had to get ready for dinner.

'It was lovely meeting you Jan. Hope to see more of you now that you are living here,' Candy said while slipping a turquoise silk georgette Alia Bastamam tunic over her swimsuit.

'Likewise, Candy. See you around.'

Chapter 16

To an outsider looking in, it appeared that Candy Fong was a woman who had everything. Fine-boned and slim-bodied with a flawless, porcelain complexion, she was pretty by any definition—not in the beauty queen kind of way but through an innate elegance that was the result of her pampered and privileged upbringing. Cultivating an air of hauteur, Candy exuded a prissy kind of glamour—slightly aloof yet enigmatic—a trait some people found off-putting while others found strangely appealing. But while her aura might have been illusory, there was no illusion about her pedigree. Anyone looking at her would surmise that she came from a well-to-do family. From the top of her professionally-coiffed head to the tip of her Christian Louboutin-shoed feet and everything in-between, she spelt wealth. The way she accessorized, dressed, or looked couldn't have been achieved without deep pockets. Educated in an international school and then shipped off to university in the UK, Candy really had her life mapped out for her from the day she was born.

Of course, she had been expected to marry someone of equal wealth and stature and of a similar background. And she didn't disappoint her parents when she tied the knot with Terence Fong, the eldest son of a construction tycoon. Giving birth to fraternal twins—Max and Melissa put the plump cherry on top of her well-decorated cake. She did all that was expected of her and fulfilled her life's purpose, all at the grand old age of thirty-six years.

But was this it? Isn't there more? Anything else to strive for? *Yes, no and maybe.* The answers came to Candy in a flash.

She didn't really have a career because she wasn't expected to have one. She had worked for a short while in her father's property development company when she'd first came back after graduating. Armed with her psychology and counselling degree, she had toyed with the idea of starting her own business, probably in fashion or beauty but then she'd gotten pregnant soon after getting married and any germ of a business had to be put on the back burner.

She could go back and work for her dad, but her elder brother was doing a fine job, and she didn't want to interfere. Furthermore, property development wasn't where her interest lay. She had the luxury of choice but sometimes having too many options was also a disadvantage. It made her catatonic and impervious to any ambition she might have had.

But for the time being, she was content attending fashion shows and meeting her friends for two-hour lunches, picking up her kids from school, and getting her nails done. Empty? Well, if one were judgemental then maybe it was meaningless. Nevertheless, it was a life less ordinary, undoubtedly privileged, and indulgent but evidently not cheap, simple, or meaningful.

But what it lacked in substance, Candy made up for with superficial follies.

* * *

When Zainal got home, Azizah was sitting in the living room watching TV. He could smell the delicious curry wafting out from the kitchen. Azizah didn't get up to greet him but that was alright. Zainal noticed that his wife had been out of sorts of late. Forgetful, repeating herself, agitated easily and occasionally bad tempered. He put it down to her menopause. What else could it be? They didn't have money problems. He wasn't cheating on her. Their daughter was doing okay at university.

The only thing he had to gripe about was her spending. It was getting out of hand. Her credit card bills last month amounted to the high five figures. So far, he hadn't brought it up, but he thought he better put out a warning signal soon before it escalated into something serious.

'How was your doctor's appointment today?' Zainal asked his wife while seated at the dining table. 'All clear?'

Helping herself to some *sambal petai* with prawns, Azizah answered reluctantly, 'Dr Rahaina did some tests and we're waiting for the results but from the symptoms I told her she thinks it's just hormonal changes my body is going through,' Azizah replied. 'She might refer me to some other specialists.' Azizah didn't just yet want to tell her husband that it was a psychiatrist who her gynaecologist was referring her to.

'And are you up for the top job any time soon?' Azizah asked with a tinge of sarcasm and in effect deflecting her husband's attention away from her health issues.

'My time will come when the time is right,' Zainal replied patiently, his tone indicating that was the end of the matter and he didn't want to talk about his career prospects with her any longer, or at least on this occasion.

As the Chief Operation Officer (COO) of his insurance company, Zainal was the second-in-command to the CEO. He was in charge of executing the CEO's vision for the company and managing all its internal operations. It wasn't just a supervisory role even though the day-to-day operations of the company fell very much within his purview.

But being second fiddle wasn't good enough for Azizah. Her competitive streak was still intact despite having left the labour market years ago. She didn't like the fact that Zainal had to report to Datuk Wahid Abdullah, the current CEO. All those company dinners she'd had to attend and butter up Wahid and his odious wife made her sick to the core. But as the dutiful wife whose husband was a cog in the wheel, she knew her role and how to play the game.

Her mind begin working overtime. She thought about the similarity in Zainal and Wahid's ages and how both of them had started around the same time at the company. Yes, both of them rose through the ranks and managed to scale the summit but while Wahid got to the top and planted his flag, Zainal remained a step behind, the Sherpa to Wahid's pioneer. There was no glory in that. Zainal was just playing a supporting role in the big picture, the back-up chorus in a rock concert.

'We can't wait forever, you know. Time is against us. Look at our ages. You have reached the peak of your earning potential already. Wait any longer and you'll be due for retirement. Why don't you put out feelers to see if there are any top jobs out there? You have already got a vast wealth of experience at Tawfik. If Wahid doesn't budge, you'll be his assistant forever!'

'I'm not his assistant!' Zainal exclaimed, his voice edging a notch higher. 'I'm the COO and that's an important position.'

'Yes, it is important, but does the board know that too? Sorry to say this but you are not indispensable. If the tide turns against you for whatever reason, they'll get rid of you in a minute. A call to any headhunter would tell you that a COO can be as easily replaced as a punctured tyre. Please think of the long-term picture and look out for your, our, interest. Tawfik Insurance will easily survive with or without your contribution.'

Whoa! That was a torrent of career advice coming at Zainal and after a long hard day at the office, it was the last thing he needed to hear. As usual he kept silent and uttered some fillers for Azizah's sake, just to acknowledge that he had noted what she was saying.

Later that evening while getting ready to go to bed, what his wife had told him played through his mind again. Disposable, indispensable, and easily replaced sounded a lot like the loud banging gong in his head. He admitted that there was a kernel of truth in what she had said. The corporate world was full of skulduggery, and backstabbings. Azizah was right; one slight disagreement with Wahid and he could perceive it as disloyalty and then scheme to obliterate him. He'd seen Wahid do it to other people before, so why not him too?

On Azizah's part, she felt like she had crossed the line a little bit but not much. The truth had to be told and the facts laid out, otherwise Zainal wouldn't or couldn't see the bigger picture and would just plod along aimlessly. It was true that none of them were getting any younger, and with her menopausal symptoms being a constant reminder of time slipping away, she had to shake her husband up. Sometimes one gets so engrossed in daily matters of what's right in front of you that one forgets to look up and see what's beyond. This was Zainal's problem. He didn't have foresight, the ability to view things from a macro perspective. *This is probably why he didn't become the CEO*, she thought to herself.

But all was not lost, as Azizah had a plan which might help him get to the top spot. It wasn't complicated or difficult. But it was the last resort. Sometimes you couldn't do everything by yourself and needed a little help. With that thought, Azizah put Zainal's career aside and focused on inviting a few friends over for tea the next day. She had to catch up with the other ladies staying in Harmony Heights, if only to have some companionship, otherwise she might just as well go out of her mind. Who would she invite and what would she serve? Widya was competent enough to prepare anything she asked. In that department, Azizah felt lucky. Thinking of Widya, she remembered that she wanted to ask her maid if she had seen her gold bracelet from Habib Jewels—an anniversary gift from Zainal—that she had placed on her dresser a few days ago. Azizah was certain she had taken it off before her shower and placed it on a tray on her dresser. But today when she'd been looking for it, she couldn't find it.

Chapter 17

When Terence Fong dropped by the management office the next morning to sign some documents and cheques, Arumugam briefed him on several issues regarding the renewal of contracts with several service providers. As the chairman of the management committee, Terence was inundated with hundreds of issues pertaining to the general maintenance and upkeep of Harmony Heights. It was almost a full-time job for him, which consumed a lot of his time, except that this job was voluntary and unpaid.

Anything as major as repainting the building or installing fibre optic cables to improve the speed of the internet for all the residents, to something as minor as repairing a leaking water pipe or replacing the CCTV cameras in the car parks, had to be mooted and discussed with the other committee members and given the green light by Terence. As a building contractor, Terence had an edge over the rest, as he knew about all these issues and how he would go about dealing with them.

Today, he had to deal with the replacement of the floor tiles in the lobby. When any major repair work had to be done and a third-party contractor had to be appointed to carry out the job, it was usually done through an open tender system. This meant that any contractor could submit a tender to bid for the job in question. But as the replacement of the floor tiles was an urgent need, a selective tender was agreed upon, wherein contractors who had worked with the management committee previously and done work for the condominium before, were invited to bid. In this case, Terence's family construction company of which he was the CEO was one of the few selected and they, not surprisingly, won the bid.

Some nitpicking residents might wonder if the chairman of the management committee would be the ideal person to carry out these repairs and renovations, as there might appear to be a conflict of interest. However, so far, no one at Harmony Heights queried this arrangement, as his family's company was the contractor that had built the condo.

'The new owners for apartment 25-D have just moved in,' Arumugan informed Terence while he was signing some documents.

'Oh! That's quick, the Chan's moved out already?' Terence asked.

'Yes, it was a quick sale,' Arumugam told him without mentioning that the flat was in pre-foreclosure.

'Who are they?' Terence asked without looking up from his papers.

'Hmm . . . it's two ladies with a child.'

'Oh, I see. I'll have to organize a gathering for them then. Could you give me their names and contact number so I can WhatsApp them?'

Just then, Ms Chew walked in and gave Terence several cheques to sign. It was part of the standard operating procedure that any withdrawals from the condo's bank accounts had to be signed by two people, namely the chairman and the building manager. As Terence looked through the cheques, he saw that they were for the monthly expenses and fees to the service providers such as the security company that supplied the guards, the gardening company that Iqbal worked for, the property management company that employed Arumugam and Ms Chew as well as utility bills for the electricity, water, and internet amongst others.

When Terence got back to his penthouse, he WhatsApped his wife to see if she was home. As it happened, she was in and watching TV in the upstairs hall.

'Hi darling,' he called out as he reached the top of the curved staircase and saw Candy. She was lying supine on the L-shaped sofa with Coco, who immediately jumped down and ran to Terence.

'Hi Terence, you are home early, a quiet day in the office?' Candy enquired as she sat up and turned to face him.

'I was just in the management office signing some cheques. You know I won the bid for replacing the tiles for the lobby.' Terence said while bending down and scooping up the fluffy white toy-like dog in his arms.

'Oh God! You mean you bid for it? You know what the residents here are like? The slightest chance they get, they will jump at you. It's not worth it. You don't need this job, do you?' Candy asked.

'No, I don't, but as it was a selective tender and as our company built the condo and pool, I was entitled to bid.' Terence replied. 'By the way, we need to invite the new owners for 25-D. Apparently, they just moved in, as they bought the apartment in a quick sale.'

'The Chan's moved out already? I didn't know that.'

'They just managed to sell the unit before the foreclosure by the bank.'

'Oh dear! That's so sad. The poor Chans. They were a nice family. Their kids were always asking about Coco when I saw them in the lift. I hope that they have found a place to stay.'

'Yeah, I spoke to Mr Chan a few times too. I think he was made redundant by his company. Can't be easy.'

'Who are the new owners?' Candy asked her husband.

'Arumugam told me it was two ladies and their child.'

'Oh! Gosh! Yes! Now I remember. I think I met them at the pool a couple of days ago! Her name is Jan and she's got an adopted daughter.'

'Are they a couple?' Terence asked while giving his wife a mildly quizzical glance.

'I don't know Terence, I just met one of them. But if we are inviting them over for dinner then we'll soon find out.'

* * *

It was customary for the chairman of the management committee of Harmony Heights to invite any new owner of a unit to dinner to welcome them into the building. As both Terence and Candy were planning an anniversary party, they decided to combine it with the welcoming dinner.

Candy enjoyed the time she had spent planning for her eighth wedding anniversary party despite the usual minor hiccup, which, in her case, was that of not being able to secure the caterer she normally used. She had enjoyed chatting with Jan when they met at the pool and was looking forward to seeing her again. She had shortlisted several new caterers and had also booked a pianist to entertain her guests. She had a Steinway baby grand which was placed at the entrance of the foyer of her penthouse, just at the bottom of the curved staircase. The poor thing hadn't been played for aeons and she wanted to hear its keys tinkle again.

Eight was an auspicious number for any Chinese couple and that being the number of years she was married meant it called for a celebration. She took a few days to draw out her guest list, which included a mix of good friends and acquaintances. It couldn't be as small and intimate as she would have liked, as she had to invite the management committee of Harmony Heights as well as some of the residents.

But it had been a long time since she had thrown any sort of party in their home, and she wanted to bring out her Halcyon Days and Noritake China dinner service and was keen to engage the new caterer that everyone had been talking about.

Specializing in combining different cuisines (she hated the word fusion) to create something fresh and unique, Klute Kitchen was making waves in all the smart and beautifully decorated homes of KL for the past year, and Candy just couldn't wait to try them out.

Chapter 18

There were just three qualities that Padma looked for in a son-in-law. That he be healthy—so he could spawn her grandchildren; wealthy—so her only daughter would live a comfortable life; and wise—so he would realize what a good match Shivana was for him. So simple, yet it had been so difficult. The previous boyfriend Shivana had left a lot to be desired in Padma's mind. She had hoped and prayed that her daughter would come to her senses and realize that Kevin was not a suitable partner. He wasn't husband material. How could a personal trainer support her daughter, and if they had children, be the breadwinner for the entire family?

Heaven forbid that she and Gopi would have to support them if they ever tied the knot. No, no, no! The divinities must have heard her pleas and prayers and when Shivana broke up with Kevin, she was over the moon. When Shivana met Dinesh, she couldn't believe her luck. Shivana might have thought it was a chance meeting, but it wasn't really.

Padma had known that the scion of the Lakliani clan would be present at a wedding in Bali and she managed to acquire an invitation for Shivana. She then arranged for a friend's daughter to introduce Dinesh Lakliani to Shivana. After all that planning, she prayed hard that they would hit it off. Again, the gods must have been listening to her because Padma was beyond thrilled when they kept in touch after Shivana returned from Bali. She egged and pestered Shivana to call Dinesh and even asked her to invite him over for dinner one night.

As a young, dutiful daughter, Shivana was wise in some aspects of her life but still quite naïve in other aspects. Easily manipulated by her scheming mother, Shivana always thought both her parents only wanted the best for her and to that end, she never questioned their motives for getting her to do this or that. In a way, she was right. But sometimes, parents like Padma don't realize that children must make important life choices on their own, even if they know it's a huge mistake.

* * *

After reading Sonya not one but two bedtime stories—tonight it was *Perfect Soup*, a cute story about a mouse with perfectionist tendencies going in search of making soup and the different characters he meets along the way. And the other was by a Malaysian children's author, Emilia Yusof, called *My Mother's Kitchen*. Jan had unpacked Sonya's belongings earlier and took out the book *Heather Has Two Mummies* but was saving it for later, when they were more settled.

After Sonya had drifted off to sleep, Jan left the child's room to join Erika in the living room and thus began her favourite time of the day (or night). This was the time when both Jan and Erika could talk about how their day went, what happened, their joys and frustrations as well as discuss their plans for the immediate future.

'I met a really nice resident at the pool yesterday while taking Sonya for a swim,' Jan began while Erika logged off her MacBook Air.

'Really? What's her name?' Erika asked. 'Which floor does she live on?'

'Candy and she didn't say, but she saw me picking up Sonya at kindergarten, as her twins go to the same school.'

'Great, did Sonya play with them?'

'No, her children weren't with her, but we did agree to introduce them.'

Apart from Lillian, whom Jan and Erika had bumped into while she was snooping around in their flat, they hadn't really met anyone else yet.

Jan's part-time job allowing her to pick up Sonya from school and work from home on some days was a godsend. But she couldn't do everything she wanted without these flexi-hours. She thought about hiring a maid and going in full-time but until she found a trustworthy one, she would rather do it herself. Her anxiety disorder made her very particular about who she allowed in their home.

Erika usually left matters of the home to Jan, as she knew she was perfectly capable. Unless, of course, there was something major that needed Erika's input. This was where the balance of responsibilities lay in their relationship.

When they'd first met each other at a self-improvement workshop, Jan had just broken up with a man she'd been in a long-term relationship with. They were supposed to get married, but things hadn't worked out when he'd said that he wanted to return to Malaysia to join his family business while Jan had wanted to stay on in Sydney. At that time, Jan had not been ready to come back home and something in her had told her to stay on. That was when she met Erika and her world just turned around.

She'd never felt the same way with any man; the way she felt with Erika. Everything felt real and right. She didn't feel the need to justify anything. She knew deep down that all her past experiences with men had prepared her for this relationship. She'd had fantasies about being with other women even before this but had dismissed them, as she hadn't been ready yet. Now, when she had come into her own, she knew there couldn't be anything else.

'When's the rest of the furniture arriving?' Erika asked, breaking her from her reverie. 'We're lucky the previous owners just renovated the apartment and put in a brand-new kitchen before they sold it.'

'Yes, we are lucky. Everything should be delivered in the next two weeks. We have to get a few more things for our bedroom and the guest room but the main things have been ordered already,' Jan replied.

'Great. I'll go to the management office tomorrow to meet the manager. There was a letter in our mailbox informing us that there are a few things we have to sign and collect.'

* * *

'Just SHUT UP!' Desmond Choo yelled at the top of his voice to Hway Ping. No one irritated him as much as his wife and tonight she was particularly annoying. She had started whining about needing help with the housework and how late Desmond seemed to come back every night from his clinic and about Yi Wei constantly locking herself up in her bedroom and not helping out at all with the household chores. Yi Wei, her mind occupied with her coursework and content for her OnlyFans, just sat there looking belligerent.

Hway Ping had wanted Desmond to employ a maid for her, but Desmond felt she was capable of taking care of everything on her own. After all, she was a full-time homemaker. If they employed a maid, what would his wife do with all the spare time she had on her hands? Continue to overthink things and then nag him when he came back from work? No siree!

Bringing out her ginger and cilantro steamed fish dish and stir-fried *choy sum* to the dining table, Hway Ping remained silent after being shouted at. But her passive-aggressive stance didn't serve her well, not tonight anyway.

'Where's the *kam heong* chicken from last night?' Desmond asked curtly. Shrugging her shoulders, Hway Ping didn't look at her husband who was growing more impatient by the second. Taking her seat at the dining table, she just helped herself to the food and started eating.

'I asked you where last night's chicken is!' Desmond demanded.

Hway Ping continued to eat and just ignored him.

Desmond felt a fireball of anger rise from the pit of his stomach and move rapidly to his head and then his limbs and hands. That's when he swung his arms and struck Hway Ping on her face.

'Owwwww!' Hway Ping exclaimed in pain.

Just then, Yi Wei jumped up from her seat at the dining table and ran towards her mother who was, by now, holding her face, shielding herself from Desmond whose face had turned bright red. Yi Wei grabbed her mother and pulled her away from her father. She felt anger mixed with shame and fear. Angry that her father would resort to violence towards her mother and shame that this was what her parents had resorted to when they could not resolve their differences. Her fear came from knowing what the repercussions of this altercation would be—Desmond would withdraw emotionally from them and punish her mother by financially starving them. Money was Desmond's weapon of choice. And so were his hands.

Chapter 19

Azizah used to be on the management committee of Harmony Heights until the last annual general meeting when she had decided to resign. She didn't particularly enjoy spending hours discussing and arguing over humdrum matters like replacing water filters or rectifying sewage pumps. But she did enjoy the friends she had made on the committee, particularly with the other women.

The women committee members used to meet informally once a month either for lunch or tea when time permitted, and even after Azizah left, the four women continued to meet. All four took turns to host and today it was Azizah's turn. She invited Lillian Gan, Sukhminder, and Nisha to her place for tea and she was looking forward to seeing them.

She liked to get updates about the committee and what else was happening, but if the truth be told, it was the gossip which she relished and delighted in, and the three other women provided that in bucketfuls.

She had asked Widya to bake a pound cake for this occasion, but the other three ladies also usually brought food as a courtesy. Lillian was the first to arrive at 3 p.m. sharp, bearing a box of curry puffs. Ten minutes later, Nisha turned up with her home-made chocolate brownies that were also a best-seller from her home baking business. She was followed by Sukhminder, who brought an assortment of Indian snacks like vadai and samosas.

After Widya served them tea, they settled down in Azizah's comfy living room with its teak furniture and fluffy cushions. It was located in front of the open balcony, thus allowing a light breeze to blow in. Naturally, it would be Lillian to break the news about the new residents on the twenty-fifth floor.

'There's a new family that just moved into 25-D,' she said excitedly. 'I bumped into them in the midst of them moving in,' she continued, conveniently omitting the part where she had trespassed into their flat to snoop around.

'The Chans moved out so quickly already?' Sukhminder asked.

'Yes, it was a quick sale, as the bank was about to foreclose on the apartment. I wonder how much they bought it for!' Lillian wondered aloud.

'Who are the new owners?' Azizah asked, curious because even though she lived four floors below, she hadn't seen them yet.

'Okay, this is it. It's two women and their daughter.' Lillian stated, trying her best to keep any judgment out of her statement.

'Two women and their daughter?' Nisha repeated, raising her arched eyebrows and thereby enlarging her already huge, kohl-lined eyes.

A momentary silence followed until Sukhminder's first crunch into a deep-fried curry puff broke it.

'I'm sure they are not from here,' Nisha said. 'Where are they from?'

'Okay, the masculine one is *Mat Salleh*, the feminine one is Chinese, and their daughter is Indian.'

With three pairs of eyes looking quizzically at Lillian, it began to sink in that a same-sex couple had moved into Harmony Heights and a modern family would be living amongst them.

At this point, Azizah, who enjoyed a good bit of gossip as much as the next person, spoke. 'You're sure the two women are a couple?' She asked Lillian who was devouring a slice of Azizah's pound cake.

'200 per cent sure,' came Lillian's reply. 'I met them and introduced myself.'

Changing the subject at this point would have been the proper thing to do, as the three ladies could see that Azizah looked uncomfortable. But what she said next flummoxed them.

'If they bought the flat then it would mean they will be staying here for a good measure of time. They will live amongst us and become our neighbours. We all should welcome them with open arms,' Azizah said.

'Of course, we should!' Sukhminder said while Nisha nodded in agreement after taking a sip of her Boh tea that was sweetened with a drop of condensed milk.

Lillian who had remained non-committal and factual the entire time, even though she was the one who broke the news, still sat on the fence. 'The Chans just renovated the entire flat before Mr Chan lost his job, so the flat is as good as new.'

The other women, of course, knew, better than to ask Lillian how she knew all these personal details of the former owners. Although Azizah found Lillian a tad too much sometimes, crossing thresholds she had no business to step over—in this case literally as well as figuratively—she knew her heart was in a good place and that she didn't mean any harm. But despite it all, Azizah revelled in all the juicy gossip and secretly loved hearing about the comings and goings of the residents of Harmony Heights.

'There's nothing wrong you know. We are living in the twenty-first century. I don't know if you remember but a couple of years back there were two guys who lived here too, and they were the nicest people. One drove a Porsche and the other a Mercedes,' Nisha added.

'Yes, I remember! They were also a mixed-race couple! They, however, were just renting while their new home was being built in Tropicana.' How Lillian found out and retained so much information baffled Azizah, Sukhminder, and Nisha.

'Do you know what these two women do for a living? Did you get their names?' Sukhminder asked.

'I think it was Jan and Erika, if I remember correctly. And no, I didn't find out what they do. But I will the next time we meet up!'

All four of them started laughing. What's a ladies' tea without someone like Lillian to inform and entertain, revealing juicy scoops and divulging spicy titbits.

'Oh! And let us tell you my dear about our run-in with Padma in the lift the other day!' Lillian continued looking at Nisha. Although all four of these women came from different backgrounds, they bonded over several common interests, chiefly their dislike for Padma. 'Lillian put her in her place!'

'Good job!'

'Well done!'

'Bravo!'

Came the chorus from all the women, who found Padma uppity and snooty.

'She complained that our driver parked our car in the guest car park but she herself breaks the house rules by placing all her potted plants along the corridor outside her flat!' Azizah told the other three.

'She's just jealous that you have a driver and she had to let hers go when her husband retired,' Nisha said.

'That sanctimonious hypocrite!' Sukhminder bellowed. 'With a constipated look on her face!'

All four of them had had run-ins with Padma and most of their quarrels had something to do with the house rules. 'Does she think she is the condo police? Going around complaining and sticking her nose up at everyone?'

Nisha had fallen out with Padma after the latter ordered a Sugee cake from her and then complained that Nisha used inferior ingredients and thus compromised the cake's taste and quality. She also told a few people that she was overcharged, as she could have bought a better-tasting cake at another bakery for a cheaper price.

'You know her daughter is dating a distant relative of mine?' Nisha said.

'Noooooooo! Goodness Nisha! What if—' Sukhminder stopped just in time before voicing out a catastrophic situation.

'Perish the thought Sukhminder! That can never happen! I can't even bring myself to think about it!' Nisha said, halting all speculation amongst the three women of her becoming a relative of Padma dead in their tracks.

In two and a half hours, the four of them managed to demolish three quarters of the pound cake, all four curry puffs, almost all the chocolate brownies, the *vadais* and all the *samosas* save three! Needless to say, time flew by and before they knew it, it was already dusk and time to leave.

Chapter 20

When Lillian opened the door of her flat, she smelt something burning. She quickly ran to the kitchen and there standing in front of the stove was her skinny father, his left hand holding his right arm that appeared to be red and swollen. A frying pan emitting black smoke was on a gas ring, which was still turned on.

'What are you doing Pa?' Lillian yelled out, rushing to turn off the fire and lift the frying pan to the sink to douse it with water. She brusquely pushed the old man aside in case the hot frying pan burnt him during the transfer from cooker to sink. 'Look what you have done!' She hollered again, her voice registering anger mingled with irritation.

Looking blankly at his daughter, Uncle Gan lifted his right hand and showed Lillian where he had burnt his hand. Lillian immediately calmed down and grabbed some ice from the freezer. She wrapped it with a tea towel and gently pressed it against her father's burnt hand. While nursing her father's burnt hand, she noticed that there was a raw piece of chicken drumstick with a bite taken lying on the countertop.

She pieced it all together—her father must have been feeling famished while she had been out and being too impatient to wait for her to return and make him something to eat, he had tried unsuccessfully to cook something and feeling frustrated that he couldn't, he had just eaten the raw chicken!

Being at an advanced stage of Alzheimer's, Uncle Gan's condition was fast deteriorating. He could barely walk now and was confined to his bed most of the time. Apart from the more common symptoms like memory loss and confusion about past events and mixing up timelines, Lillian also noticed a drastic change in his personality, which had shifted from being fearful and suspicious of everyone in the early stages of his diagnosis to now becoming quiet and withdrawn. Hardly uttering a word, let alone carrying on a conversation, Uncle Gan only spoke intermittently when he wanted something, like when he needed to go to the bathroom to relieve himself or when he was cold or hungry. His speech was for the most part monosyllabic and sometimes incoherent, usually mumbled or yelled out, depending on his mood, as complete sentences were no longer within his grasp.

Sometimes, when Lillian looked at her father struggling to put a spoon into his mouth and eat or when he started shaking for no reason whatsoever, she felt a pang of pity for him. He had been so energetic and vibrant in his younger days. A gung-ho individual with a can-do attitude about everything he took on. How could he change so drastically in just a couple of years? No doubt, the ravages of time took their toll on everyone, but this disease of the mind must be one of the cruellest afflictions to strike anyone, as well their caregivers and family. Memories erased, thinking obliterated, mobility curtailed. How much more helpless could anyone be rendered when this dreaded, brain-degenerating disease struck?

* * *

Like most entrepreneurs and businessmen, Terence was a visionary who was very much focused on the bigger picture. He dreamed big and had large plans. From making business deals, investing in start-ups, expanding the family business or dabbling in the stock market, when there was a buck to be made, Terence was there.

Naturally, this came at a price. He had his fingers in a lot of pies and, as a result, he often spread himself too thin. Overextending himself in more ways than one had made Terence run into cash-flow problems on numerous occasions.

But when you have your eye on the big prize, you don't let trivial matters like having enough cash stop you from pursuing your goals. Money should take care of itself and shouldn't prevent you from getting what you want. That was Terence's mindset.

So, when the opportunity arose whereby his bid for a tender was guaranteed to be chosen (read: bribing an official to get a tender), Terence jumped at the chance. He asked his accounts manager how much cash they had in the current account and was told it was around RM 300,000 which wasn't enough for this 'donation' he was planning. The company, just like any other, had monthly expenses to pay including the salaries of the staff and other miscellaneous outgoings and the money in the current account was reserved for this.

Having invested in a cloud kitchen as well as a food delivery service recently, not to mention a start-up which was creating an e-wallet app, Terence had already reached his quota for any funds that were available for 'business opportunities'. He had his own money stashed aside but he didn't want to dip into that. Maybe he could sell some laggard stocks but then he would lose out.

Putting this conundrum aside for a while, Terence decided to switch his attention to something else. Quite often, he found that bright new ideas came to him after he stopped thinking about them. Just like the time when he ran into a roadblock while negotiating the purchase of a plot of land. He thought and thought about the way to circumvent it but couldn't. Finally, when he went on holiday with Candy and his twins, it suddenly occurred to him one morning by the resort's pool that the solution would be to give the seller one unit in the development he was planning to build on the land, as a sort of sweetener. Of course, that was welcomed favourably by the seller, and he managed to buy the land at the price offered.

* * *

Manoeuvring his yellow Lamborghini Huracan into the first level of the car park at Harmony Heights, Terence felt exhausted after a hectic day at the office. But there was nothing a few lines of coke wouldn't fix. He had managed to get hold of a stash earlier and was planning to snort it after dinner. So far, he'd managed to keep his cocaine habit from his wife. He snorted it in the bathroom, in his office, at a friend's place, and once at a restaurant bathroom.

He didn't see it as a problem, as he knew he felt he had it under his control. It was just for recreational use, nothing more. *What's the harm in that?* Obviously, he was indulging in self-deception of the grandest scale. But, then again, most addicts and alcoholics do. Of course, Terence wasn't in control. He was just deluding himself. He was floating on the longest river in the world, the Nile.

Just as he had parked his Lambo and gotten out, he saw Erika walk towards the car park exit. She had also just come back from work. As Terence knew all of the residents, he gathered as much that she was the new owner of flat 25-D. Although Arumugam hadn't spelt it out, he alluded to the fact that the couple who moved in were a same-sex couple.

Terence didn't even blink or give it a second thought. He was a businessman first and foremost. Same or opposite sex couples were equal in his eyes. If he could make money from anyone, he would do it. Didn't matter what their gender or sexuality was. LGBTQIA+ was A-OK by him. At university, he and a few of his uni buddies set up a gay bar which made him quite a lot of money. It might have been called the pink pound in the UK but those pastel notes helped pay for his university fees and then some. They also bought him a second-hand Volkswagen Polo, which was his first ever car.

As Terence entered Harmony Heights, he caught sight of Erika waiting by the lifts.

'Hello! Have you just moved in?' Terence flashed Erika a smile. 'I'm Terence,' he extended his right hand.

Shifting her briefcase to her left hand, Erika smiled back. 'Yes, you are right. How are you? My name is Erika.'

'Nice meeting you Erika, and welcome to Harmony Heights! Oh yes, perfect timing. Are you and your partner free next Saturday night?'

'I'll have to check but I think we are. Why?' Erika asked, curious that someone she had just met would invite her anywhere.

'That's great. I'm the chairman of this condo's management committee and it's been a tradition here that the chairman invites any new owner for a dinner.'

Erika nodded at his explanation, which satisfied her curiosity.

'It'll be at 8 p.m. next Saturday at the penthouse. The entrance is on the thirty-fifth floor. Look forward to seeing you then!'

Chapter 21

Having returned home from work a little earlier than usual, Terence remembered the WhatsApp message he received from the building manager Arumugam to pick up a few documents pertaining to renewing the security guard company's contract as well as to sign several cheques.

He glanced at his Piaget Polo Chronograph and saw that it was already 5 p.m. He knew both Arumugam and Ms Chew left on the dot, but he was willing to try his luck. They could have stayed back for a few minutes to finish off some paperwork. After all, they just had their monthly management committee meeting and there were lots of follow-up tasks to complete.

As it happened, Terence was in luck, as both Arumugam and Ms Chew were in the office. Ms Chew was on the phone probably handling a complaint from a resident while Arumugam was typing on his laptop.

Placing his black Aigner briefcase on the floor beside Arumugam's desk, Terence then signed the contracts and cheques to pay all the services providers Harmony

Heights engaged. Halfway through, Terence's phone rang. It was Candy wanting to know where he was. While still chatting with his wife on his mobile, Terence gestured to ask Arumugam if that was all once he had signed the last cheque, and Arumugam gave him the thumbs up. Walking out of the management office while chatting on the phone, Terence told Candy he was already back at Harmony Heights and would be up in a few minutes.

Arriving at his penthouse, Terence used his key fob to open the front door. Having just installed it, this electronic access system utilizing radio frequency identification technology to allow entry into his home had made life much easier for everyone. He could use his smartphone to enter or use the access card. It was also linked to the home security system and alarms as well as the security cameras that were placed at strategic points around his home.

Candy was in the open-plan kitchen with their maid Lucia when he walked in. Coco scurried to him as soon as she saw Terence walking in. 'Come here, my baby! I missed you!' Terence cooed. Even his own children didn't elicit such an affectionate response from him. Coco jumped into his arms when he bent down to pick her up and covered Terence's face with wet, sloppy kisses.

'Can I have a cognac?' Terence asked his wife while walking to the living room. 'I'll open Penfold's Grange 2016 for our dinner. Join me for a glass if you wish,' he told his wife who was busy preparing their dinner.

'In a minute, I'm just going to sear these scallops. I bought them today from this new seafood import place in Hartamas. I also got some *engawa*, large *bara uni*, and lobster tail and claws . . . which cognac do you want? The Hennessy Paradis or Louis Tres?' Candy asked.

Apart from their love of travelling, Terence and Candy also shared a common love of food. From French cuisine to Japanese, this couple indulged as much as their tummies would allow.

Bringing her husband a side plate of freshly seared garlic scallops on crostinis, sprinkled with chopped chives and topped with Beluga caviar on one hand and an etched crystal tumbler containing the king of cognacs, Louis XIII. It was Terence's favourite drink and he enjoyed savouring one after work while he winded down from the day. He looked at his wife. It didn't look like Candy had been slaving away in the kitchen at all. Her hair was pulled back in a ponytail, and she looked fresh even without a trace of make-up. Dressed in a colourful print Melinda Looi one-shoulder top and paired with skinny Roberto Cavalli jeans, she looked much younger than her thirty-six years.

Just as she was about to join her husband for their aperitif, Terence suddenly realized he was missing his briefcase.

'Oh shoot!' Terence muttered, 'I left my briefcase in the management office!'

'Were you there?' Candy asked while taking a sip of the cognac.

'Yes, I went to see Arumugam to sign a few cheques and must have left it there.'

'Not in your car?'

'No, I'm sure it was in the management office. I'll have to go there now, as I need some stuff from there tonight.'

Nothing or no one was going to disturb Candy's evening pleasure, so she nodded and waved Terence off while tasting her scallop crostini and taking another sip of cognac.

As Terence walked along the corridor in the basement of Harmony Heights leading to the management office, he realized why most residents didn't like going there—it was dark and dingy and the flickering fluorescent lights which supposedly lit up the place, gave it an eerie feeling. Just before Terence got to the door of the office, he heard a low moaning noise coming from inside so he slowed down and when he got to the door, he realized that the lights in the office were all off except for one coming from the far corner. As the door had a glass panel with blinds on the inside, he peered in and couldn't believe his eyes.

On the desk at the corner of the office was Arumugam with his pants down around his ankles humping away at Ms Chew who was lying in a missionary position. Her skirt was hitched up around her waist and she was moaning with each thrust.

Terence immediately threw himself to the side of the door, just in case either one of them would see him but with the placement of the desk at the corner of the room and at the angle towards the door, it wasn't possible for this amorous couple to spot him. Further, Arumugam was facing away from the door while Ms Chew's line of vision was obscured by Arumugam's heaving body.

Quick as a whistle, Terence fished out his iPhone from his back pocket and turned on the video recording. While still standing beside the door, he just extended his hand to the glass window and recorded this lustful couple in their after-office activity.

* * *

Growing up as a little girl, Jan always envisaged herself as a little princess or mermaid swimming in an ocean of love. On her fifth birthday, the age her adopted daughter Sonya was now, her parents had thrown her a birthday party where she dressed as a fairy tale princess, not unlike Cinderella but without the wicked stepmother and the two jealous stepsisters.

With balloons and cake and other yummy treats, it was a birthday party any five-year-old would have dreamt of. Of course, she was too young then to think about a handsome Prince Charming and ask her parents why there wasn't one. Spoon-fed this fantasy, Jan grew up believing that one day she'll meet and fall in love with someone who will fulfil all her emotional needs. This fantasy wasn't really too far-fetched— she did fall in love with someone except it wasn't Prince Charming but another princess.

Although not exclusive to Jan, she hoped that her daughter would not fall victim to the Prince Charming Syndrome. She would try to instil in Sonya the belief that meeting a soul mate, twin flame, or whatever one wishes to call it doesn't mean living happily ever after. Relationships are hard work and inevitably, problems will arise. How would she prepare Sonya to handle this perpetuated myth? It was all part and parcel of being a parent.

Jan couldn't be blamed for searching for her ideal man. She had three boyfriends prior to meeting Erika and each one was a huge revelation to her. No, they were not knights in shining armour but normal men with imperfections and flaws just like her and anyone else. When her third serious relationship ended, Jan was about to throw in the towel. She saw all her friends getting married by then and questioned why she found it so difficult to meet a potential partner. Was there something wrong with her? Was she unlovable?

Experiencing an existential crisis at the grand old age of twenty-eight led Jan on a soul-searching mission. She read books by self-help and relationship gurus and attended various self-improvement courses. From Tony Robbins to Bert Hellinger, Jan spent her weekends attending workshops and courses in the hope of finding out what she really wanted in a relationship.

Some courses gave her a little insight into the human condition while others like tarot card readings offered light relief and an alternate way to how she normally viewed life. But it was one particular self-improvement course, InnerWork, which dealt with the repressed and unconscious parts of one's personality which turned out to be a life altering revelation for Jan.

Not only was this Jungian psychological realization beneficial for Jan to see why she kept picking on the faults of her past boyfriends, it also orchestrated her meeting with Erika and that changed her life forever.

But Jan and Erika didn't form a union immediately. They knew each other for a year before they started dating. It was a slow dance for both of them—Jan was cautious after three failed relationships, while Erika took a slow-burn approach when it came to matters of the heart. Being a same-sex partnership also meant that they had the added burden of their family's approval to think about.

But all that went out of the window once they realized that no matter how much they thought about it, they weren't going to get everyone's approval. So, they decided to live their lives according to their own rules and moral compasses.

'Who cares what others think anyway,' Jan would say to Erika when she was in one of her feisty moods. 'They are not God! What right do they have to dictate to us how we should live our lives?'

As long as they weren't harming anyone else, they had as much right to live their own lives as anyone else. Enough said.

Chapter 22

While Nisha sold her cakes and cookies to residents of Harmony Heights as a side hustle, Sukhminder taught yoga in their condo once a week. Attended mostly by women, there was the occasional male yogi who turned up to practise sun salutations and various *asanas*.

Roping in all her buddies or *kakis*, Nisha, Lillian, and occasionally Azizah would put on their Lululemon stretch tops and Alo Yoga leggings while hugging a rolled up Manduka yoga mat and make their way to the multipurpose hall, a separate building located near the swimming pool.

It was an oppressive and hot late Tuesday morning when the three ladies made their way to Sukminder's yoga class. Walking along the garden path edged with red ginger and green hedges, they chatted about their plans for the week and Candy and Terence's upcoming dinner party. Azizah who was feeling out-of-sorts that day—in fact she hadn't been feeling her best for a couple of days prior—had initially wanted to cancel but thinking that some exercise might make her feel better, had ultimately decided to attend. She looked slightly pale and wasn't as talkative as she would have usually been.

Arriving at the hall, they were all greeted by Sukhminder who had left earlier to set up the space for her class.

'It's going to be quite hot and sticky, and the two fans are not working!' Sukhminder announced to the three of them as they walked towards her. 'I've already told Ms Chew about it, but she said the repairman can only come this afternoon.'

Grimacing, Lillian quickly walked towards the window then unfurled her yoga mat on the floor with annoyance, securing her spot and ensuring that her place was the best, as she might enjoy a cool gust of wind, if any, might blow in.

Nisha took her place next to Lillian and whispered to her yoga neighbour that the management office was slacking of late and she had noticed that several light bulbs in the car park and in some common areas were blown but not replaced. Lillian naturally nodded and agreed wholeheartedly, quoting a few more complaints of her own about the state of the condo.

Azizah who was silent throughout this interaction was left with the spot farthest from the window. She really didn't mind where she planted herself as she told herself it was only an hour-long class, and that they weren't going to be there forever.

As the three ladies sat cross-legged on their mats facing Sukhminder, they heard the door open behind them and turned to see who else was attending the yoga class. It turned out that both Jan and Erika, who had seen the advert for the yoga class on the notice board and decided to join.

Egged on by Jan, who had been practising yoga since her university days, Erika had decided to go along on her day off work, but only after she ensured that there was someone to look after Sonya—on this day her adopted daughter was in a playgroup. Smiling at Sukhminder, Jan greeted everyone while Erika remained reserved.

Trying to be subtle, but failing miserably, Lillian quickly eyed Nisha and gestured with her facial expressions to indicate that Jan and Erika were the couple who had just moved into Harmony Heights. Afraid that the same-sex couple might see Lillian's gestures about them, Nisha quickly nodded and then brought a finger to her lips, telling Lillian, in effect, to shush.

As Erika unrolled her yoga mat behind Azizah, she greeted Azizah with a polite smile. Jan broke the iceberg made up of these four friends by asking why the fans were not turned on.

'They are out-of-order,' Sukhminder replied matter-of-factly. 'I can give you a rebate on the class fee if you like.'

'Don't be silly,' Jan said. 'It's fine . . . have any of you done Bikram Yoga?' Jan asked, referring to the cultish style of hot yoga.

'Oh God, no!' Came Nisha's reply. 'That's torture!'

'This class might just become one!' Lillian yelped out while rolling her eyes. Both Jan and Erika smiled at each other. They found these women trivial at worst and amusing at best, but harmless all the same. Yet, at the same time they wondered what kind of quirky people they were living amongst.

'Shall we begin?' Asked Sukhminder rhetorically while eyeing the one thing that was working in the room—the clock.

Starting with a short grounding meditation where everyone closed their eyes, the part-time yoga instructor then proceeded to guide them through several stretching poses before beginning the sun salutation sequence. Beads of perspiration formed on Jan's forehead, while Nisha huffed and puffed almost suffocating in the stuffy and sweltering room. Dark patches of sweat were visible on Lillian's leotard while her face turned to a shade of pink.

Erika soldiered on, her endurance level almost tested to the limit, even though she had run the Sydney Marathon a few years back. All the women noticed the droplets of sweat falling on Sukhminder's yoga mat while she demonstrated the Adho Mukhga Shvanasana or downward dog pose.

Suddenly, just as Sukhminder was about to move into the standing poses—beginning with the Warrior One asana—a sudden thump was heard from the corner of the room. Everyone turned to see where the sound had come from. Azizah—who had complained the least amongst this lot, in fact she hadn't even uttered a single word—had collapsed and was now lying on her side, her yoga outfit drenched in sweat and her mat slippery from her perspiration.

'Oh my God!' Lillian shouted out while Nisha covered her mouth with both her hands. Sukhminder quickly grabbed her phone and dialled 999 while Jan ran to Azizah's side. But the person who really showed up was Erika who motioned for Jan to move aside and let her take over. The Australian had been a former New South Wales State Emergency Service volunteer back when she was in her twenties and thus knew precisely what to do in such a situation.

Keeping calm, unlike Lillian and Nisha who were both in panic mode, Erika gently rolled Azizah on her back and asked Jan to get a chair from the pile at the far end of the hall. She then lifted both of Azizah's legs onto the seat of the chair. She checked Azizah's pulse and luckily, although it was on the high side, it was still within the range of a normal heart rate.

She asked Jan to run up and get some ice from their apartment while she ordered the rest to clear off and not crowd around Azizah, to give her some room to breathe. Grabbing a towel, Erika then proceeded to fan Azizah, cooling her down and in effect reviving her from her sudden black-out.

When Azizah opened her eyes and regained consciousness, she immediately knew what had happened. The heat combined with the lack of air in the room plus her hot flashes and insomnia—typical symptoms of menopause— had all come together, making her dizzy and light-headed. The downward dog asana, while good for a healthy individual, didn't help, as this popular inversion pose threw Azizah off-kilter.

'The ambulance should be here soon,' Sukhminder announced.

'*Puan*, how are you feeling?' Erika asked Azizah, adopting the local lingo as a sign of respect.

'Still slightly giddy and weak but I don't need the ambulance, please cancel it! I don't want to go to the hospital!' Azizah replied, embarrassed and defiant at the same time.

'It's normal to feel like that, but your temperature is slightly high, and your heart is beating quite fast,' Erika responded in a gentle and soothing tone, trying to comfort Azizah.

'You don't have to go to the hospital but just to give yourself some peace of mind, why not go and make sure everything is alright?' Erika added, hoping Azizah would see some sense in her explanation.

Lillian chimed in to ask what the worry was, after all, she was heavily insured by her husband and any medical expense—large or small—could be claimed; her voice tinged with a slight degree of bitterness.

Just then, Jan arrived back at the multipurpose hall, panting and covered in more sweat, with an ice pack and a hand towel.

'Here you go,' Jan said while placing the wrapped ice-cube bag on Azizah's forehead gently, bringing immediate relief to her.

'Thank you so much,' Azizah said, looking at Jan, then Erika. 'Both of you are so kind.'

'It's nothing,' Jan said reassuringly and smiled at Azizah while pressing the ice pack against Azizah's forehead in case it slid off. Looking up from her supine position, Azizah saw Jan immediately above her holding the ice pack in place against her forehead while Erika stood a few feet away fanning her with a towel.

It was an unusual first meeting but the way Erika and Jan had treated Azizah made her feel all warm and fuzzy inside, the way anyone would feel when a stranger extends a helping hand at a time of crisis or when one feels vulnerable and out of control.

Azizah felt touched, and this act of kindness by both Jan and Erika, restored her faith in humanity, as these two women, who until a few minutes ago, had just been strangers, known only to her from her neighbours' gossip, were now showing concern for her and caring for her like she was their mother.

Chapter 23

While browsing the racks of clothes in Zara, Padma spotted a scarf amongst the accessories displayed on a table. As there was only one of its kind, she knew she would have to have it. She grabbed a couple of blouses from the rack and carefully buried the scarf underneath the clothes and walked calmly to the ladies' changing room.

Once inside, she carefully folded the scarf into a tiny square and put it into the zipped compartment of her handbag. She had no intention of trying on the two blouses but nevertheless waited for a good ten minutes before she emerged from the changing room and returned them to the assistant seated at the entrance.

Later, while making her way to the accessories section, she spied a necklace hung on a hook and quickly made a beeline for it before anyone took it. Putting it against her neck, Padma shifted her upper body at several angles, all while looking at herself in the mirror. The colourful beads would look good against any of her black outfits. Studying the reflection of her surroundings in the mirror, she made sure no one was looking before casually slipping the necklace into an open shopping bag she was toting.

All this was just foreplay in her mind, the appetizer to whet her appetite before the entrée and the prelude to the performance. The rush she felt only came after she walked out of the store with the stolen items, and she managed to get away with them.

The irony of this peculiar affliction of Padma was that she didn't really need or want the articles she stole. And it wasn't like she couldn't afford them. It was just for the sheer thrill of being able to do such a risky act and being able to get away with it. Maybe she was bored with her life and needed the spurt of endorphines in her brain. Whatever it was, it was her dirty little secret.

* * *

Calling his right-hand man, Mr Siew to his office, Terence logged out of his bank's app after checking his balance. After asking his finance manager the amount his company had in their current account, he wanted to know how Mr Siew's meeting with the representative from the company putting out the tender had gone.

A middle-level manager who had been working with Hing Chong Construction for nearly twenty years, Mr Siew was a loyal soldier who did all the groundwork needed for all the construction or building projects carried out by Terence's family construction and property development firm. From negotiating with landowners when they purchased land for development to applying for permits before any construction commenced, Mr Siew was well versed in each and every step of the official bureaucratic procedures.

He was also updated on the informal part of any construction and development projects and that included all the palms that needed to be greased to ensure a smooth workflow and unhindered progress. Having met the representative of the company who was putting out a tender for subcontracting the construction of a warehouse, Mr Siew had to report to Terence how much was required to ensure Hing Chong Construction won the bid.

'RM 800k was his price,' Mr Siew told Terence as a matter of fact.

'Did you bargain?' Terence queried.

'Yes, I did but he wouldn't go lower.'

Mentally calculating the amount of cash they had— all payments of these sorts had to be in cash so that they couldn't be traced—he was RM 300,000 short. As there was a deadline to meet, Terence pondered on how he could raise that amount in three weeks' time.

He dismissed Mr Siew and went through his personal bank accounts again. After checking, he once again came to the conclusion that it wasn't enough. It would be ideal if the representative could wait till the project was completed, but he knew that was not going to happen. What if he reneged on his promise? Then the representative would have given him the contract and not obtained any payment for it. No one would ever do that for fear of being played out. Plus, there was no legal redress, as the whole set-up was illegal.

Terence could borrow from Candy, but he felt ill at ease about that thought. Coming from a business background herself, she would know how things worked but it would still bother his male ego to borrow money from her. He also didn't want to borrow from his father because he knew most of his money was invested in the company already.

Just as he was about to give up and withdraw his bid for the tender, a sheet of paper sticking out from the Harmony Heights file on his desk caught his eye. It was the bank balances for the management accounts for Harmony Heights. Glossing over the maintenance account which was used to pay for the monthly expenses incurred for the general upkeep of the condo, Terence's eyes zoomed in on the sinking fund amount. RM 2.3 million! He knew that all residents contributed each and every month towards the sinking fund, but he hadn't realized it had grown to such a sizable amount.

As the chairman of the management committee, Terence could access the money in the sinking fund, but he would also need the signature of Arumugam if he were to write out a cheque to withdraw money from that fund, as both of them were joint account holders of the sinking fund account.

Of course, him 'borrowing' RM 300,000 or any amount of money from the sinking fund was illegal by any definition. But Terence reasoned with himself, thinking that no one would know, as the bank accounts were not revealed to the residents and the minute he was paid for completing the warehouse, he would return the money. To carry out this feat, however, there was one obstacle he would have to overcome—getting the building manager's signature on the cheque.

* * *

After dropping Candy off at the medi-spa where she had an appointment for a SilkPeel Microdermabrasion, Shamsul would usually park on a side street nearby, turning the air-con of the Vellfire on full blast while he took a nap or scrolled through his Facebook. Today, however, he had a ton of things to do while waiting for his lady-boss. From her past visits to this medi-spa, Shamsul knew she would be a good two hours, if not slightly longer, which gave him plenty of time to run his errands.

He'd met Tiger through some mutual friends, who were also chauffeurs of some other VIPs in town, while waiting for Candy at an upmarket shopping mall in town. Friendly banter turned into more meaningful conversations. Bonding over a cup of *teh tarik* at a roadside *warung*, they became fast friends. Tiger had asked Shamsul one day to help him ferry an envelope across town as a favour, and since he wasn't doing much that afternoon, Shamsul agreed. Tiger was, of course, charming to the core and Shamsul was taken aback when, after doing the favour, Tiger gave him a tip of RM 300.

He didn't expect to be paid at all so this was a nice surprise. The next few deliveries Shamsul did were also handsomely rewarded, and he started getting used to the extra money he was earning. Having worked for Terence and Candy for just under two years, Shamsul hadn't reached his maximum pay yet and he needed as much extra financial help as possible.

He hadn't questioned Tiger about what was in those envelopes. He figured that the less questions he asked, the better. It did occur to Shamsul that he was taking a risk, but he reasoned with himself by telling himself that driving for a living was also a big risk, which he took every day.

Today, however, was different, as Tiger had a bigger job for him. He had two cardboard boxes which he had to deliver. Shamsul hesitated at first but when Tiger waved RM 2,000 in front of him, all his hesitation and resistance whittled away.

It seemed like easy money. All Shamsul had to do was deliver it to a house in Cheras, which wasn't that far from where he had just dropped Candy off. Factoring in the traffic, who could resist earning a month's salary doing a thirty-minute side hustle? Certainly not Shamsul who had three hungry mouths to feed.

Using Waze to navigate the streets of KL, Shamsul knew he could be back on time to pick Candy up. An hour was all he needed. She hadn't called or WhatsApped him yet. *So far so good.* The lunchtime traffic would have dispersed by then and it would be a fast and efficient delivery, just like all the previous ones.

But, of course, Tiger didn't just pay Shamsul or any of his mules such a high price for nothing. He was a gangster who preyed on people's greed and vulnerability and made them do his dirty work. Shamsul was just one of the many he'd victimized and once Shamsul got caught in his sticky web, it would be difficult to extricate himself.

Arriving at the address, Shamsul sat in the MPV and waited for someone to come out as per Tiger's detailed instructions. He waited and waited and after ten minutes or so, nothing happened. He then WhatsApped Tiger and waited again, looking at the clock ever so often. Finally, Tiger replied.

'Sorry but there's a change of plans. No one is there now. You keep the two boxes and return them to me tomorrow.'

Change of plans? Keep it until tomorrow? What was this? He was paid to courier packages, not to store them! Even if he could, where would he keep them?

With all these questions swirling around his head, Shamsul had to turn off the engine and get out of the car to smoke a cigarette. A burst of nicotine should help him think better and calm his nerves. Glancing at the clock again, he was in good time. He had another ninety minutes or so before his lady-boss called him. Inhaling the smoke from his cigarette, Shamsul thought more about Tiger's request. No wonder he had been paid RM 2,000 this time. Not only was the delivery bigger, it also came along with extra requests. *Dang it*. He shouldn't have agreed but he'd thought it would have been a straightforward delivery just like the others. He should have known.

Suddenly, an idea came to him. The storeroom in Terence and Candy's penthouse was in his charge. He used it as a resting room when he didn't have to drive Candy about, and it was used to store some household stuff which wasn't needed. Only he and Terence had the keys to go in. He could probably store it there. After all, it was just for one night before he shipped it out again.

Just as he took the last drag of his cigarette, his phone pinged. It was Candy. She was ready and wanted to be picked up. Shamsul threw the cigarette butt on the ground and put it out with his heel. It would take at least thirty minutes to get to Candy so he had to think of a good excuse to tell her why he was late. That and hiding the two boxes at the back of the car so she wouldn't notice them. Two thousand ringgit now was hard earned money for Shamsul.

Chapter 24

Padma had just gotten back from the management office after filing yet another complaint about a fellow resident. This time it was about cigarette smoke that she could smell in her bathroom. She was sure the smell was coming from the flat below. So far, she had complained about Lillian, Azizah, and Sukhminder, amongst other residents, for a range of wrongdoings, most of them petty and trivial. She had even complained about Coco barking at her in the lift.

In a perverse way, Padma enjoyed policing Harmony Heights and trying to correct every wrong she saw. She didn't see herself as a vigilante, just someone who was morally superior and therefore had every right to tell anyone who was acting out of order or who broke the house rules off. If someone was using a drill during the weekend, she'd be the first to ring up the security guards to complain. If a resident threw a cigarette butt in the car park, she'd rush to the management office to lodge a report. Complaining and keeping an eye out for rule-breakers gave her a sense of purpose and made her feel useful and wanted. She made herself feel important by being the voice of the moral majority, not realizing that this very act made other residents hate her. Telling people of all the 'good' that she had done—either for charities or within her family and small circle of friends—boosted her self-esteem.

Padma's fondness for virtue signalling was only one part of her holier-than-thou persona. She felt the need to constantly assert her moral superiority over others.

As a young girl, she had been told what constituted 'good' and 'bad' behaviour and she was shocked when she found out that she wasn't perfect. There were aspects of her personality that her parents and teachers told her off or punished her for. So, she repressed them and denied them in herself. Her ego didn't allow her to acknowledge those aspects, as she only wanted to be seen in the best possible light.

Of course, these unsavoury parts of her personality were buried by her, but they never disappeared completely, like she wanted them to. She just constantly denied their existence and soon she became unconscious of their presence. But not acknowledging her shadow caused her major problems in life, chiefly with other people. Manifesting as projections on to others, their existence was made evident through Padma's habit of constantly criticizing, judging, and condemning other people—particularly the community at Harmony Heights—for their actions and behaviour.

What Padma failed to see was that she was turning a personal character trait into a perceived moral deficiency in someone else. The very thing she disliked about others was the thing that she disliked—and had disowned—in herself. Her need to demonstrate or show-off her moral values to others stemmed from an incident that had occurred in her childhood. During her schooldays, she had been selected as a school prefect and she found that she got a kick out of telling her classmates off for slacking in their schoolwork or horsing around. This extra responsibility that was placed on her made her feel morally superior to the other students even though she was secretly envious of them at times because she couldn't let her hair down and have fun like they did.

It was hardly a surprise when later, she sought out Gopi as a husband, what with him being a lawyer—a criminal prosecutor at that—and working in the Attorney General's Chambers. What better way to demonstrate moral grandstanding than being the wife of a public prosecutor?

But, to an outsider, she was an uptight and self-righteous woman, who oftentimes felt it was her God-given right to tell others off for their so-called moral shortcomings and lecture them on how they should behave. This was exactly what she had been doing today, this time to her own daughter, Shivana.

* * *

Naturally, Dr Rahaina advised Azizah to go for several tests, including a Pap smear and a mammogram as well as blood and urine tests to check on her general health and determine her menopausal status. Her symptoms—the hot flashes, insomnia, forgetfulness, and mood swings—were all textbook. But it wasn't the physical symptoms that Azizah was here to seek treatment for. It was the mental and emotional ones— her mood swings and irritability as well as her uncontrollable spending sprees that gave her a temporary high. She really needed to see a psychiatrist or psychotherapist for this but the association with these mental health specialists was something that she wasn't particularly keen on.

She certainly wasn't crazy or off her rocker to begin with. Neither did she struggle with suicidal ideation. She felt depressed occasionally, but who didn't? There were some days when she could barely keep her head above water, days when she was overwhelmed with negative thoughts, days where Azizah felt that if she didn't paddle vigorously enough, she would drown. Then there were other days when she was cruising along swimmingly and everything, including her emotions flowed smoothly.

Azizah knew her spending had been through the roof of late, Zainal had made sure she was well aware of it. But how was that related to her mental health? Surely the liberal use of her credit card had nothing to do with her emotional well-being. Or did it? Shopping to fill an emotional void? Whatever! This was why she had come to see Dr Rahaina again and she hoped that the doctor would be able to provide a solution this time.

'Have you given any thought to my recommendation from the last time we met?' Dr Raihana asked Azizah.

There was a pregnant pause before Azizah answered hesitantly.

'I just need to ask you a few more questions. You recommended that I see a mental health specialist the last time, and by that, you mean a psychiatrist, right?' Azizah asked.

'That's correct.' The gynaecologist replied before adding, 'Do you have any reservations about seeing one?'

It was at this point in their consultation that Azizah's mind went blank. It took a few minutes for the words she was hearing from her doctor to sink in.

A psychiatrist. I need to see a psychiatrist. Do I need to consult with a psychiatrist? After that initial shock, Azizah's mind went into overdrive. *Is there something really wrong with me? What will Zainal think? What if word gets out? His boss might think he's married to a nutter. That certainly would harm his prospects for promotion. No, no. NO! I am not mad and do NOT need to see a psychiatrist!*

'*Puan* Azizah? Are you alright?' Dr Raihana asked, and in effect, brought Azizah's ruminations to a halt.

'I'm fine, I'm fine,' Azizah answered even though from the slightly troubled expression on her face Dr Raihana could tell she was not.

'You don't have to give me an answer right now but do think about it. Many functioning people see psychiatrists and mental health counsellors when they fall into a slump. It's not unusual.' Dr Raihana might as well add mind reader to her credentials because she had done just that.

'Yes I know but . . . ' collecting her mile a minute thoughts Azizah paused to regain her composure.

'I can assure you most psychiatrists are very discreet and professional. You don't have to worry about anything.'

By referring Azizah to a psychiatrist, Dr Rahaina was hoping to help her with her mental health issues, particularly to alleviate her mood disturbances. Medication would help her but so would talk therapy and this was what Azizah needed, as she frequently felt lonely. With Zainal away at work and her daughter abroad, Azizah didn't have many people she could turn to. Talking about her feelings and sharing how she felt and what went on in her head were good ways for her to let off some steam. A psychiatrist would provide Azizah with the help and support she needed, regardless of the stigma attached to seeing one.

* * *

Yi Wei aka Sherilyn had surprisingly amassed a sizable number of subscribers on her OnlyFans in the short while since she created her account. Surprising not just because it was the first time she ever did anything as audacious as this but also because the content she posted wasn't as explicit as that of other—specially Western—creators. Shimmying around in lacy undergarments was tame by today's standards and so it took Yi Wei by surprise when the numbers of subscribers started to climb, and the money started to flow in.

Yes, the money. That was the main reason why Yi Wei did it in the first place. From a young age, she recalled her father using money and his position as the head of the household to control her mother. The acrimony in their home that she had experienced since she was a child still reverberated in her head like it was just yesterday. For as long as she remembered her mother had been unhappy but only recently had her father raised a hand to hit her mum.

Yi Wei had made many attempts to become financially independent in the past—she had worked part-time as a barista at a hipster café for a few months until the harassment from the customers got too much for her to bear. Married men would hit on her constantly and she got tired of it. Then she tried to do some online sales where she bought make-up from Korean brands and resold them on Shopee but the profits she made were a pittance. It hadn't even been enough to cover the next few shipments of sheet masks and nail polish from Seoul.

Being a Christian—she used to go to Sunday service every week until recently—she might have said that it was divine timing that someone told her about OnlyFans but somehow, she didn't make this connection in her mind. Yi Wei checked her bank account every day, more frequently when she posted a new video, and the growing amount somehow assuaged any guilt she might have harboured.

She would delete all the videos and photos once she got enough to move out of her parent's apartment at Harmony Heights and was able to find a place for herself. She fantasized about buying a car and maybe even asking her mother to move in with her if it became unbearable. But those thoughts were still pipe dreams, as so far she had only accumulated four-digit figures in her bank account.

On this day however, Yi Wei was transforming herself from a demure college student to a vampy temptress with the help of Maybelline, Revlon, Nudestix, Rimmel, and NYX Cosmetics. Brushing out her long dark tresses and backcombing the hair on her crown to make it look more voluminous, she then reached for the burgundy lace La Senza Oh La La Cheri unlined bra and panty set which she had splurged on in the shopping mall. As the bra was see-through, Yi Wei remembered to put on her nipple covers so they wouldn't show.

Studying herself in the full-length mirror, Yi Wei almost couldn't recognize herself. At nineteen years old, she had blossomed into a woman with curves that would no doubt elicit envious stares from other women. Yi Wei, on account of being a late bloomer, had just begun to discover her sexuality after repressing it for years.

Turning on the ring light and adjusting her iPhone, Yi Wei thought she was quite adept at this by now. She had already filmed a dozen short clips and was planning to add a few more minutes for this new content. Sure, it would be more risqué and titillating but that was what was needed if she was to get more subscribers. But no matter how daring it was, Yi Wei drew the line at being nude. Some might argue that the transparent lingerie she wore, albeit with nipple patches already left nothing to the imagination. Nonetheless, she didn't want to expose herself any further than showing bare skin and underwear. It made her feel too vulnerable, and she didn't like that feeling.

Studying various explicit music videos was easy enough but whether or not Sherilyn could emulate what she'd seen the women in the videos doing, was another matter. She was by no means as agile and flexible as those female rap superstars. But when she slowed the video down, she could incorporate the moves better. She felt comfortable performing like this and it didn't look half bad. She decided to record her video to 'Bang Bang' the hit song by Jessie J, Ariana Grande, and Nicki Minaj on this particular day and she wanted to get it done before her father returned from work.

Lip syncing to Ariana Grande's high pitched soprano voice, Sherilyn got carried away by the song. Her body enjoyed moving to the upbeat rhythm and she was so engrossed in her performance that she didn't even notice her nipple patch slipping off and exposing her left nipple through her lace bra. It was something that she should have spotted while editing the video later, but in her haste to post it (and hopefully get more subscribers), she overlooked it, a slip-up which was going to cost her dearly.

Chapter 25

Meeting Iqbal at their usual place under the shade of the rain tree during their lunch break, Widya wasn't her usual calm self. Not only was she frazzled from the morning's chores, her employer had lost a pair of pearl and diamond earrings and she had spent the entire morning looking for them but to no avail. This, of course, meant that the rest of the housework was held up, and she would have to double her speed in the afternoon if she was to finish all the cleaning, cooking, and ironing.

Widya had been looking forward to seeing Iqbal and when he finally arrived, all sweaty from performing his gardening duties, she felt elated. She was so happy to see him that she didn't mind the sweat at all. He always looked so optimistic and happy, unfazed by what was happening around him. This was one trait that she wished she, too, could have.

'Here, I picked this for you,' Iqbal said sweetly while handing her a pink and white frangipani flower. This touched Widya's heart deeply, as this was the first time any man had given her anything. It was worth more than any jewel because she knew how pure Iqbal's heart was and that the sincerity behind the gesture could not be questioned.

'Thank you so much, Iqbal.' Her eyes started to water but she didn't want him to see her tearing up. Her fondness for him was a mixture of compassion and sympathy, a combination of emotions that she found hard to process and reconcile with.

Unpacking the lunch that she had packed for both of them, she gave Iqbal the bigger share of fried chicken and rice while she made do with the smaller one. After all, he did more strenuous work and needed more fuel than her. As a treat for their lunchtime rendezvous, she had also brought some nice Malay *kuih* that she had made the night before.

'Are you enjoying your new duties as the pool boy?' She asked him. 'Is it too tiring for you?'

'A little bit,' Iqbal replied, chewing his food while beaming at Widya, his bright smile belaying any weariness he might have felt from his extra duties. 'But I like it because I get to go into the swimming pool while cleaning it! It's nice to go in on a hot day!'

It was then that Widya noticed the rough and scaly rash on Iqbal's hands. 'What's this on your hand?' Widya asked, looking concerned. 'When did it appear?'

'I don't know,' Iqbal answered while pulling his right hand away, feeling self-conscious all of a sudden. 'I think it appeared after I started cleaning the pool.'

Noticing his embarrassment, Widya changed the subject.

'You get to go in the pool? That's great! What time do you do it? I can look down from the flat to see you next time you're cleaning it.'

'Sometime in the afternoon, Arumugam said I have to clean first after doing my gardening otherwise I might make the pool dirty.'

Soon after, Iqbal left and Widya cleared up and thrown away the remnants of their lunch, she remembered to take the frangipani Iqbal had given her. She placed it on her bedside as soon as she got back.

* * *

After making her rounds of the grounds of Harmony Heights, including poking her nose into the multipurpose hall and then dropping into the management office to see Arumugam about some issues pertaining to the upcoming annual general meeting, Lillian took a leisurely walk back to her apartment, only to find herself thunderstruck.

As she opened her front door and stepped into her flat, a strong gust of wind blew across her face and body, slamming the wooden door shut with a loud bang. Next, the bright light flooding her flat almost blinded her. She was accustomed to darker interior lighting, as she always had the curtains drawn. After her eyes adjusted to the brightness, she saw the curtains on the balcony doors flapping in the wind.

With her failing eyesight, she just about managed to make out the figure of her father standing on the raised concrete balcony ledge and holding onto the metal railing. Lillian immediately dropped her basket and rushed towards her father, grabbing both his arms and pulling him away from the edge. With the force and momentum Lillian exerted, both of them fell backwards and rolled onto the balcony floor.

'What the hell are you doing!' Lillian yelled out after she managed to upright herself and gain some composure. Her father's eyes were closed, and he just lay on the balcony floor motionless. Lillian slowly helped him stand up and supported him while he hobbled into the flat and sat down on an armchair.

It was pretty obvious what Uncle Gan had been attempting to do and Lillian was shaken to the core at this realization. She was about to lose her temper at him, but she controlled herself. Uncle Gan didn't want to live anymore. He wanted to end his life. He wanted to end the pain, the suffering, the confusion he felt. The quality of his life was slowly diminishing, and this was something he found hard to accept.

Lillian had thought of placing him in a nursing home for the elderly but the ones she looked up were beyond their means. Texting her elder brother and younger sister to ask if they could help out financially and contribute to their father's care yielded no response from both her siblings. Lillian's meagre pension wasn't enough to even hire a maid to take care of her father, let alone use a home-care service. What else could she do? It was unrealistic for her to watch over her father 24/7. No one in their right mind could undertake such a daunting and draining task.

After making her father a cup of Chinese tea, she went into her bedroom and retrieved a bottle of Tiger Balm muscle rub. She wanted to massage the cream onto the bruises caused by his fall. Her back and hips were aching too but she wanted to attend to her father first. He was probably suffering in silence, robbed of words that could express his pain.

She tried not to hold on to any resentment she felt toward him but when she recalled how he used to treat her, his unfairness in showing his disparity in love as well as his taunts about her not being married, she found it hard to do so. Uncle Gan would be so blatant in his favouritism toward her two siblings. When she was younger, Lillian would often feel emotionally neglected by her father who was unavailable, withholding, and distracted. She would be a saint if she didn't begrudge him now, especially when all she could think of when she looked at him were sad and painful memories of her childhood.

Just then, an idea flashed across her mind. She may have found the solution to keep her father safe when she was out or not able to keep an eye on him.

It may sound cruel and barbaric to others, but she didn't plan on letting others know. Firstly, no one would know anyway unless they came into her flat and she never ever had any visitors. Secondly, without enough money, what choice did she have? Lillian was in a no-win situation. So, she did the next best thing. Yes, she would go to the hardware store tomorrow and buy what she needed—a chain and lock so she could tie her father to his bed when she wasn't around, so he wouldn't wander about and hurt himself or attempt suicide again.

Chapter 26

'Has Dinesh called you yet?' Padma demanded as soon as she saw Shivana walk into the kitchen.

Ignoring her, Shivana poured herself a glass of iced tea from the fridge and quickly walked out of the kitchen while Padma lifted the lid of a pot of vegetarian avial that was stewing on a low flame.

'Don't ignore me, Shivana. I asked you a question!' Padma said, slamming down the lid and raising her voice an octave or two higher.

'You asked me that yesterday and I told you that he hasn't!' came Shivana's curt reply from the dining room. Her mother's meddling was really getting on her nerves of late and coupled with her neurosis, Shivana was almost on the brink of losing it.

Walking out of the kitchen to confront her daughter, Padma persisted. 'Why don't you give him a call then! How long has it been since you last saw him? Who waits so long to call back? Your father kept calling me when we first started dating.'

Okay, the last statement was the proverbial straw which broke the camel's or in this case, Shivana's back. She spun around so quickly to face Padma, the iced tea spilt out of the glass and splattered on her blouse and the floor. Irritated by the spilt tea, Shivana couldn't hold it in any longer and yelled back at her mother.

'If you are so keen on Dinesh, then why don't *you* call him!'

'I only want what's best for you,' Padma stated, lowering her voice and summoning patience. She was trying to be as calm as possible.

'You mean you only want what's best for yourself!' Retorted Shivana, quick as a flash. It was a comeback uttered without thought but searing nonetheless because of its inherent truth.

Storming in to her room, Shivana then slammed the door shut. She could only take so much in a day and the only thing more annoying than an interfering mother is one who thinks she knows better than you.

Padma was furious that her daughter would answer back and yell at her. But what hurt her the most was the last statement. It implied that Padma was self-serving and didn't have her daughter's best interest at heart, qualities which were not what Padma identified herself with. When did Shivana become so disrespectful and rude? Her mind started to race back and forth trying to recall the other times Shivana had shouted back at her or answered sarcastically. Didn't her daughter know that all she wanted as a mother was best for her? How ungrateful could she be? Padma's own mother never did as much as what she had done for Shivana, but that was because Padma came from a large family—she was the sixth child in a family of seven children.

She was going to have a word with Gopi that night about Shivana's attitude. This wouldn't do. As her thoughts escalated, so did her heartbeat. Padma needed to calm herself down. She went into the kitchen and made herself a cup of masala chai. There was nothing a little tea couldn't solve. She decided to give it a rest for now. She would speak with Shivana later.

In her room, Shivana took off her clothes and studied her body in front of the mirror. She didn't like what she saw. Her belly protruded and she felt that her bum looked too big. She had what some would call a pear-shaped figure and it didn't appeal to her. Putting her clothes back on, she realized she was hungry. The argument with her mother and the pressure she felt had triggered her appetite. Eating was the only way she could comfort her ragged nerves. The only problem was that during her binge sessions, Shivana would overdo it and soon after she would have to induce herself to throw up.

* * *

After dropping Candy at the lobby of Harmony Heights, Shamsul quickly drove the Vellfire to the residents' multi-level car park. As it was just 4 p.m., he was glad to see that hardly anybody was around. He had covered the box with a blanket at the back of the Vellfire but Candy wouldn't have noticed it anyway, as she sat in the front.

Carefully removing the box from the car, Shamsul furtively glanced around to make sure the coast was clear as he carried it and walked to the car park exit and towards the lifts. As luck would have it, Lillian was also at the lifts, having just returned home from her grocery shopping. She smiled at Shamsul and looked inquisitively at the cardboard box he was carrying. Curiosity got the better of her and she asked Shamsul, 'Carrying something for your boss?'

Not wanting to answer her, Shamsul feigned that he had left something in the car and turned around to walk back to the car park without acknowledging Lillian. 'What a rude man,' she said under breath as the lift door opened.

After Lillian had gone, Shamsul waited for the next lift and hoped no one would see him. The ride to the thirty-sixth floor seemed like an eternity. When the lift finally reached, Shamsul breathed out a sigh of relief. Fumbling for his keys, he felt quite lucky to have encountered an empty lift. He'd even managed to evade Lillian's question. Letting himself into the storeroom, Shamsul placed the box at the far end of the room, near the window. It was out of view from the entrance, and he sure hoped that no one would notice it.

As only he and Terence had the keys to the storeroom, Shamsul felt that it would be safe to keep the box here overnight. He would remove it discreetly when he got instructions from Tiger tomorrow about where he was supposed to deliver it. No one would know and he'd be RM 2,000 richer.

* * *

After she saw Shamsul, who had ignored her, Lillian didn't go back to her flat but instead went to the twenty-fifth floor. She wanted to see if Jan and Erika had settled into their flat and wanted to know how they were doing. As a member of the management committee, she also took it upon herself to invite the new residents to the dinner hosted by Terence and Candy to welcome them. That would be a good excuse as any to pay them a visit and take a look at what they had done to their flat. Walking past their front door, she initially tried to see if they were home by listening intently for any conversations or noise coming out of the apartment, but she found that she couldn't hear anything. She then rang the doorbell.

Jan opened the door and recognized Lillian immediately from their yoga class. 'Hi! I didn't catch your name the other day at yoga,' Jan asked, her memory jolted by Lillian's utilitarian grey bob and the wicker basket Lillian was cradling. 'How is Azizah doing? Have you seen her since?'

'It's Lillian,' Lillian replied, not wanting to answer Jan's query about Azizah. Despite being inquisitive herself, Lillian very rarely gave information away, unless it was a juicy piece of gossip. Now that, she would gleefully share.

Jan smiled at Lillian and persisted. 'Where is Azizah now? I hope the hospital gave her the all clear.'

'I'm not sure,' Lillian replied with deliberate vagueness. Apart from having perfected the art of digging information from others, Lillian was also adept at pretending not to know something, just to test other people's knowledge and check if their version matched hers. 'What about you? Have you heard anything?' She in turn asked Jan.

Not wanting to play this childish game, Jan took the high road and answered in the negative.

'I'm here to ask if you are free next Saturday, as the chairman of the management committee is hosting a dinner and would like to invite you and errr . . . hmm . . . ' Lillian couldn't find the words to address Erika.

'Me and Erika,' Jan said, bemused that this little old lady was befuddled.

'Yes, you and Erika. The dinner will be at the chairman's flat on the thirty-fifth floor. It's the penthouse,' Lillian said, her eyes now moving beyond Jan's silhouette to look inside their apartment. Just then Sonya came running to the door. 'Who is it mummy? Why are you taking so long?'

'Alright, thanks for dropping by to let us know,' Jan said. 'I'll see you there.' And with that she closed the door. By closing the door, Jan missed the look of disappointment on Lillian's face, as she had expected that she would be invited in.

Chapter 27

Informing her husband that she was seeing a mental health practitioner wasn't something Azizah wanted to do, as she usually kept her health issues to herself. Furthermore, the stigma attached to anyone getting help from a psychiatrist or psychotherapist was still ingrained in Malaysian culture. Sadly, the circles Azizah and Zainal moved in still shamed people who had mental illnesses. Seeking help or treatment was seen as taboo.

Dr Raihana's recommendation had plagued her ever since she had left the consultation room of the clinic. It worried her no end that of all the people she knew, she would end up on a psychiatrist's couch. How could that happen? She always saw herself as someone stable and secure. Self-sufficient and strong. Even if there wasn't anything seriously wrong with her, mentally or otherwise, the fact that her doctor had recommended her to consult with a psychiatrist went against everything Azizah believed herself to be.

How could she tell Zainal? Must he know? Would he find out? He would if she agreed to go, as any claim on her health insurance policy would involve her husband. She couldn't hide it from him. There was too much on her mind and all this thinking brought on another malady.

Suffering from yet another migraine and dizzy spell, Azizah lay in her darkened bedroom with the air-con on at full blast. She recalled her fainting spell at Sukhwinder's yoga class earlier today and felt embarrassed. Something like that had never happened to her before. With an ice pack placed on her eyes, she was just drifting to sleep when she heard a gentle knock on her bedroom door.

'*Masuk*,' Azizah called out and her maid Widya came in.

'*Puan*, I made a drink for you. It's to relieve your headache,' Widya said softly, careful not to speak too loudly.

'Why, thank you Widya, just leave it on the bedside table,' Azizah replied without moving an inch. 'What is it?' Azizah enquired, curious about the orange–golden liquid, which was giving off a fragrant aroma.

'It's made from some herbs and spices like Secang tree bark, *cengkeh*, *jahe*, *serai*, *kemukus* and *kapulogo* which I brought back from my hometown in Indonesia. They help cool the body and relax the mind. I'll just leave it here,' Widya said, pointing to the bedside table.

'*Terima kasih*, Widya, That's so kind of you.' Azizah said again, 'I'll just let it cool down before I drink it.' Azizah was keen to try anything that would get rid of her head-splitting migraine.

'*Sama-sama*,' Widya politely replied while leaving the room and closing the door.

After Widya left, Azizah thought how lucky she and Zainal were to hire Widya from the maid agency and how well everything turned out. Shelling out RM 18,000 to pay the agent's fees wasn't a small amount but having had Widya for almost a year and a half, Azizah would be the first to agree that she was worth every cent. Hard working, considerate, and polite, Azizah really couldn't find any fault in Widya. Azizah had never had to raise her voice or scold her. *Finding a good maid was just like marrying a good man*, Azizah thought to herself. It all depended on the luck of the draw and in Azizah's case, she had hit the jackpot.

* * *

After being told off yet again, Nurse Ho felt irritated and frustrated. Why was Dr Desmond on her case of late? It wasn't that she was slacking more than usual. Sure, she had her down days but they never interfered with her performance. She then wondered if he was finding fault with her because he wanted to get rid of her. That was the usual modus operandi of most bosses. First, they undermine your work to make you lose confidence, then they make it virtually unbearable for you to stay so you resign on your own accord.

Nurse Ho had seen this happen with her own eyes when she first joined Dr Desmond's OB/GYN practice. Her predecessor, Nurse Yap had been treated very badly by Dr Desmond, as she was getting on in years (she was almost fifty) and kept making small mistakes. But instead of terminating her, in which case Desmond would have to give her severance pay, he wanted her to resign so he wouldn't have to pay her anything. To do this, he made life impossible for her—it was the oldest (and dirtiest) trick in the employer's handbook and one that only the lowest of the low would resort to. So, eventually, Nurse Yap resigned on her own accord, and she was replaced by Nurse Ho, who now found herself in the same predicament. In Dr Desmond's case, history always repeated itself.

Sure, Nurse Ho was careless too and made mistakes, but they were only little mistakes, not big or negligent enough to constitute grounds for dismissal, or a termination with just cause.

Having assisted Dr Desmond with patients for the entire duration of that morning, Nurse Ho thought it best to lie low for the time being. She needed to think carefully about what she could do next. If her boss didn't want her anymore, then she would be better off searching for alternative employment. No point hanging around and facing Dr Desmond's wrath and scolding. *Life is too short to endure such unpleasantries*, she thought to herself.

As it was the end of the day and closing time, Nurse Ho started tidying up so she could leave. Dr Desmond had left already, and it was her duty to lock up. While she was in Dr Desmond's office putting his instruments away, she suddenly saw a pile of papers in the rubbish bin. They hadn't been shredded or squashed up, but just thrown in. Out of curiosity, she picked one up to see what they were. To her astonishment, they were receipts issued to various patients for gynaecological tests and dated for the past three months.

Nurse Ho looked more closely at the names of the patients and couldn't recognize any of them, which made her even more curious, as she knew most of the patients who walked through the doors of Dr Desmond's practice. A light bulb went off in her head. She knew instinctively what the receipts were for and where they came from. She gathered all of them from the wastepaper basket and stuffed them into a large brown envelope. If Dr Desmond was going to play dirty with her, then it was game on.

* * *

With a child in their lives, it was now a big production whenever the three of them went out somewhere. Jan had to make sure she took a bag containing Wet Ones, tissues, a bottle of water, and some snacks just in case Sonya needed them. And yes, she also packed in a spare pair of jeans and underwear for Sonya, in case of an emergency.

So, a weekend jaunt to the mall became an expedition worthy of one almost to the opposite ends of the earth, which took the joy out of spontaneity and impulse shopping for these two parents. Clutching Sonya's padded amenity bag, her own handbag, and a reusable cloth shopping bag, Jan, along with Erika and Sonya, made her way to the lifts outside their apartment.

When the lift doors opened, the three of them got in. Jan who was slightly claustrophobic felt a pang of anxiety being in such a small and confined space. After an unfortunate incident back in Sydney where she'd been trapped in a malfunctioning lift and had suffered a panic attack, she always prayed that she would not be stuck in a situation like that ever again.

Stopping on the third floor, the lift doors opened and standing right in front of the lifts were Padma and her husband Gopi. While Gopi got in without delay, Padma hesitated for a bit then reluctantly stepped in. Looking at Erika first, Padma's gaze then shifted to Jan and finally she lowered her eyes to take a look at Sonya. Not able to stifle her curiosity, Padma asked Jan, 'Are you the family who just moved in the apartment on the twenty-fifth floor?'

'Yes, we are,' Jan replied curtly, sensing what was coming next.

'Three of you are a family?' Padma asked, incredulous at Jan's answer.

'Yes, we are,' Erika took the liberty to reply to Padma who, by now, was not only looking surprised but a bit disapproving too. Erika noticed this and just to add a little spice, she decided to give out a little more information than was necessary. 'She's my wife,' she motioned to Jan with her head, 'and this little angel here is our daughter.'

Raising her eyebrows, Padma not-so-subtly nudged Gopi, who, during this entire conversation, had been facing the other direction. Three different races within one unconventional family was more than Padma could stomach at this early hour of the day.

'My name is Erika Saunders and my wife's name is Jan. What's yours if I may ask?'

'It's Datin Padma Ramakrishna,' Padma replied. Her tone tinged with superiority and snootiness.

'Well, nice to meet you Padma, what's your husband's name, by the way?' Erika replied civilly, being, by now, well versed and experienced in dealing with such situations.

'It's Datuk Gopi Ramakrishna,' Padma replied, putting emphasis on her husband's honorific title.

With that, Erika couldn't resist going for the kill.

'Wow! A Datuk and Datin, how honoured to be sharing a lift with such esteemed people. But I heard you can buy these titles in Malaysia. Is that true Padma? Oops, I'm terribly sorry, I mean Datin Padma!'

As the lift door opened, Gopi meekly shuffled out while Padma was rendered speechless by such a witty comeback. Feigning a fake smile, Padma walked out with a huff while Erika and Jan burst out laughing and gave each other a high-five.

Chapter 29

It was a strange day for Yi Wei as she prepared to go to college. Intuitive by nature, she felt that something was not quite right in the pit of her stomach. Usually calm and collected, and unfazed by anything, she was surprised to find herself feeling slightly tense and edgy that morning. Having found her mother crying in the kitchen, Yi Wei had spent some time comforting her, letting her know that she did have a choice if she couldn't take her husband's abuse any longer. She then wondered what sins she must have committed in her past life to warrant being born into such a dysfunctional family. No doubt she suffered from some trauma, being a child raised in a household with a bad-tempered father and a neurotic and anxiety-riddled mother. Blocking it out of her mind was her only coping mechanism, until the next time she was triggered, whereby the pains and wounds of the past would resurface as if everything had happened just yesterday and not years ago.

Leaving her mother alone, she retreated into her bedroom and did something to soothe her frayed nerves. She applied make-up. Her beauty arsenal had recently been upgraded from drugstore brands to more luxurious ones, purchased using her earnings from OnlyFans.

Taking a brush from her dressing table, she looked at all the new bottles, tubes, compacts, and colour palettes laid out in front of her—Tarte, Two Faced, Urban Decay, Fenty Beauty, Hourglass and Benefit Cosmetics. These were the tools that she deployed to transform herself from college student to seductive temptress, from dancing on TikTok to twerking on OnlyFans, and from Yi Wei to Sherilyn.

As she was only going to college, she applied a minimal amount of make-up. A little concealer under her eyes, a little blush on her cheeks, some mascara and the final touch, her favourite nude Viva Glam lipstick from MAC Cosmetics. She had bought it because she loved the fact that 100 per cent of the selling price of the lipstick was donated to organizations that empowered women and girls, supported the LGBTQIA+ community, and provided aid to those living with HIV/AIDS. But what she didn't like was the attention she got from some male students as well as some lecherous lecturers when she came to college in full make-up. Hence, the toned-down lip colour. Putting on a pair of baggy jeans and a loose-fitting t-shirt under a hoodie, she was ready to leave the house.

While waiting for the lift, she checked her messages and there were at least fifteen unread texts in her inbox. Since she started her OnlyFans account, she had been getting quite a number of messages from her fans who were mainly local, although some were from overseas. As the lift door opened, Terence, who was in the lift, looked up at her and smiled.

She had seen him around the condo and knew who he was—who wouldn't when you drove a yellow Lamborghini?

'Hi! How are you today?' Terence asked her when the lift doors closed. Still facing her, he continued. 'Going to school?'

'To college, yes,' she replied briefly but formally, as she didn't really want to start any conversation with him. Her gaze shifted up and she saw the way Terence was looking at her and it made her uncomfortable. Furthermore, she remembered what her father had warned her mother and her about. He'd told them to not engage or talk to anyone in the lift. This had happened after an incident when they'd been stuck in a lift with Lillian, who pumped all three of them with question after question, mostly personal ones.

'We're having a party to welcome the new people who moved into Apartment 25-D next Saturday night. You are welcome to attend if you like. Do bring a friend.'

'Next Saturday. Okay, let me check and I'll let you know,' Yi Wei replied. She knew the family who had just moved in, as she had seen them in the car park and by the pool. An interracial, same-sex couple with a Bangladeshi child. Yi Wei thought they were the coolest people to move into Harmony Heights. How much more progressive could you get? If she accepted Terence's invitation, it would be just because she wanted to meet Jan and Erika and get to know them.

'I'll WhatsApp you the details,' Terence said, smiling broadly at Yi Wei again. 'Can I have your mobile number?'

'I'll call the management office to RSVP, if that's alright,' Yi Wei quickly answered, although it was obvious to Terence that she didn't want to give him her number.

'Sure thing! Hope to see you at the party. It's in our penthouse on the thirty-fifth floor.'

'Yes, I know,' she replied and was relieved when she heard the ping of the lift, signalling they had reached the ground floor.

Yi Wei knew neither she nor her mother or father would attend.

* * *

Shamsul was getting anxious as he hadn't received any WhatsApp messages or calls from Tiger the following day. His attempts to contact Tiger had also failed. There was no reply to any of his calls or messages. What was he going to do with the cardboard box? His worry was slightly placated by the fact that no one ever went into the storeroom.

Driving his employer's two children to school was the first thing he did on the job. Afterwards, he had a few minutes off before he had to ferry Candy to lunch. He had been hoping that Tiger would contact him later that day so he could cart the box to its rightful owner and dust his hands off it. *Who knows what was in that box?* His mind felt like it would explode with worry when thinking of this question, so he quickly dismissed it. It wasn't his business to find out; he was getting paid two grand to deliver it, nothing less and nothing more.

By 5 p.m., when he still hadn't heard from Tiger, he started to get panicky. He didn't have to pick Terence up from work, as his boss usually drove the Huracan to work himself. Thinking of what to do next, Shamsul tried one last time to contact Tiger but to no avail. *What is Tiger playing at?* Surely those people wanted that box and its contents, otherwise they wouldn't have paid so much for the delivery fee.

* * *

It was going to be a long day for Azizah and the fact that she'd hardly slept a wink the night before didn't help. At least she could doze off in the car. She had been planning to visit this kampong for a while now, but she just hadn't been able to bring herself to do it until now. She had asked her husband if she could use the chauffeur for the day and when he'd agreed, she had set out to get directions to the place.

The two-and-a-half-hour drive was pleasant enough and using Waze, her driver managed to find the little wooden house built on stilts. She had called them a few days prior to make an appointment and had prepared all the things they'd told her to bring along.

'*Assalamu alaikum!*' Azizah called out after she got out of the car and stood at the bottom of the stairs leading up to the house.

'*Walaikum asalam!*' Came the reply and as the door creaked open, Azizah was taken aback to see a young man.

'*Ini rumah* Pak Sidek *ke?*'[1] She asked, making sure she had come to the right place.

'*Ye ya! Sekejap, saya panggil bapa.*'[2] As he didn't ask her to enter the house, she stood on the porch waiting. Looking around the garden, she saw lots of fruit trees such as mangoes, rambutans, and bananas. A beat-up Datsun which

---

[1] In Malay, 'Is this Mr Sidek's house?'

[2] In Malay, 'Yes, yes! Wait while I call father.'

must have been sitting in the garage for at least thirty years or more contrasted sharply with her sleek and shiny Mercedes, which was now parked under a merbau tree.

'*Salaam, Puan* Azizah!' A man in his sixties called out while making his way down the stairs. As Azizah was surveying her surroundings, she turned around to greet the man with both her hands in a prayer pose. Adjusting her dark blue silk Duck head scarf—she usually didn't wear one but as she was going to a Malay kampong, she'd decided it was the most sensible thing to do. Pak Sidek looked exactly like how she had imagined when she spoke to him on the phone.

He pointed to the back of the house and led her behind it to where a small wooden hut was located at the edge of the jungle. Azizah's heart started to pound slightly faster as scary thoughts ran through her head. The distinctive sound of crickets emanating from the jungle just a few feet away added to the eerie atmosphere. As Pak Sidek unlocked the door of the hut with a bunch of keys he held in his hands, Azizah peered in but couldn't see a thing, as the interior of the hut was engulfed in darkness. Pak Sidek pulled a chain hanging from the ceiling and a solitary light bulb came on, illuminating the small room.

'*Masuk, jangan takut*,'[3] the man said to Azizah, sensing her fear. She gingerly stepped in, clinging tightly to her Gucci Jackie Mini Hobo handbag. He pulled out a well-worn rattan chair for her to sit on while he walked across the room to a cupboard which he proceeded to unlock. It took some time for Azizah's eyes to adjust to the darkness of the hut but when it did, she realized that there were no windows. The hut

---

[3] In Malay, 'Come in, don't be afraid.'

was barely furnished, having only a table, several chairs, and one cupboard.

Removing a clay incense holder, Pak Sidek asked Azizah for all the paraphernalia he had specifically asked her to bring along. She unclasped her handbag and took out a manila envelope and placed it on the table. She questioned whether this was the right thing to do but even if it wasn't, it was too late now. She was at the point of no return. A numbness crept over her body, and she closed her eyes for a few seconds to regain her composure.

As Pak Sidek lit the incense burner, a trail of white smoke rose up and curled around the both of them. He then asked Azizah to open the manila envelope and when she did, she realized her hands were shaking. She removed various items, amongst them a name card, a few letters, and a photo.

'*Ini orang ya?*'[4] Pak Sidek asked her, pointing at the coloured photo of a man dressed in a tie and suit.

'*Betul*,'[5] Azizah replied, nodding while looking at the photo of Datuk Wahid, her husband's boss, and the CEO of Tawfik Insurance.

---

[4] In Malay, 'This person, huh?'

[5] In Malay, 'correct'

Chapter 30

Candy was just putting the finishing touches to her perfectly made-up face when the first guest arrived at her penthouse. Sweeping on her Laura Mercier lip gloss in the Baby Doll shade, she slipped on her eight-carat, pear-shaped De Beers Forevermark diamond engagement ring and checked her outfit for the last time in the mirror. Tonight, she decided to wear Ivan Young, a new discovery of hers—a floaty blush pink silk chiffon blouse with bell sleeves that were adorned with ostrich feathers. She had paired this with matching silk-satin, high-waisted trousers. The delicate ostrich feathers fluttered gently whenever she moved, giving her an ethereal quality. It was the perfect attire for a home dinner soirée. With her glossy black hair slicked back into a bun, Candy oozed glamour and elegance. It was a high-maintenance look, which commanded attention from some, drew admiration from others, and evoked envy from the rest.

She snapped a photo of herself posing in front of the full-length mirror. She would post this later on Instagram. This highly popular social media site was the perfect platform for

Candy to showcase her personal style and exquisite taste, not to mention the ideal vehicle to chronicle her well-coordinated outfits that were culled from her extensive, designer-laden wardrobe. With over 30,000 followers and counting, most of them young girls—all eagerly waiting to see what new designer handbag or dress she was wearing—Candy might not have considered herself an influencer or KOL in any way but she definitely was one, albeit a micro one.

Candy had initially decided to limit this evening's dinner guests to twelve people, which was the maximum number of guests her dining table could accommodate. But her list just grew and grew and when Terence told her he wanted to combine their anniversary party with the management committee's welcome dinner for Jan and Erika, she decided to opt for a buffet dinner instead.

Candy, of course, didn't object to the merger of celebrations. Why would she? She had met Jan at the pool and was pleasantly surprised at how amiable and friendly Jan was and was looking forward to seeing her again. She was also keen to meet Jan's partner Erika.

The intercom from the kitchen rang just as Candy was spritzing her Frederic Malle's Portrait of a Lady eau de parfum. Grabbing her phone, Candy yelled out to Terence to hurry up. He was still in the shower. *Men have it so easy,* she thought to herself. They just had to wash, rinse, and dry, and they were ready. Women, on the other hand, not only had to decide what to wear and doll themselves up to look presentable, they also had all this maintenance work to do— facials, manicures, pedicures, hair colouring and treatment, and those were just the basics. Never mind if you wanted to get a Brazilian wax, laser treatment, or cool sculpting.

As she descended the curved staircase from the thirty-sixth floor, where her bedroom was, to the thirty-fifth floor, she saw that it was the event planner Raja Adam who was the first to arrive. Accompanying him was the socialite Juliana Rahmat, a former model who Candy knew from the social scene. Adam had asked if he could bring her along and as Candy also knew her vaguely, she acquiesced.

'Hellloooo my dah-link!' Adam cooed as he wrapped his arms around Candy. 'You look absolutely FAB-ulous! Thank you soooooo much for inviting me! Here's a little something for your anniversary!' Adam then shoved a tissue-filled paper bag into Candy's hands. 'I hope you like it! Oh! And you know Juliana!'

Juliana then smiled sweetly at Candy who leaned forward to air-kiss her.

'Of course, I do, thanks so much for coming. Lovely seeing you again, Juliana.'

'Your home is beautiful!' Juliana said as she stepped away from Candy on the black and white chequered marble flooring of the entrance foyer and surveyed the view from the double-volume glass windows. 'You must give us a tour later.'

'Is that an Ivan Lam?' Adam asked, pointing to the large and shining abstract resin painting hung on a wall just to the left of the entrance hall.

'Yes, it is. Well spotted, darling! It's one of his earlier works. I wasn't quite sure at first, but Wei-Ling was so convincing,' Candy said, referring to the gallerist who represented one of Malaysia's most prolific contemporary artists. 'Have you got a drink yet? What would you both like?' Candy then gestured to the caterer's waiter to bring some drinks.

She then led them to the living room, which was decorated in a contemporary style. It wasn't minimalist by any definition, but it looked modern and current with two black Corbusier armchairs placed facing a grey linen sofa. A triangular glass and wood Noguchi coffee table was bestowed the pride of being placed in the centre, while built-in shelves illuminated with LED lights lining the wall and contained an assortment of books, objects d'art, and crystal ornaments. But again, what stole the attention of guests who visited was the commanding view from the floor-to-ceiling-glass windows.

'This is astounding!' Adam exclaimed, a sentiment that was closely echoed by Juliana. 'Who else is coming for dinner? Do I know anyone?' It might have been gauche for anybody else to ask the hostess such a question, but from Adam, it seemed not only appropriate but also pertinent. After all, he was the event planner extraordinaire and such a question was the norm in his line of work.

* * *

By 8.30 p.m., most of Terence and Candy's guests had arrived. Some congregated in the foyer where the hired pianist was playing a medley of soft pop hits interspersed with easy melodic classical music on the baby grand, whilst others sat in the spacious living room. Some even drifted out to the balcony, drinks in hand and for the smokers, a cigarette in the other.

Being the wine connoisseur that he was, Terence was keen to let his guests taste his latest find, Perrier-Jouët champagne. Having ordered a dozen cases of both the Grand Brut and the Blason Rosé and half a dozen bottles of the exceptional

Belle Epoque 2013 just for himself and Candy, there was no worry that they might run out of this elegant bubbly during their dinner party. Although he greeted all his guests and turned on his charm, this was really Candy's crowd, save for the few people Terence had invited from Harmony Heights' management committee. After all, if he were to claim this evening's expenses from the condo's coffers, it was only fitting that he invite all the committee members, no matter what he thought of them.

And the committee members turned up in full force— Lillian showed up with Sukhminder on the dot at eight. Nisha Vaswani came with her husband and brought one of her specialities, a black forest gateau, which she had spent the afternoon baking. And why not? Apart from praises, she might just get a few orders from some of the guests that night. Both Tan Wing Shing and Karim Abdullah came with their respective spouses. Azizah and Zainal had sent their apologies to Terence and Candy a few days before. They had initially RSVPed but considering Azizah's fainting spell and the fact that she was still feeling a little weak, they had decided not to attend. The other committee members, who didn't know many of the other guests, stuck together in a corner of the living room, chatting amongst themselves.

When Jan and Erika arrived, the party was already in full swing. Jan felt a slight wave of social anxiety sweep over her but after a few sips of the pink champagne, she managed to relax a little bit. As both of them didn't know many of the guests, Erika looked for Terence whom she had met in the lift. Jan then happened to spot Candy and waved to her.

Making her way through the crowds, Candy had her younger brother with her, who was visiting from London.

Lucas Liew was the youngest child in Candy's family and having just graduated, he was doing an internship at an investment bank in the city of London. Of course, he would be expected to return to Kuala Lumpur to help the family business eventually, but right now he was having too much fun in the UK to even think about any familial obligations. After all, their eldest brother, William, who was the heir apparent, had the family business under control.

'Hi Jan!' Candy said as she approached both Jan and Erika. 'Thank you for coming! Lovely seeing you again!' Just as Candy was about to clink champagne glasses, Jan turned around to look for Erika who was just a few steps away.

'I'd like you to meet my partner Erika,' Jan felt comfortable enough with Candy to introduce Erika as her partner. Their chance meeting at the pool, even though short, made Jan feel like Candy was an open, liberal-minded person.

'Hi Erika, lovely meeting you!' Candy smiled warmly at Erika and extended her hand. 'And welcome to Harmony Heights! Where's your champagne? Do you drink?' Candy asked while taking a swig from her glass.

'Lovely meeting you too! Yes, I do! Jan told me about you after she met you and I was looking forward to meeting you myself.'

Candy saw a waiter whizz by with a tray of freshly filled champagne glasses and motioned him to offer Erika one. 'We had such a nice time by the pool. I met your lovely daughter too. I believe she's in the same school as my twins. We can coordinate it so all three of them can go to school together in my car.'

'That would be great, but we wouldn't want to impose,' Erika replied.

'Not at all! It's no problem! It'll be more fun for Max and Melissa, and they will be excited to make a new friend. Now, where's my brother? I want both of you to meet him. He's just flown in from London for a visit.' Looking around for Lucas, she spied him chatting with a group of people in the distance. 'There he is. Talk about being quick at making friends! He didn't want to come at first because he said he didn't know anyone! But look at him now!'

Both Jan and Erika erupted with laughter. 'He seems as friendly as you are!' Jan commented, nodding toward Lucas who was talking in an animated fashion, both of his hands flailing about. A natural-born raconteur, he had Candy's friends and some residents of Harmony Heights in stitches, recounting some of his experiences of living in London as well as those of growing up with Candy. Adam, Dinesh, and Shivana could be seen laughing, and they were just few of the many who had been drawn in to Lucas' web of storytelling.

'I think he's shyer than me,' Candy joked. 'Both of you are the guests of honour tonight as this party is to welcome you both to this condo. It's a tradition at Harmony Heights that the chairman of the management committee throws a dinner for any new owner.'

'Oh! That's so lovely,' Erika said. 'We really appreciate the gesture. It's a great way to meet our neighbours and other residents as well.'

'Have you met anyone yet apart from me?' Candy looked at Jan.

Jan and Erika both looked at each other. 'We met several other residents at the yoga class and we met Lillian who was in our flat on the day we moved in,' Jan said.

'She was in your flat? Who let her in?' Candy asked, already knowing the answer.

'She let herself in. She said she was looking for the real estate agent.'

'Alright my dears. I'll have to give you the low-down on some of the residents at Harmony Heights but now is not the time. We could meet for lunch,' Candy told both of them. 'Now please excuse me while I go check on the food.'

Chapter 31

Standing on the intermediate landing of their curved marble staircase, Terence gently tapped a fork against his crystal champagne glass, which was half-full of champagne. All the guests had been ushered to the black and white chequered marble-floored foyer right in front of the staircase. The pianist, who was tickling the ivories with an Elton John number, had stopped.

Candy stood next to her husband, to his right, while Arumugam and Ms Chew stood to the left, and the other five committee members stood behind him. With the noise level still high, Terence had to tap his glass one more time before the guests quieted down. Even though the guests were fragmented and congregated into social cliques, most of the people present were having a great time talking, gossiping, and catching up with one another.

'I'll be quick, as I know how famished you all are by now and we don't want the food to get cold,' Terence began. He had planned to deliver a short speech as the current chairman of Harmony Heights' management committee. 'Firstly, I am so happy that all of you made it here tonight, as it's been some time since we managed to organize a gathering with all the committee members and residents. This party is to welcome our new residents Jan and Erika who moved in a few months ago.'

Terence lifted his glass to toast both Jan and Erika who were standing at the bottom of the staircase. Both of them smiled and waved at everyone.

Turning to face the couple, Terence continued. 'I speak on behalf of all the committee members and staff at the management office to welcome you to Harmony Heights. And I'm sure the residents here—those whom you have met already and those who you have yet to meet—also extend the warmest welcome to the both of you and to your daughter.'

Everyone applauded and this genial and friendly gesture brought tears to Jan's eyes. 'We think you are an exceptional family.'

Someone in the crowd cried out 'Hear, hear!' And this was followed by another round of applause. Wiping a tear that had rolled down her cheek, Jan leaned against Erika who wrapped her arm around her wife's shoulders.

'Thank you so much for this party and the kind words . . . we really appreciate it.' Erika managed to say.

'Wonderful, I said I won't take long so finally, just to say that tonight also happens to be Candy's and my eighth wedding anniversary,' Terence revealed to the crowd, some of whom expressed surprise. Terence then lifted his other hand that held a red leather box trimmed with gold accents, a box which could only be from Candy's favourite jeweller.

'Darling, here's something for all you have done for me and for putting up with me for the last eight years!' The guests who stood below them were in raptures. Some were applauding loudly and others were whistling. Candy, who had been quiet all this while, reached out her hand to accept this generous gift from her hubby. One of her friends shouted out for her to open the red Cartier box and she did so. Someone else standing at the back asked what was in the box.

'Oh my God! It's a Cartier watch! Thank you so much honey!' Candy wrapped her arms around Terence's neck and kissed him. Slightly embarrassed by the public show of affection, Terence quickly broke up their embrace and told everyone that the food was laid out in the dining room, and they could start eating.

When everyone had dispersed and gone to get the food, only Terence and Candy were left standing on the staircase landing.

'It's an automatic Ballon Bleu, darling,' Terence whispered in Candy's ear. 'Here, let me put it on your wrist for you.'

Terence carefully removed the watch from the box and slowly put it on Candy's slender left wrist. Once the clasp was securely fastened, Candy lifted her hand up towards the chandelier to admire the gold and diamond-encrusted watch.

'It's in rose gold . . . my favourite!' She excitedly exclaimed, this time holding nothing back and allowing her emotions to show. 'I love it! LOVE IT! Thank you so much my darling!'

He bowed his head slightly forward to kiss her hand and smiled at her, looking intently into her eyes. It was a rare and tender moment shared by two people who were normally so caught up with their own lives and agendas. It was a timely reminder of why both of them had formed this partnership in the first place.

* * *

The food, which was served buffet-style at Terence and Candy's party, was eclectic and diverse, reflecting the guests and their different backgrounds. Japanese inspired sushi dishes were mixed with Mexican ingredients like chorizo and jalapeño peppers while French croquettes had fillings normally used in Chinese dumplings. Bite-sized Spanish tapas like *patatas bravas* were garnished with spicy tandoori sauce.

Strictly speaking, it hadn't really been Candy's idea to serve such a profusion of innovative dishes. She heard about Klute Kitchen from a few socialites in town and then Renee, who went to a store opening at the Pavilion Mall, was deeply impressed with the canapés served there. Renee, a keen party hostess herself, wasted no time in finding out who the caterer was and passed this information to Candy when she heard that her good friend was organizing a dinner party. That was how introductions and recommendations worked in this town, usually by word of mouth, or in this case, by a taste of the trap.

But apart from their culinary skills, what intrigued Candy was that Klute Kitchen was known not just for their mouth-watering and inventive fare but also for the handsome waiters they would supply. Renee did mention to her that plenty of the ladies, and some of the men for that matter, hired Klute Kitchen as much for their food as for their servers, who were certified eye candy. And judging from the few Candy had seen so far, she wasn't disappointed.

Of course, there were the typical Malaysian dishes which no party on this peninsula could be complete without. Fried *bee hoon, satay, roti canai* and *roti jala* with chicken and potato curry, *nasi kunyit, beef rendang,* and *chendol* all took the place of pride at the centre of the dining table. But for those with a more adventurous palate and audacious taste buds, the fusion fare was placed on a sideboard for them to help themselves. Roast beef served from a carving station as well as salmon in filo pastry completed this casual dinner.

As Padma didn't want to go, she sent her daughter Shivana who brought Dinesh along. They hadn't seen each other for some time and this party would be a nice way to deepen their blossoming romance, or so Shivana thought. With such delicious food laid out before her, Shivana was tempted to gorge herself but that would mean she would have to make a discreet trip to the bathroom soon after to throw everything up again.

With her glass of rosé champagne in hand, Candy stood at the entrance of her living room and surveyed the scene in front of her. Residents of Harmony Heights were grouped together on one side while her friends were gathered on the other side of the spacious living room. All guests were scattered in cliques. Amongst her friends and acquaintances, she saw all the different types whom she had come to know and learnt to accept, flawed and quirky as they might have been.

There was Herman Koh, jeweller to KL society and the bearer of bling to the Tungkus, Che Puans, Puan Sris, and Datins. Sucking up to VIPs was part of his business strategy, which made him highly unpopular with normal folks. Always trying to get new customers to come to his store, those in the know steered clear of him, as he would bad-mouth those who bargained too much or didn't buy anything at all. His modus operandi would be to target a VIP, inveigle an invitation to a high society event, twist someone's arm to introduce him, then charm the living daylight out of his target, whoever that might be. Tonight, the unsuspecting focus of his attention was Tengku Fauziah who he hoped would become his next customer.

Haris Ridzuan was the interior designer du jour, who designed Terence and Candy's penthouse as well as half of their friends' homes. Snobby, snooty, or simply *sombong,* he considered himself the ultimate tastemaker in town and turned his surgically altered nose up at anyone he didn't consider chic, stylish, or in possession of even a fraction of his good taste. Arrivistes engaged his services for an ulterior motive—so they could gain entry into KL society. What they didn't know was that as long as they hired him and were willing to pay his high fees, they could have entry to heaven or hell or anywhere in between. He didn't mind one single bit.

Chong Mei Sze, a former manager of a fashion chain but now just a glorified housewife, was keen to associate herself with the young *tai-tai* set and the in crowd. She had tried to ingratiate herself with Candy and Candy's BFFs, like Renee and Pam, but she was neither as pretty nor as fashionable as them. She was also totally oblivious to the fact that most people laughed at her behind her back for trying so hard. In her mid-forties, she was married to a man twice her age and half her height.

Samuel Loo was a small-town boy totally out of his depth in a big city. A university friend of Candy's younger brother, it was Lucas who had invited him to the party. In his eager attempt to fit in, he had made himself stand out even more—that too in the most unflattering way possible. His social media posts reeked of pretentiousness while his affected manner of speaking revealed his deep-seated insecurity. With his frizzy, permed hair, pierced ear and

Mao-style glasses, mean girls (and guys) called him an *ah lian*. That's right. An *Ah Lian*, not an *ah beng*. Other names he was called? A wannabe, a poseur, and a shrimp who fancied himself a lobster.

As a psychology major, Candy was acutely aware of human relationships and how they were formed. She was interested in studying the specimen laid out in front of her and the various behaviours that they exhibited. She could see all the archetypes and personality traits that she used to read about in her textbooks.

Candy could tell almost immediately which friendships were genuine and which ones were were transactional or forged with an ulterior motive. There were friendships whereby both parties befriended each other for mutual benefit, almost like a marriage of convenience. These were bonds that were built with hidden agendas. Then there were one-sided friendships where one party hoped to gain a favour or an advantage by cozying up with the other, whatever that favour or advantage might be—career prospects, business interests, or social advancement. They were those who ingratiated themselves with important people, famous people, or wealthy people thinking that their own status might somehow be elevated by mere association; the social sycophants who thought nothing of kissing the *derrières* of those who had more than them, somehow thinking that by hobnobbing with those of a higher social status, a little gold dust and fairy glitter might rub off on them and they too might glow in the dark.

Candy didn't particularly like the word social climber because she believed everyone was guilty of behaving like one to a certain extent. Placing a premium on human relationships based on popularity and status was universal and her Instagram and Facebook were full of these kinds of people. Using other people's existence or achievements to boost their own self-worth was a psychological construct as old as time. *Everyone has a right to be whatever they choose to be,* Candy thought. She just wished they would be clear about their intentions and not mask it under a guise of authenticity. But she maintained her sanity by being friendly to all, close to only a few, and trusting none.

Suddenly, Candy heard the sound of breaking glass followed by a high-pitched, expletive-laden outburst coming from the balcony. She looked at everyone around her and they looked back at her too. She quickly made her way to the sliding balcony doors, pulled them open, and stepped out. Two women whom she hardly knew were having an argument, the shorter woman looking more agitated than the other one, who towered over her and stood with her arms akimbo. It was obvious the angrier one had had just a little too much to drink and had become aggressive.

'I'll sue you for slander!' The shorter one yelled out in anger at the taller woman.

'You can only sue if it's false . . . a true statement is NOT considered defamation! Get that into your thick skull!'

Who the hell were they? They were the plus ones of two acquaintances and although Candy had welcomed them into her home, she didn't know them. Not wanting to get involved in two strangers' quarrel, Candy turned around and luckily saw Terence nearby.

She called out to her husband and Terence came out. 'Darling, can you please help out here?' She asked her husband in a hushed tone. 'And be careful, as there's broken glass on the floor.'

Nodding in a reassuring manner, Terence asked Candy to go back in and then closed the balcony door. Because of the loud chatter inside, no one heard the fight and he wanted to keep it that way. Diffusing the volatile situation between the two women would require some tact and skill on Terence's part and with a sprinkle of his masculine charm thrown in, Terence felt confident he could restore peace between the two women.

Chapter 32

Shivana couldn't help herself this time despite her attempt at self-control. The spread was just too tempting and her willpower, weakened by a few glasses of pink champagne, had dissolved. Piling her plate high with the mouth-watering starters, she soon moved onto the Malaysian fare—upping her fill of *roti jala* with chicken curry, *satay, rojak, otak otak,* and *fried beehoon.* Two slices of roast beef with Yorkshire pudding dripping with gravy was followed by some salmon in filo pastry and mashed potatoes. The Peking duck went down a treat as did the bowl of *chendol,* which almost filled her up and satisfied her sweet cravings but then she saw the dessert table and couldn't resist a slice of basque burnt cheesecake.

In the midst of her gustatory orgy, she lost track of time as well as of Dinesh who she'd last seen in the living room. She walked back to the living room but couldn't find him. Having satiated herself, she now felt disgusted and wanted to purge out everything she had devoured. Shivana walked quickly to the guest bathroom but found it occupied.

She asked a passing maid whether there was another bathroom and was told it was one floor up, in the guest bedroom.

She made her way up the curved marble staircase, wobbling from the uneasiness she felt from overeating while her high heels just barely held firm on the marble stairs. Landing on the thirty-sixth floor, she found that it was a quiet respite from the noisy chatter and music of the floor below. This was where Terence and Candy's bedroom was located as well as their twins' and two spare guest rooms. She ventured to a room on the first left and opened the door. To her surprise, she found the lights on and so she walked in and looked for the bathroom.

Shivana spotted a door at the far end of the room. Assuming it was the bathroom, she made her way there and twisted the knob to open the door. What she saw next was probably a blessing or a nightmare, depending on how one interpreted it.

Sitting on the toilet facing the door was Dinesh, his head thrown back as he moaned in ecstasy. His trousers and underwear were pooled on the floor around his ankles. Kneeling on the marble bathroom floor between his legs was one of the hunky waiters from Klute Katerers whose head was bobbing up and down and leaving very little to the imagination as to what the two men were up to.

'What the hell is this?' Shivana yelled out in total shock. Dinesh jumped up in shock, scrambling to pull up his pants and zipper up while the waiter fell to the side, ending up seated on the bathroom floor. In total shock, and traumatized by her discovery, Shivana ran out of the bedroom, tears streaming down her perfectly made-up face. Dinesh tried to run after her but just as he got out of the bedroom, Coco, who had been sleeping on Terence and Candy's bed and was now awake due to the commotion in the room next door, jumped off the bed and ran out.

Seeing a man running while pulling up his trousers up in the hallway, Coco made a dash towards Dinesh and bit his trouser leg, shaking it vigorously from left to right while growling, not letting go. Attempting to kick Coco off his leg, Dinesh lost his balance and fell, hitting his knee on the marble hallway floor. He howled in pain. Meanwhile, Coco released Dinesh's trouser leg only to attack him on his arm, this time sinking his sharp fangs into Dinesh's biceps. Who knew a docile and pampered Pomeranian could suddenly turn into a ferocious beast?

Running down the curved marble stair in her sky-high heels, Shivana was crying and sniffling at the same time, her eyeliner and mascara now streaking her face in black rivulets. With tears clouding her vision, she lifted a hand to wipe it off when she missed a step and tripped, rolling down the stairs. She let out a piercing scream and landed at the bottom with a loud thud. A waiter who was walking by ran to her aid. He tried to lift her up, but it appeared that Shivana had been knocked unconscious by the fall. The waiter quickly summoned Candy's maid and asked her to call an ambulance.

* * *

As a foreign student in Malaysia, Zhang Jinhui enjoyed some of the freedoms which were denied to him when he lived in China. Hailing from Kunming in the Yunnan province of the PRC, Jinhui won a scholarship from the state government to study abroad and chose Malaysia because he wanted to stay in

Asia as opposed to going to the US or Australia, which were his other options.

Being new to Instagram and Facebook—as these two highly popular social media apps are banned in his homeland—Jinhui had a whale of a time scrolling through these apps as well as YouTube, Twitter, and Google. Yes, China has its version of these apps such as WeChat, Weibo, and Baidu but somehow it didn't feel the same. Heavily censored by the authorities in China, everything appeared so tame and innocuous behind the Great Firewall of China.

When he wasn't attending his lectures or classes, Jinhui was glued to his smartphone and apart from chatting online with his friends from back home or with the new friends he had made in Malaysia, he indulged in the dopamine-producing activity of posting, liking, and commenting on Instagram and Facebook, and fuelling his fantasies with porn.

It was through sheer chance that one day, when he was just scrolling mindlessly through the internet, he came across some social media influencer's profile with a link to their OnlyFans account. Curious to find out what this subscription-only platform was all about he dived into it without a second thought. After all, he was a nineteen-year-old teenage boy. Holed up in his university hostel, Jinhui was nimble with his fingers as he navigated the OnlyFans website. There were thousands of men and women offering explicit content of themselves for a monthly subscription fee. Most of them were Caucasian from countries like the UK, Australia, and the US but there was a sprinkling of Asian creators on OnlyFans and those were the ones Jinhui was interested in.

His eyes nearly popped out of their sockets when he saw someone resembling a student he had seen frequently around campus. With her statuesque body and pretty face, Yi Wei stood out amongst all the other girls in her university. It was no surprise that she caught the roving eye of Jinhui and many other male students and some lecturers too.

Spotting a Chinese girl called Sherilyn clad in a bright red Victoria's Secret lingerie was what made Jinhui pay the RM 25 monthly subscription fee. That was the same as the price of a small pizza, which Jinhui ate almost every alternate night. If it gave him that much pleasure and relief, why not? He wasn't hurting anyone, in fact he might even be helping the creator monetarily.

After looking through several posts on Sherilyn's account, he chose the one of her dressed in a lace burgundy bra and panties. It must have been his lucky day because that was the one which Sherilyn had edited and posted in a rush and, in her haste, she had forgotten to carefully screen the eight-minute video, which exposed not just her face but also her bare boob. Even though it was only a flash, Jinhui managed to screenshot this blink-and-you'll-miss it split second and saved it in his smartphone. They say haste makes waste but, unfortunately, in Yi Wei or Sherilyn's case, the waste she had made was not something that could be cancelled, cleared, or deleted.

Chapter 33

Getting more jittery by the minute, Shamsul was a bundle of nerves by the time he heard from Tiger. However, Tiger's words weren't the ones he wanted to hear. Luckily for him, no one had entered the storeroom on the thirty-sixth floor of Harmony Heights since the day he had placed the box there. At this point, all he wanted was to deliver the box to whoever it belonged to, finish the job, and get his money. Plain and simple.

But of course, things weren't that clear cut. The latest instruction from Tiger was to open the box, take everything out and then go to another address to pick a few things up before he would be paid. This deviated from the original agreement, but he should have known who he was dealing with. Gangsters very rarely kept their word and Tiger was no exception. Working for a drug lord who controlled nearly half of the methamphetamine market in the Klang Valley, he really must have been cursed the day he'd been unfortunate enough to meet Tiger.

The WhatsApp from Tiger was in all caps but was concise and short. 'LEAVE THE BOX WHERE IT IS AND GO TO THIS ADDRESS TODAY TO PICK UP SOME EQUIPMENT. JUST WAIT FOR MY INSTRUCTIONS AFTER YOU PICK IT UP.'

Shamsul's head was spinning when he got the message. He had to take his bosses' kids to school then drive Candy for her lunch appointment, wait for her, then take her to the hair salon. If she was doing some hair treatment or colouring, he could probably speed off and pick up whatever Tiger wanted him to pick up. If not, he had to do it later, in which case he would have to inform Tiger who would be none too pleased.

Another WhatsApp from Dato' Sri Terence instructed him to go to a wine importer in Bandar Sri Damansara to pick up several cases of champagne and place them in the Fong's storeroom. *Adui!* Why was there so much to do on the day Tiger decided to contact him? He practically had nothing to do for the last three days except take the kids to and from school and suddenly, wham! A thousand assignments.

He glanced at the cardboard box he had hidden under the table; he was dying of curiosity about its contents. But nerves needed calming first and a dose of nicotine was the answer. He carefully locked the storeroom and took the lift down to the ground floor where he walked quickly to the car park to have a smoke before starting his day.

* * *

After a quick breakfast of shredded chicken *hor fun* and a few *siu mai*, Terence was ready to leave for the office. Candy was, of course, still asleep. She rarely woke up before noon unless she had a lunch appointment and if it was with her BFFs, they would know better than to meet before 1.30 p.m. Terence on the other hand was an early riser. In his thirties, he would squeeze in a workout before going to the office but ever since he had hit forty, he had started slacking off. The services of his personal trainer were dispensed with, and his gym sessions had been replaced with a monthly round of golf. He wasn't overweight by any definition, but his six-pack and chiselled torso was now all but gone, replaced by a spare tyre and soft layer of fat.

Terence rarely used Shamsul for his daily errands, as he preferred to drive himself. Unless he was using the Bentley, he let Candy—who didn't like to drive—use Shamsul. His yellow Lambo Huracan was his pride and joy and he looked forward to driving it at every opportunity he had.

As he grabbed his keys, he realized that a couple were missing. The bunch appeared lighter than usual. But as he was in a hurry, he dismissed it and simply reminded himself to look into it later.

* * *

When Candy was ready to leave, she WhatsApped Shamsul but she didn't hear back from him. He was usually very attentive, and she wondered what might be delaying his reply. Finally, after ten minutes, he replied, and she took the elevator down. After a few minutes in the car, Candy noticed Shamsul was out of sorts. He had also not been very responsive when she had asked him about where he'd been earlier.

But it was at a set of traffic lights, which he tried to speed through in order to skip the red lights, that Candy knew something was wrong. Shamsul, despite speeding, wasn't able to make it in time and he slammed the brakes hard to avoid running the traffic light. The car came to a screeching halt, jolting both the driver and the passenger. Luckily, both of them had their seatbelts on, otherwise the momentum would have thrown them forward.

'What was that, Shamsul!?' Candy asked, raising her voice.

'I'm sorry, ma'am!' He replied, a few beads of sweat forming on his temple despite the arctic air-conditioning inside the car. 'I'm so sorry,' Shamsul repeated. 'I was trying to beat the red light. It won't happen again. I promise. Please don't tell Dato' Sri.'

Straightening her blouse and putting back the contents of her yellow Nano Celine luggage bag, which had spilled out, Candy was a little shaken. She, however, regained her composure as soon as the Vellfire got back to normal speed and she heard Shamsul continue to apologize profusely.

'Just don't do anything like that when the children are in the car, okay Shamsul?'

'I promise I won't, ma'am. Please forgive me. I'm so sorry.'

The next twenty minutes were spent in silence. Candy didn't really want to tell Terence, as nothing detrimental had happened and it would definitely get Shamsul in trouble. *Everyone has their off days and Shamsul is no different*, Candy thought. She quickly diverted her attention and looked forward to meeting her BFFs Pam and Renee. It had been some time since the three of them had met and she had so many things she needed to update them on. She was also looking forward to hearing about what had been up in their world.

Candy got out of the car at Pavilion KL, and she reminded Shamsul to stand by and wait for her WhatsApp as she didn't fancy waiting on him again, like she had this morning.

Chapter 34

After doing her morning chores, which consisted of preparing breakfast for both Zainal and Azizah, washing up, changing their bed linen, cleaning the bathroom, and mopping the floor, Widya found a moment of respite. All the work was done and the apartment was quiet. Soon, she would have to prepare lunch for Azizah before the round of her afternoon chores began—cleaning and dusting the numerous ornaments in the living room and around the flat, hanging up today's laundry and then ironing yesterday's, polishing Zainal's leather shoes and completing any other special tasks from *Puan* Azizah before she began preparing dinner. It was a cycle which was repeated day in and day out until sometimes Widya wondered if she was in a time loop, going through the motions mindlessly and on autopilot, without any bearing on what day or month or year it was. It was an unrelenting Groundhog Day of cleaning, washing, ironing, cooking, and finally sleeping.

Surely there was more to life than this? Yes, housework was dreary and tedious—ask any housewife, homemaker, or domestic helper and chances are they would be the first to say that they were doing it only because they had to and not because they enjoyed it. But when Widya had signed up for it, she'd had only a slight inkling about what her job would entail but never did she envisage how soul-draining and dream-shattering it would be.

The only solace she had was that her contract with Zainal and Azizah was for two years. She had already completed twenty-two months and with bigger plans in her mind, she saw a light at the end of the tunnel. So, it was a bolt of sunshine in the dark, dreary tunnel of her life, when she got a reply by email from the University of Surabaya, accepting her as a student in their Pharmacology course. She hadn't told a soul when she'd applied eight months ago and had almost forgotten about it when the acceptance email arrived.

She naturally had her doubts when the germ of this idea had first gotten hold of her mind. With her limited education and lack of funds, why on earth would any college or university even consider her? None of her family had gone to university. They were farmers and rural folk who made their living toiling the earth to grow crops. How dare she break the family tradition? Did she think she was better or smarter than her siblings?

She had finished her high school or Sekolah Menengah Atas and had obtained a diploma. Despite this, she would need to attend a foundation course first before she could start her degree. All this needed money and even though she had scrimped and saved for the past twenty-two months when she had been working in Zainal and Azizah's household, it wasn't quite enough. She thought of ways and means to get funding, including borrowing from her relatives or getting a loan from the bank, but her chances were slim.

Even with the odds stacked against her, Widya remained hopeful. She possessed something far greater and more powerful than any obstacle that was hindering her. With complete trust in herself and her ability to manifest what she wanted, Widya believed that the only thing that would stop her from achieving her goal and prevent her from getting what she wanted out of life was herself. She was convinced she deserved a better life. And the universe responded—as it sometimes does to those who are kind and pure of heart—and decided to serve it to her.

* * *

When Terence called Harmony Heights' management office to speak to Arumugam and was told by Ms Chew he was on sick leave, Terence seized the chance to see Ms Chew while she was alone in the office. Zooming home in his yellow sports car was a breeze at 4 p.m., as the rush hour hadn't begun yet.

Entering the management office, Terence noticed that Ms Chew was standing beside the photocopy machines with several piles of paper scattered around her, which she was stapling to distribute to all the residents to inform them of the annual general meeting that was to be held in a couple of weeks' time.

'Dato' Sri, how can I help you?' Ms Chew asked while shuffling a few sheets of paper, stapler in hand. 'Arumugam will be back tomorrow.'

'He's not well? I need to discuss a few things with him about the upcoming AGM. Is that the agenda and statement of accounts you are preparing?'

'That's right. He's come down with the flu. I'll let him know you want to see him when he gets in tomorrow.'

'Great. Do that.'

Expecting Terence to leave, Ms Chew wondered why he took a seat behind her desk.

'Is there anything else I can do for you?'

Reaching for his iPhone in his back pocket, Terence ignored Ms Chew's question and instead focused on navigating his media library, swiping through the photos and videos he'd stored.

'Yes, as a matter of fact, there is,' pressing play, Terence turned the phone around to show Ms Chew the clip he had recorded of her and Arumugam *in flagrante delicto* on the very desk he was now sitting at.

Terence could see the colour from Ms Chew's face drain out. She became as pale as the white walls surrounding her. A few seconds later her lower lip started to quiver. She dropped the sheets of the financial statements she was stapling on the floor, and they all separated and fanned out around her, with the last sheet touching Terence's shiny black leather Bally loafers. She felt the room start to spin around her. Ms Chew grabbed the photocopy machine for support as her knees buckled.

Pulling herself up, she muttered something incoherent, but Terence wasn't interested in what she had to say or what her explanation was. He was expecting one of two reactions— either she flew into a blind rage or she cracked under the embarrassment. He was kind of glad it was the latter.

To distract and comfort her, he made sure that he spoke clearly and slowly, so she could take in everything he said.

'Ms Chew, firstly I haven't shown this video to anyone . . . yet. I am not the moral police and neither am I here to scold or judge you. I will delete this video of you and Arumugam if you just do one simple thing for me.'

Ms Chew looked at him without blinking. What was running through her head at that moment was sheer panic and fear. As a married woman with a family, everything was at risk. She wanted to know what Terence wanted.

Terence got up from his seat and walked over to the photocopier. He bent down to pick up a few sheets of the financial statements that Ms Chew had dropped on the floor. She stood frozen beside the photocopier and could do nothing but look at him.

Glancing through the printed sheets of paper, Terence found what he was looking for.

'There, I see it says here we have RM 2.6 million in our sinking fund,' he said while pointing to the figure on the sheet of paper. 'Now I need you to let Arumugam sign a cheque for RM 800,000, which you will pass to me,' Terence said clearly, deciding on the spur of the moment he needed more than RM 300,000.

'I can't do that! It's a crime! That's too much to ask!' Ms Chew blurted out.

Cool and calm, Terence snickered at her reply. 'It's not a question of can't or too much Ms Chew. You will do it. Your entire life is at stake and will be ruined if this video of you and Arumugam goes viral. Don't forget that you will have to explain . . . this . . . to Arumugam's wife and family too.'

Studying Ms Chew's face, Terence noted that while she was in the denial stage, a look of compliance showed in her eyes, so he continued. 'It is not a crime if nobody knows. I am not asking you to steal that money. It is just for a loan which I will pay back in full in a couple of months. Only me, Arumugam, and yourself are privy to the monthly bank statements so if you are smart and able to hide it from Arumugam, then no one will be any wiser about the money being withdrawn.'

Ms Chew gave Terence a slight nod. 'And you promise, no swear, that you will delete the video after I do it?' She asked.

'After you bank in the cheque, which I will give you in a few months' time, yes.'

Clicking his phone off, Terence placed the loose sheets of financial statements on the desk and started to walk out of the management office. As he reached the door, he turned around to look at Ms Chew who looked to be in a really sorry state.

'I need the cheque in a few days' time. I will be in touch with you. And, oh yes, have a nice evening with your husband and children.'

Chapter 35

Candy followed-up and did not renege on her promise to take Jan and Erika out for lunch. A week after their welcome dinner party, she decided to meet them at Marini Grand Caffè & Terrazza, which was located just in front of the Mandarin Oriental Hotel in the heart of town. After her Pilates session in the morning, Candy rushed home to shower and quickly change into a light mauve Elisabetta Franchi crop-top paired with a dark pink Self-Portrait boucle mini skirt. She decided to go for a natural, no-make-up look which took all of twenty minutes to achieve. Grabbing the nearest pair of shoes which caught her well-trained eye—in this case, it was a pair of Roger Vivier wedge sandals—she grabbed her new Fendi Baguette in burgundy and left her penthouse.

Being dropped just at the entrance, she instructed Shamsul to wait for her call and alighted from her car. Although she loved the open terrace outside, her outfit and vanity prevented her from sitting there. A waitress led her to her table and just as she was about to sit, she saw someone waving at her from a corner table.

Turning her head, she recognized Adele Foo, a frenemy whom she normally strived to avoid at all costs, but as the restaurant was empty, there was no way out for Candy. Competitive and envious, Adele hailed from a prominent family too and was someone she had known since high school. But the worst thing was that she had dated Terence previously and could never seemed to get over the fact that her first love had married Candy. She was someone Candy hardly saw except at social events here and there, even though Candy wished it would be never and nowhere.

Candy really didn't want to make the effort and was hoping a small wave would suffice but now Adele, garbed in a sleeveless Tyrolean-inspired Prada gingham check dress with a black Balenciaga Hourglass bag slung on her forearm, was making a beeline for her.

'How are you, Candy? It's been some time. What are you up to these days?' Adele cooed, her voice reeking of insincerity.

'I'm fine, and you?' Candy hesitantly replied, knowing what question would follow.

'And Terence? How are he and the twins? Sorry I forgot their names. What were they?'

'It's Max and Melissa,' Candy managed to utter before adding, 'and Terence is doing great!'

'Wonderful! You know what? We should really get together with my boys, Terence still plays golf, correct?'

Candy really didn't want to continue this conversation, especially with someone whom she vehemently disliked. But she had been brought up well and had good manners, so she played the game and obeyed the social rules, despite the fake affectations.

'Yes, we should . . . but don't you travel a lot? Might be hard to get a hold of you if you are in and out of town,' Candy replied with a saccharine smile plastered on her face, the subtext being that she really didn't want to make the effort.

'Are you still living in Harmony Heights? It's been so long! I thought you and Terence were building a proper house in Damansara Heights,' Adele asked, dismissing Candy's question.

Just as Candy's limit on how far etiquette could keep her civil was being tested, she was saved, not by the bell but a holler of her name from someone walking up behind her. Spinning around, she saw both Jan and Erika, a true sight for sore eyes and saviours who were—unbeknownst to them—rescuing her from this awkward social situation.

'Hello! Thank God you are here! I was just thinking I might have forgotten to WhatsApp you the venue!' Candy said to Jan who bent forward to give her an air-kiss. Dressed in her school mum attire, a simple Cotton On sundress, she had just picked Sonya up and deposited her at a relative's home.

'You didn't forget and here we are!' Erika replied. Looking at Adele, there was a momentary silence, as Candy didn't really want to introduce them but social etiquette demanded that she does.

'This is Adele, someone I've known since high school,' Candy said, the words sour in her mouth. Adele's eyes darted between Candy, Jan, and Erika, her brain now working overtime, trying to figure out who these two people were and, more importantly, what their relationship to Candy was.

'Nice to meet you, where are you from?' Adele asked Jan while also simultaneously eyeing her from head to toe with disapproval. Turning her gaze towards Erika without even waiting for Jan to answer, she asked, 'Are you visiting, or do you live here? What work do you do? Oh! Are you two a . . . '

Adele stopped short of prying into two stranger's lives and in effect saved herself some embarrassment, because if she had continued, Erika would have had no qualms about putting her in her place.

'Is this the Spanish Inquisition or are we playing 21 Questions? Because I'm Aussie and I'm starving!' Erika exclaimed.

With her tail between her legs, Adele retreated to her table while a smirking Candy, Jan, and Erika sat down at theirs.

'What was that all about?' Erika asked. 'Who the hell is she?'

'She's a fucking bitch!' Candy said, dropping her guard and letting loose, all traces of civility and decorum thrown out of the floor-to-ceiling glass windows.

Nodding in agreement, Jan added, 'No need to hold back Candy, I didn't like her energy either.'

Taking a sip of the refreshing Chandon Garden Spritz, Candy regained her composure, then smiled at Jan and Erika. 'She's not a friend, just someone I know. My husband, Terence, was her first boyfriend but he dumped her, and she never got over that. She feels like she's above everyone, as she comes from old money . . . her grandfather founded the first steel mill in Malaysia,' Candy revealed, making sure she spoke in a hushed tone.

'Old money?' Erika exclaimed, her voice tinged with incredulity.

'That's right, old money here means their wealth can be traced back to two or three generations at most,' Jan echoed with a straight face while looking at Candy who wasn't sure if she was being facetious or serious.

'That's laughable if you think about it!' Erika blurted out, then looked slightly sheepish, remembering she was in Asia. 'It doesn't matter if she's a nouveau riche or an aristocrat, her attitude sucks!'

Candy ordering a Caesar salad and a margherita pizza for starters for the three of them. What she liked about this café was that it offered both European fare as well as Asian dishes, which was a treat for Jan and Erika, who opted for the *nasi lemak* with *wagyu beef cheek rendang* and seafood *cartoccio* style linguine pasta, respectively.

Sipping her citrus-flavoured sparkling wine, Candy asked Jan and Erika if they had enjoyed the party at their penthouse a week ago.

'Yes, we did . . . but we never saw the drama!' Jan replied either referring to the cat fight between the two ladies on the balcony or Shivana's fall.

'Which drama? There were several! OMG! I hope both of you don't think that all our dinner parties are such spectacles!'

Both Jan and Erika laughed. 'Oh no! Believe me, we have had our fair share of drama too! I'm referring to your guest who tumbled down the stairs. Poor kid! Is she alright now?' Jan asked, more concerned than nosey.

'Yes, thank God she is! Luckily, she didn't break anything It was just a sprained ankle and concussion.'

'Who is she?' Erika enquired further.

'Her name is Shivana, and she lives in our condo with her parents. Her father is a retired judge and her mother, well, she's her mum,' Candy answered, her expression revealing her inner thoughts about Padma.

'Oh them!' Jan exclaimed. 'We met them . . . no, we had a run-in with them in the lift!'

'A run-in? What happened?' Candy asked. This lunch was getting more interesting by the minute and both Candy and Jan had an inkling this was just the tip of the iceberg.

'She was bloody rude and snobbish is what happened!' Erika didn't pull any punches when it came to offensive people.

'She insisted we call *Datin* Padma and gave us disapproving looks when Erika told her we were a couple,' Jan elaborated.

'Ah, that sounds like her alright. Padma loves to complain about everyone in the condo. If you look at the complaints file, 90 per cent of it would have come from her! But do you know what happened with her daughter and her fiancé at the party?'

'No, we missed out on all that action!' Jan said.

'Shivana caught her fiancé with another man, one of the waiters in fact, having sex in the guest bathroom!' Candy said.

'That's very brave of him!' Jan exclaimed, to which Erika added, 'I guess there is no holding back when nature calls!' The three ladies all burst out in rapturous laughter, which echoed throughout the restaurant.

'What about Lillian?' Jan asked Candy. 'What's her story?'

Taking a deep breath, Candy began, 'Lillian is quite a character; the busybody of Harmony Heights, a *kei poh*. But if you can stand her nonsense, she's really quite harmless except she likes to mind other people's business and gossip. A few years ago, a resident threatened to sue her because she was spreading rumours about them. But they moved out, so I don't think they did sue. Just be careful about what you say to her. I, for one, try to avoid her as much as possible.'

'Yes, we found her inside our apartment the day we were moving in, snooping around,' Erika stated.

'She lives with her elderly father whom she takes care of. I haven't seen him in ages. Someone told me he's not very well and has dementia.'

'That's a hard job, taking care of someone with dementia, it can be overwhelming,' Erika said, stopping short of telling Candy about her own struggles as a caregiver to her mother who also suffered from dementia.

'We met Azizah at the yoga class, she fainted in the middle of the class,' Jan told Candy who raised a well-plucked eyebrow in surprise.

'She fainted? What happened?' Candy asked.

'She wasn't feeling well to begin with, and it was an exceptionally hot day and the fans were not working in the hall. It all added up.' Jan was going to continue but Erika chipped in.

'She's fine now. Sukhminder called an ambulance, and she was brought in to the hospital for a check-up and she was discharged on the same day.'

'No wonder she didn't come to our party, she didn't tell us why, but it makes sense now. You know she was a famous singer back in the day. I remember hearing her on the radio all the time. But her singing career came to an abrupt halt. Word is she couldn't take the pressure and decided to quit soon after she married her hubby.'

'A famous singer! Wow! Does she have any kids?' Jan enquired.

'A daughter, I think, but she's studying abroad and rarely returns. Azizah seems quite lonely. She used to be a member of the management committee and invited us over to her flat for dinner. That's all I know about her, nothing much.'

And with that, the three women bonded over pizza, *nasi lemak*, tittle-tattle, pasta, sparkling wine, and gossip. Isn't that how all friendships start?

Chapter 36

After dropping Candy off for her lunch appointment, Shamsul drove to a dodgy part of town, but thank goodness for Waze because he found his destination without a problem. It was a row of derelict shophouses beside a brown and polluted river and hidden from the main road in Puchong. He WhatsApped Tiger to tell him he had arrived and waited for a reply. There was none, so he got out of the Vellfire and lit a cigarette.

Inhaling deeply, just as the effects of the nicotine were beginning to hit him, the ping of his phone went off. 'WAIT A FEW MINUTES AND SOMEONE WILL BRING SOMETHING TO YOUR CAR. JUST SIT TIGHT.' He continued smoking. Just as he'd thrown the butt of his cigarette on the ground, he saw two men walking towards him carrying four boxes.

As the two men in their late twenties approached him, they asked if his name was Shamsul and when he answered in the affirmative, they motioned with their heads for him to open the back of the MPV. *What the bloody hell!* Shamsul thought to himself. *More boxes! What am I getting myself into? Tiger better pay me more.* After the two men left, he WhatsApped Tiger and waited. Surprisingly, he got a reply almost immediately.

Tiger's instructions were for Shamsul to bring the four boxes back to Harmony Heights and store them together with the first box and then wait for further instructions. *Sial ah!* He swore under his breath. *When can I get my money? How many more favours must I do? Kimak! I did not agree to do all this for RM 2,000. Who the fuck does Tiger think he is? Celaka! He's NOT my effin Boss!!!*

Despite all the cursing and swearing, Shamsul really had no choice in the matter. He was now knee-deep in excrement and there was no way he could extract himself out of it.

* * *

After putting the laundry into the washing machine, Widya packed a small lunch for herself and Iqbal consisting of some rice, a fried *kembung* fish each and stir-fried water spinach with shrimp paste. It was the simplest meal anyone could make yet it possessed a richness that went beyond its basic ingredients because it was made with love.

She looked toward the day with trepidation because it was the day she was going to tell Iqbal about her acceptance into the University of Surabaya to study pharmacology and her decision to leave her current place of employment. She didn't know what to expect. She didn't know how he would react to this news. She had grown close to him during the past year, and it was with a heavy heart that she had to tell him about her leaving.

Making sure everything was turned off on the cooker, Widya took her keys and phone and left through the back door of the apartment where the service elevator was located.

Carrying her packed lunch and the turmeric and aloe vera paste she had concocted herself in the kitchen, Widya made her way along the shady path behind Harmony Heights that led to the tennis courts. When she got to their usual meeting spot, she found that Iqbal wasn't there, so she unpacked their lunch and waited. Very soon, she could see Iqbal descending the stairs holding a flower and beaming at her.

'This is for you,' he said, handing her a single bright red *bunga raya*. The gesture was so pure and genuine, it melted her heart.

'Thank you so much, Iqbal. It's so kind of you to think of me. Now, come, let's eat!' Widya handed him the packet of food she had wrapped in banana leaf and newspapers earlier.

'Wow! This looks so delicious . . . so yummy . . . What a nice treat : . . Thank you!' Iqbal said loudly in a staccato rhythm while opening his lunch. 'I was late again for work today and Rajen wasn't happy.'

Renting a room from a distant relative in a PPR (People's Housing Project) flat in Selayang, Iqbal had to wake up at 6 a.m. in order to catch the bus to get to work at Harmony Heights. Public transport was infrequent and erratic in his area and sometimes, especially when it rained, the buses were so full, they didn't stop at all to pick anyone up. He also had to make four changes of buses to get to work and sometimes when one bus was late, he would miss the connecting bus and had to wait another half-hour or so to catch the next one, which would invariably make him late for work.

Her heart sank when he told her that his supervisor was going to cut his pay for his tardiness. She wished she could help him in some way, but she really didn't know how.

'Here is the medicine for the rash on your hands,' she said. 'Rub it on when your skin starts to sting and make sure to put it on before you go to bed.' Widya handed him the small container of yellow paste that she had made herself. It was the chlorine granules, which he constantly dipped his hands into to sprinkle into the pool, as well as the chafing from sweeping the lawn and driveway that caused the rash and the skin on his hands to peel and eventually bleed.

'Iqbal, I have something to tell you.'

'What is it?' He looked up at her with an innocent gaze.

Widya paused for a moment to gather her thoughts before she continued.

'I've been accepted by the University of Surabaya to study pharmacy.'

For a minute, Iqbal stared at Widya without any expression. She didn't know if he had heard her or if he was just having trouble comprehending the news. She decided to continue.

'My course starts in three months' time and my contract working here ends soon,' Widya continued while Iqbal still looked at her blankly.

'I will have to leave and return to Indonesia.' Tears started to well up in her eyes as she saw Iqbal's face drop. It seemed as though a dark cloud had drifted across the clear blue sky and now it was grey and gloomy under the shade of the rain tree.

Finally, after a pregnant pause, Iqbal broke the silence. 'So, you will be leaving Malaysia for good?'

Avoiding eye contact with him, Widya looked down and answered softly, 'Yes, I will.'

Chapter 37

Having had a week of sleepless nights, Ms Chew looked worse for wear with dark circles under her eyes and a pallid complexion. It was a day she dreaded, as she had to get Arumugam to sign the cheque because Terence wanted it that afternoon. She toyed with the idea of coming clean and telling Arumugam everything but then she felt embarrassed at the prospect. So, she devised a plan in her mind as to how she would pull the wool over her manager's eyes. If all went according to plan, then Terence would get the RM 800,000, and in a few weeks, pay it back and no one would be the wiser. All evidence of her amorous activity in the management office would be erased and everything would go back to normal.

She then began to agonize over why she had been so reckless. What had she been thinking? A grown and responsible adult doesn't give in to temptation so easily. Or do they? She was married with kids and had responsibilities. Why was she so reckless? She was now paying a hefty price for a fleeting moment of weakness. She thought how unlucky she was to have been caught. While some got away with murder, she couldn't even get away with having a fling.

Turning up for work on Monday, Ms Chew had no appetite and decided to forgo lunch and stay at her desk in the office instead. She had a lot of work to complete and many documents to prepare for the forthcoming AGM. One silver lining for her was that this week was the time when she usually printed out the cheques for both Arumugam and Terence to sign to pay the various service providers of Harmony Heights. With that comforting thought, Ms Chew went about putting together the stack of documents and cheques, which required both Arumugam and Terence to sign as co-signatories.

Waiting till a quarter to five—the time when Arumugam would be preparing to switch off his computer and go home—Ms Chew walked into his room with a file bulging with documents and cheques. She timed it so that he would be tired from a hard day's work and thus would most likely rush through the signing without being too meticulous.

Looking up at her from his laptop, Arumugam asked, 'What's this? Can't it wait till tomorrow?'

'Some can, some cannot,' she replied as calmly as possible. 'I have to bank in the cheques to pay the contractors first thing tomorrow so those need to be done now.' Ms Chew then removed all the cheques from her folder and placed them in front of Arumugam. 'I'm going to Terence's home later to get his signature,' she volunteered.

In front of Arumugan was a stack of cheques, paper-clipped to their respective invoices and discreetly inserted amongst them was a blank one. Her heart started pounding hard and fast as she stood in front of Arumugam while he uncapped a pen and started to sign each cheque. Ms Chew closed her eyes as her boss flicked through the cheques signing each one. As she opened her eyes, Arumugam's phone rang, and he stopped what he was doing to answer the call.

She saw that he was at the third last cheque, the one before the furtively slipped in blank cheque. 'Yes, Dato' Sri,' Arumugam spoke into the phone. 'I'm just signing them now and Ms Chew will bring them up in a second.' As it turned out, Terence's timing had been impeccable, and his call had interrupted Arumugam from examining in detail the remaining cheques to be signed.

Ms Chew gestured with her hands to ask him to quickly finish signing and he did so for the last three cheques while still speaking to Terence on the phone. Ms Chew quickly grabbed the cheques and left the room.

After Arumugam left the office, Ms Chew took the file containing the cheque and went to meet Terence in his penthouse. As the lift door opened on the thirty-fifth floor, she was met with a strange acrid smell wafting around the corridor. With her mind preoccupied with the matter of Terence deleting the video clip of her and Arumugam, Ms Chew was too busy to think about the smell.

One of the maids answered the door when Ms Chew rang, and she was led to Terence's study. With her nerves getting the better of her, Ms Chew's hands became cold and clammy, dampening the folder she was clutching tightly. Sitting in the study, she observed the various objects in the room—a large painting of a mythical animal in full flight and in combat mode by Malaysian artist Sean Lean stared down at her. Various business and self-improvement books lined up the built-in shelves. *The Art of War* by Sun Tzu, *The Subtle*

Art of Not Giving F*ck by Mark Manson, *Rich Dad, Poor Dad* by Robert Kiyosaki and *What They Don't Teach You at Harvard Business School* by Mark McCormack were the few which caught Ms Chew's attention.

Just as she was shifting her attention to the window, Terence came into the room, his walk slightly skewed, having just taken a hit of coke.

'I've got the cheques for you to sign,' Ms Chew told him, adding quickly, 'And the blank one as well from the sinking fund account.'

'Fantastic,' Terence replied while sticking his hand out, eager to get hold of the cheque.

Ensuring that the door to his study was closed, Ms Chew continued, 'You have to delete the video first before I hand it over to you.' She then opened the folder and removed the blank cheque with Arumugam's signature and waved it in front of him.

'Let me see,' Terence studied the cheque then added, 'Only after it clears which should be about two days' time.'

Her heart sank but she nodded in agreement. *Dang! Another two tortuous days and nights.* She then passed the other cheques for Terence to sign.

'Come back in two days' time and I'll delete the video in front of you,' Terence said with a grin. 'And remember, no one has seen the video except for me . . . and you, of course, and no one will if everything goes according to plan.'

* * *

When she got to college, Yi Wei felt a strange vibe permeating the campus. She tried to brush it off when she walked into her classroom, but she felt even more alienated because her close friend Valerie wasn't around. Yi Wei wondered what had happened to her. If she was ill, Valerie would have WhatsApped her, but she hadn't got any such message.

In her second year of her bachelor of arts honours degree in Design Communication, Yi Wei had excelled in some modules like Digital Photography and Motion Graphic Design—the theory of which she applied and put to use in her OnlyFans content—while other modules like Design Enterprise, she struggled with. She wasn't the top student, but neither was she at the bottom. As of now, she was just coasting along until she graduated in another year and a half's time.

At lunch break, she looked around for Valerie but still couldn't find her. Sitting alone in the cafeteria having her lunch, she heard a few boys laughing and joking in a corner but dismissed it, thinking they were just being obnoxious and loud. It was only when the laughing got louder that Yi Wei turned around to see who and what the amusement was all about.

To her surprise, she saw a group of male students gathered around Jinhui who was holding his phone and pointing crudely at the screen. One of the boys in the group turned around and saw Yi Wei looking at them and he nudged his friend next to him. The five boys then started snickering and whispering amongst each other, followed by a chorus of chortles.

Yi Wei instinctively knew it was something about her. Summoning up all the courage and strength she could muster, she got up from her table and walked across the cafeteria to where they were sitting. When Jinhui saw her approach, he motioned for the others to scram, which they did instantly.

'What were all of you laughing at?' Yi Wei asked Jinhui who rolled back the chair, so it was balanced on its two back legs.

'Laughing? Who's laughing? We were enjoying a show,' came Jinhui's reply.

Looking puzzled, Yi Wei enquired further. 'Okay, what show were you enjoying?'

'You really want to know?'

'Yes, I do.'

'This show!' And with that Jinhui flipped his phone over so that the screen faced Yi Wei. Playing on the screen was Sherilyn dancing suggestively and twerking in scarlet lingerie to the vocals of Rihanna.

Her face turned a bright shade of red—rivalling the colour of the bra and panties set she was wearing in the video—Yi Wei tried to grab the phone from Jinhui's hands, but she wasn't fast enough. In the ensuing grab and pull, Jinhui lost his balance on the chair, and it fell backwards, taking him along. He scrambled and tried to right himself, but failed, falling, and hitting his head against the dining table. As the cafeteria table was edged with metal, it sliced into the back of Jinhui's skull, cutting his scalp and causing blood to spurt out.

He lost his grip on the phone, and it dropped to the floor, spun away from him and stopped at Yi Wei's feet. Not sure what to do, Yi Wei picked it up then looked at the video Jinhui and his friends had been giggling at. It confirmed Yi Wei's biggest fear—they were logged on to OnlyFans and it was her account, or rather Sherilyn's account that they'd found.

Moaning in pain while clutching the back of his head, Yi Wei only realized Jinhui had hurt himself when his palm came back covered in blood when he removed it from the back of his head. His friends had come to his aid by now and one of them was cussing at Yi Wei, thinking that she had attacked him.

'He fell backwards . . . I didn't touch him!' She yelled out before throwing the phone back at Jinhui and running out of the cafeteria. What did she expect? Was Yi Wei that naïve to think that no one on campus would recognize her on OnlyFans? It was definitely going to go viral, now that this bunch of rotters had seen it. What would happen to her? Would she survive such an embarrassment? Would this scandal destroy her?

Chapter 38

Cocooned in a world which was devoid of sound or any distractions, Yi Wei had never felt so liberated and free. Weightless and suspended by the buoyancy of the water, Yi Wei moved like a ballerina in slow motion, fluttering her fins to glide further downwards and deeper into the ocean. Streams of air bubbles floated up from her regulator while she looked around with curiosity at her surroundings. The underwater world intrigued Yi Wei as much as it provided her a respite from all the noise and chaos of the dry land.

Like a mermaid in her element, she twirled and spun around in the water while flitting her arms about in an elegant manner. This was better than any dance moves she had done or seen on TikTok. No one around to catch her or judge her in any way. She was in a world of her own and she relished it.

Yi Wei had booked a one-way ticket to Thailand. It had been a long journey to get to the sybaritic island of Koh Tao, known for its pristine white sandy beaches that circled lush, verdant hills. Yi Wei had flown to Bangkok, then taken a flight to the island of Koh Samui, followed by a ferry to Koh Tao. Once there, she had rented a tiny beach bungalow on Sai Nuan Beach. It wasn't just the crystal-clear waters and swaying palms that had attracted Yi Wei to this compact island on the western shore of the Gulf of Thailand. It was the scuba diving destination of choice in Thailand with dive schools and shops proliferating in clusters around Mae Haad Bay, located on the west side of the island, and *that* was the main reason why Yi Wei chose to go there.

Far away from all the trouble and strife she had left behind, Yi Wei had no plans regarding her return. She didn't know when she would return or what she would do when she went back. She just lived in the moment and took each day as it came, and this worked out for her. The present was all that she had, and it was enough . . . for the moment.

* * *

With the board meeting looming ahead, Zainal felt slightly tense that morning. The Chairman and board of directors would be in full attendance and while the weight of the meeting fell on Datuk Wahid, Zainal had to support his immediate boss to carry it through.

He had spent the last two weeks preparing all the facts and figures to present to the board and to also anticipate any left-field questions anyone might ask in addition to the usual queries. He had to put on his thinking hat and be quick on his feet. This was his chance to shine and impress the chairman and make him see that he was a strong contender for the top post, should Wahid ever decide to step down.

Forgoing his usual morning coffee, as it would make him even more nervous than he already was, Zainal had a hearty breakfast that Widya had prepared for him. Eggs, chicken sausage, baked beans, and grilled tomatoes with whole wheat bread and a cup of Milo, he had all the fuel he needed to fire on all four cylinders.

He looked at Azizah across from the dining table and noticed that she seemed to be lost in a reverie. Sipping her tea, she had a glazed look in her eyes and Zainal put it down to it being too early for her.

'So, what are your plans for the day, *sayang*?' Zainal asked her, momentarily breaking her out of her daydream.

'I have several things to do today,' she replied, still not quite sure if should tell Zainal that she had started seeing a mental health specialist.

'What things?' Zainal asked, his mind miles away.

'Things I do day in and day out, and if you are not interested, please don't ask,' she snapped at Zainal.

'Alright, you can tell me about it tonight. I have a lot on my mind this morning, my darling,' Zainal lovingly replied to Azizah, disarming his wife and diffusing the tension between them with that term of endearment.

Putting his best foot forward meant looking the part and for this it called for Zainal to wear his best suit—a bespoke dark grey lightweight wool one from Lord's Tailor with his favourite silk Hermes tie. Zainal mentally went through all the topics they had planned to bring up later at the board meeting. He said goodbye to Azizah and left the flat, riding the lift down to the lobby and getting into his chauffeur-driven Mercedes, which was already waiting for him in the driveway.

After breakfast, Azizah went back into her bedroom and planned her day. She had to bring some of her clothes for dry cleaning and alterations, so she opened her wardrobe and went through her outfits. While shuffling her clothes on the rail, she saw a half-opened blue box placed at the bottom. Bending down to retrieve it, she opened it fully and saw her pearl necklace, gold bangles, and sapphire ring together with a wad of cash. She suddenly remembered that she kept all her valuables in there and usually covered it up with some item of clothing. A sense of relief came over her, as she had thought she lost all these things.

Placing the box on her bed, she put on her pearl necklace and gold bangles and sapphire earrings and walked to her dressing table to admire them. Her gaze then shifted to her own image reflected in the mirror. She zoomed in on the fine lines around her eyes and the smile lines which ran from the corner of her nose to the edges of her mouth. Her lack of sleep had caused bags under her eyes while her slackened jaw was beginning to form jowls. There was no doubt she had been ageing more rapidly in the past few years.

She thought of visiting an aesthetic clinic or consulting a dermatologist to rectify the beauty that had been ravaged by time. But first, she had to fix the way she felt. After visiting her gynaecologist, Dr Rahaina, she had been advised to see a therapist. Her menopausal symptoms were overlapping with her mental health issues, and she was lucky she had the means and insurance coverage to seek professional help. In her case, being married to an insurance high-flyer really did have its advantages.

* * *

The huge boardroom in Tawfik Insurance overlooked the KLCC twin towers and other skyscrapers in the vicinity.

Everything was spick and span with bottles of Evian water, pads of paper, and pens at every place seating. Tan Sri Mohammad Sidek Yusof, a couple of years short of eighty years of age, was still spritely and sharp as a razor. A veteran in the insurance industry and an old hand in the corporate world, you couldn't fool this sly old fox with any sleight of hand or boardroom manoeuvring as he had seen it all before.

Using a walking stick and aided by Datuk Wahid, Tan Sri Mohammad slowly made his way into the boardroom of Tawfik Insurance in a slow and deliberate manner, his driver carrying his crocodile-leather briefcase, which contained his documents and notes. Declining coffee or tea, the chairman of the board was keen to get down to business. He was seated at the head of the long rectangular table and as he made his way there, the other board directors, who were already seated, stood up when Tan Sri Mohammed Sidek Yusof walked in.

With Datuk Wahid, the CEO, sitting on his right and Zainal, the second-in-command, seated next to Datuk Wahid, the other executive board directors were seated to the left of Tan Sri Mohammad Sidek while the non-executive directors and company secretary filled up the other seats on the left and right of the boardroom table.

As the meeting convened, Tan Sri Mohammad Sidek announced the call to order and made some welcoming remarks as well as reiterated Tawfik Insurance's mission statements. As there were no changes to agenda, the chairman moved to approve the previous meeting's minutes. Having signed copies of the minutes, it was now the time for the CEO to make his presentation and report, which included the review of the company's operations and projects.

As he stood up to speak, Datuk Wahid felt a sense of foreboding come over him. He had prepared everything—an overview of Tawfik's business outlook, trends in the industry, business updates and all the new initiatives they were planning to implement in the upcoming year. However, despite the conscientious preparation on his part, he just couldn't seem to get rid of this pessimistic feeling.

Suddenly, as he was speaking, he felt all the blood from his head rush down his body and a feeling of extreme dizziness and nausea overcame him. The boardroom started spinning and he broke out in a cold sweat, beads of perspiration forming on his greying temples. A sharp pain shot through his chest and Datuk Wahid collapsed on the floor, but not before his head hit the edge of the wood boardroom table with a hollow thud.

All the board members stood up, including the almost octogenarian chairman. As Zainal was sitting next to Datuk Wahid, he was the first to come to his aid. Someone shouted out to the staff outside to call an ambulance. Taking off the jacket of his favourite suit, Zainal bunched it up so it would support Datuk Wahid's head. Another director pushed the Herman Miller Aeron chairs aside so there was more space and Datuk Wahid could be properly aligned and straightened up on the carpeted floor. Zainal tried to feel for his boss's pulse. When he couldn't find it, he bent forward to put his ear on his chest.

Before long, the paramedics arrived with a stretcher. Everyone was cleared out of the boardroom and the paramedics performed CPR on Datuk Wahid. He had gone into cardiac arrest. He wasn't breathing and was unconscious. There was commotion in the office and even though the staff at Tawfik Insurance tried to remain calm, it seemed impossible, considering the scene that was unfolding before them. Even with the chest compressions performed by the paramedics, there was no light at the end of Datuk Wahid's tunnel. His heart had stopped beating, and he was pronounced clinically dead when he arrived at the hospital.

Chapter 39

Having submitted her resignation at Dr Desmond Choo's clinic, Nurse Ho had served the requisite one-month notice period and it was during this time that she deployed all her wiles and cunning stratagems to outsmart her employer and cause as much damage to him and his practice as possible. However, she remained as agreeable as possible, as she didn't want to rock the boat and wanted to remain under her boss's radar.

Desmond, on the other hand, had turned swiftly against Nurse Ho, who at one point in time time had been his right hand and most trusted employee. He put her in the back office of his clinic, thus barring her from interacting with any of his patients and he also forbade her from going into the dispensary, and from accessing any files on the computer. Basically, she had been sent into cold storage.

But Nurse Ho had access to Desmond's personal computer because he had forgotten he had given her the password a while back. When he was out for lunch and her replacement was busy, she managed to copy all the files that pertained to his illicit abortion practice. She also had stacks of receipts that she had managed to salvage from the rubbish bin and was planning to hand them over to the authorities as evidence.

In his haste, Dr Desmond had forgotten to shred the receipts and now she had evidence of his activities. She had a few more days to go before her notice period was up and she had already planned her next move with military precision.

First, she would report her former boss to the income tax department for under-declaring his income, both from his legitimate practice and his illegal one. She had heard of other doctors and medical specialists who had gotten into trouble with the law and specifically with the tax department for under-declaring their income. And with the evidence she had gathered, she was sure they would investigate and prosecute him.

Then, after going to the tax department, she would report him to the Malaysian Medical Council for breaching the council's ethical codes by performing illegal abortions at his clinic after office hours. If they didn't get him for tax evasion, then they would certainly nab him for performing abortions. She would also report him to the Malaysian Medical Association, which her boss was a member of, just to shame him amongst his peers in the medical fraternity.

* * *

On her last day at the clinic, Nurse Ho laid low and handed over her duties to her replacement in the most cooperative fashion. However, deep inside, she was chuckling at the carnage she was about to wreck on Desmond and his practice after she left and reported him to the relevant authorities. She hoped his medical license would get revoked and that he would end up losing his livelihood and facing financial ruin as a consequence. Hell hath no fury like a woman scorned. She hadn't been scorned in the strictest definition of the word, as she hadn't been rejected or betrayed in love, but she had been treated unjustly professionally and, in this day and age, that was tantamount to being scorned.

* * *

With a heart that felt like it was weighed down by lead, Widya walked from the back of Harmony Heights to her and Iqbal's usual meeting place, underneath the rain tree beyond the tennis courts. She knew this day would be inevitable when she'd applied to the university but she hadn't expected it to arrive so soon or that she would feel so down about it.

She also felt sad leaving both Azizah and Zainal, as they had been very good to her, and when she told them she wouldn't be renewing her contract, they had given her a leaving bonus, which consisted of two months' salary. Widya was touched by their kind gesture, and she knew what to do with this extra windfall.

When she got to the meeting place, Iqbal was already there, pacing up and down and looking slightly bothered. She waved to him as she descended the stairs and he ran up to meet her, helping her with the bag she was carrying. He would miss her and their lunchtime rendezvous for sure.

Removing their packed lunch from her bag, Widya gave Iqbal his *nasi bungkus* with a herbal drink that she had made herself. She noticed that the allergy on his hand looked much better and she took out the paste she had made for him.

'Here, Iqbal, I made extra paste for your rash,' she told him, handing him the container with yellow paste. 'Have you been using it?'

'Yes, I have, every night, and it's less itchy and red,' he replied while opening his lunch.

'That's wonderful, please continue to use it until the rash has gone completely,' she told him.

They then started eating and chatted about what she was going to do once she got home. As her university course started only in February, she had over two months before it began, time she wanted to spend with her family.

'What about you, Iqbal, do you have any plans for the future?' She asked him softly, knowing that he was different, his choices in life were limited.

'No plans, I just take one day at a time,' he replied, his innocence making her heart melt.

'We will keep in touch through WhatsApp, okay Iqbal? I want you to know I have enjoyed our friendship this past year.'

'Thank you for being my friend too . . . and for the food!'

Widya then reached into her pocket and took out a white envelope. She placed it against her heart for a minute before handing it to Iqbal.

'Iqbal, here is RM 2,000 for you to buy a second-hand motorcycle so you can get to work on time. No need for you to take the bus anymore!'

He looked at her expressionless for a few seconds before replying. 'I cannot take it!' He yelled out.

'No, take it! It's only half of the leaving bonus my employers gave to me, I want you to have it.'

Iqbal looked down to the ground. He was visibly sad and then he started to sob uncontrollably.

'Please don't cry,' Widya told him while wiping the tears from his eyes.

'I'll pay you back,' Iqbal continued between sobs. I'll start saving up each month and pay you in a few months' time. Give me your bank account number in Indonesia.'

'You don't have to pay me back Iqbal, it's a gift,' she told him.

'No, I want to. I don't feel good taking so much money from you. You need it too, to pay for your university course.'

'Alright, Iqbal but take your time. You don't have to pay me back immediately. I'll message you my bank account number later.'

Iqbal nodded and put the envelope into his trouser pocket. The clouds in the sky above them suddenly turned dark and the sound of distant thunder could be heard. It was going to rain heavily soon, and this would be the last time they would see each other.

Chapter 40

When Terence got home that day, he was exhausted and sapped of energy. He just wanted to relax with a cold beer. Ascending the stairs to their private living area located just outside their bedroom, Terence spotted Candy lounging comfortably on the cream fabric Molteni & C sofa with Coco sleeping on her lap and walked towards them. *No wonder Pomeranians are referred to as lap dogs*, he thought to himself.

Buzzing for their maid to get him an ice-cold beer, Terence then collapsed on the opposite end of the large cream sofa, muttering something to Candy before slumping into the plush cushions and falling asleep. He only woke up temporarily to take a sip of his beer before dozing off again.

With Coco on her lap and a glass of rosé in hand, Candy, who was wearing a green Juicy Couture velour tracksuit, was watching a Korean drama on Netflix. It had been a long day for her too, and the slightly dry pink-hued wine helped wind her down. She'd met up with someone from a counselling service, as she wanted to see if she could volunteer in any way. She had a degree in Counselling and Psychotherapeutic Relationships after all and it would be a shame to not to put that to some practical use.

After half an hour, Terence woke from his nap and told Candy he was going to take a shower and freshen up before dinner. Looking out of the balcony's sliding doors, Terence saw that dusk was rapidly approaching and it would be dark soon. In a half-comatose state, Terence struggled to get up from the comfy sofa, falling back a few times before he managed to languidly right himself and get up.

After her husband had left the room, Candy changed to another series on Netflix, but found that nothing interested her. With her attention only half focused on the curved TV screen, Candy's thoughts drifted off to what had happened at her dinner party a few weeks ago. What's a party without a quarrel or two? Apart from a few, at least most of her guests enjoyed themselves. She did her best to spoil her guests as much as possible and give them a good time and that was all that mattered.

It was unfortunate, what had happened between Dinesh and Shivana. However, she didn't feel responsible for it in the slightest. She may have been the hostess of the party, but she couldn't control the actions of her guests. They were all adults and knew what they were doing.

Suddenly, Candy felt something vibrating. Looking around, she didn't see anything on the sofa or the coffee table, and it wasn't her phone, as she was holding it. Putting Coco down on the carpet, she lifted the cushion to see if there was something beneath it, but there was nothing. If the vibration had stopped, Candy would have just ignored it, but it went on and on. Coco saw Candy searching for something, so she jumped onto the sofa and helped her look for it.

Sniffing around the sofa, Coco padded to the far end of the long sofa where Terence normally sat and then started sniffing at the seat and using her well-groomed paw to scratch and dig at the space between two seats. Dipping her hands between the cushioned seat, Candy fished out Terence's iPhone, which must have fallen out of his back trouser pocket and slipped between the cushioned seats. Holding it between her expertly manicured fingers, she saw that it was upside down so Candy rotated it upright. When she clicked on the side button, what she saw shook Candy to her very core.

* * *

Staring out of Terence's iPhone screen was a selfie of Lola Li, her doe-eyes looking straight at Candy while her wet and glossy lips were puckered as though she were ready to kiss whoever saw her photo. Dressed seductively in a silk Xixili dressing gown, her caramel highlighted hair tumbled down her fair shoulders, while her pose and body language exhibited a come-hither demeanour. But it wasn't just the intimate nature of the selfie which made Candy's blood run cold. At the bottom right of the photo, you could see Lola holding a pink Birkin bag, which Candy recognized immediately. It was the one that had gone missing from her wardrobe.

The room started spinning around her and all at once Candy felt light-headed and nauseous. She could feel her blood drain from her head down to her feet while her hands started trembling. This was worse than a punch in the stomach, it was a slap on her face too. She tried to stand up, but it was like the rug had literally been pulled from under her feet. As the shock and pain floored her, Candy stumbled back down on to the cream-coloured sofa, spilling her half-drunk glass of rosé on it.

Coco saw her mistress fall back and started yapping in her high-pitched bark and jumping all over Candy who was now lying on the sofa in a foetal position. Tears streamed down her face while she pressed her fingers to both sides of her head, massaging her temples as she felt a massive migraine coming on. If this wasn't the worst day of her life, then it must be the second worst day, the first being the passing of her beloved grandfather.

In most circumstances, Candy would be calm and rational, deliberating her next move while considering her options. But needless to say, these weren't normal circumstances and Candy, no matter how hard she tried, couldn't maintain her composure. It was a heart-wrenching and life-altering moment for Candy which traumatized her greatly and she began to weep. Coco had stopped yapping and was now cozied up to her, licking her face and trying to comfort her. But as cute and cuddly as her toy Pomeranian was, nothing in the world could console Candy at this moment in time.

* * *

Dressed in a polo shirt and shorts, Terence definitely looked refreshed after his shower, almost like a different man. A couple of white lines he had snorted while in the bathroom also helped perk him up. He was taken aback when he walked back into their private living room and saw Candy lying curved up on the sofa and sobbing.

'What's the matter babe?' He asked Candy, quickening his pace towards her. When Coco saw Terence approaching Candy, he jumped on top of Candy and assumed an aggressive stance, growling at Terence.

Candy looked up at Terence and then slowly sat up, moving Coco away from them. 'What's the matter? This is the FUCKING matter!!!' Candy raised her right hand which held Terence's iPhone. As the screen was blank, Candy clicked it back on and lo and behold, the image of Lola Li appeared.

'Oh shitttttt!' Terence muttered to himself. 'I can explain . . . it's not what you think it is . . . you are jumping to conclusions!'

'Really, Terence? Not what I think it is? You BLOODY LIAR!' Candy shouted at him. 'Who the hell is she and why is she holding my Birkin bag???'

'I can explain . . . just calm down and give me a chance . . . it's a misunderstanding, I swear!' Terence replied with desperation in his voice.

'Don't tell me to calm down, okay Terence? I've been looking for this pink Birkin for the past three months and now a whore is holding it in a photo she sends to you? What am I not understanding here?' Candy hollered.

'You are overthinking this . . . please don't make rash assumptions . . . there's a simple explanation to this. Believe me!'

'The only explanation to this is simple. You stole my Birkin to give it to your mistress. And stop gaslighting me!'

Just then, their maid appeared up the stairs to let them know dinner was ready but when she saw both her employers screaming at each other, she tried to make a discreet U-turn down the stairs. Candy, however, had already caught sight of her.

'What is it, Lucia?' Candy asked irritably.

'Ma'am, dinner is ready,'

'I'll be down in a minute,' Candy replied.

'Yes, ma'am.' And with that Lucia quickly scuttled down the marble staircase.

Glancing at her wrist to check the time, she saw it was almost eight o'clock on her new Cartier watch. Yes, the gold and diamond watch Terence had bought her for their eighth wedding anniversary not too long ago. In a fit of anger, Candy wrestled it off her wrist and ran out to the balcony.

'This watch wasn't really for me!' She hollered. 'It was to make you feel better!!!'

'Don't do it,' Terence said sternly, his voice lowered a few octaves.

'Watch me!' Candy exclaimed loudly to him while standing on the balcony near the railing.

Without hesitation, Candy swung her arms back and threw the gold and diamond Cartier Ballon Bleu watch out of the balcony. It flew from her hand into the dark of night where it could have landed anywhere—on the lawn, in the treetops, amongst the bushes, or even in the vacant neighbouring land. No one could have known where the watch landed, and Candy didn't want to know.

There was no hope in hell for anyone to find it. But Candy didn't want it anymore and she couldn't care less if it was never found. She knew it had been a gift to assuage Terence's guilt rather than a declaration of love. Her heart was broken, and she felt betrayed. And even if it was found, she would never wear it again. Ever.

Chapter 41

Returning home from the supermarket, Lillian Gan lugged the heavy reusable grocery bags into her flat and placed them on the kitchen floor. It had been a strain on her these past few months, taking care of her father as well as attending to her own personal work and health issues.

After putting away the perishables into the fridge, she called out to her father who was in his bedroom, asking if he wanted a cup of tea. She put the kettle on and then went to check on him. Walking into his messy bedroom, which obviously hadn't been Marie Kondo-ed, she saw him lying in bed, both his hands and feet chained to the steel frame of the bed. His mouth was covered with duct tape and his eyes were wide open. He was like a prisoner in his body and his home.

It was a pitiful sight by any definition regardless of whatever the circumstances were. To spend the golden years of one's life trapped in a deteriorating body and degenerating mind. It would be kinder to let him go but euthanasia wasn't legalized in Malaysia yet. Lillian unlocked the chains around his hands and feet and then slowly tore off the duct tape across his mouth. She really had no choice, as Uncle Gan would shout and scream at the top of his lungs when she had first chained him to his bed. What would her neighbours in Harmony Heights think? She had even had to slap him on the face a few times to stop him from shouting and becoming a nuisance. After her father's attempt at taking his own life, chaining him to the bedposts and taping his mouth shut was the only solution Lillian could think of. It was also Lillian's misguided attempt at being cruel to be kind.

Oftentimes, like today for instance, Lillian felt an overwhelming sense of guilt. Feeling guilty she wasn't doing enough for her father or for yelling at him or just ignoring him. She constantly felt like she had failed as a daughter and caregiver. But the truth of the matter was Lillian was doing the best that she could considering her own mental state, her temperament, and personality type as well as her level of tolerance.

Helping her father sit up in bed, she noticed that his wrists and ankles were chafed with bruises and abrasions. It was probably because he had been struggling and trying to release himself from the bondage. Giving him a cup of *pu-erh* tea, Lillian held it while she helped bring his mouth to the porcelain cup. A memory suddenly flashed across her mind. She had been about six or seven years of age and playing with her elder brother and younger sister when her father came home from work. He called out to Richard and Grace, and they went running to him. He took out a toy for each of them, all this time ignoring Lillian as if she didn't exist in his eyes.

Lillian remembered how hurt she had felt and the humiliation permeating every single fibre of her body. Treated like a black sheep because she wasn't as pretty as

Grace or smart like Richard, Lillian was always the scapegoat child, often blamed for things she didn't do. Later, when both her siblings had gotten married and started their families, her father would taunt her for being a spinster. Harbouring hatred and resentment, these destructive emotions festered in her causing deep emotional wounds which existed in her even today.

After he had his tea, she sat with her father on his bed for a while and read through some of her WhatsApp messages, mainly from the Harmony Heights' management committee. Halfway through reading a message, she looked up at her father and saw that he was just staring blankly at her. She realized how much her father's condition had deteriorated as his dementia progressed. He was already in the advanced stages of Alzheimer's. It was just a few years ago when he had been healthy and spritely, able to drive around, go hiking, and play Chinese checkers.

The first sign that she recalled was Uncle Gan forgetting what day and month it was. He kept repeating himself and asking Lillian the same questions over and over again, irritating her and getting on her nerves. As the disease progressed, he began to misplace things and then started accusing Lillian of stealing them, causing her a lot of stress and mental anguish. Her attempts at explaining to him that he was the one hiding his things around her flat fell on deaf ears.

That was the time she took him to a geriatrician in a public hospital and after many rounds of tests like MRIs and CT scans, he was diagnosed with Alzheimer's. Soon after, Uncle Gan was supposed to stop driving on the doctor's orders. This was a big challenge for Lillian, as he stubbornly refused to listen. A few minor road accidents and Uncle Gan finally threw in the towel and gave it up.

At this time, his personality also changed, and he became combative and grumpy, constantly finding fault with Lillian and scolding her. But, by now, Lillian already knew it was his dementia that caused all these difficult behaviours and didn't take it personally. As the default caregiver, Lillian practically had no support or help and as a result faced plenty of challenges and difficulties. Facing a highly stressful environment and put under enormous pressure, looking after her father full-time was a task that required even professional caregivers to take training or complete a degree or diploma programme. Not surprisingly, there were days when she just lost it and blew up at him; who wouldn't under the circumstances she was facing? But things quickly reverted to normal as Uncle Gan would also forget about any arguments he had with his daughter in a matter of minutes.

Uncle Gan stopped talking and retreated into his shell of a body soon after. This was when she had to sponge him daily as well as feed him and help him to go to the restroom. Lillian was astounded at how quickly Alzheimer's had hijacked her father's mind and rendered him to a pitiful shadow of his former self.

Today, Uncle Gan was bedridden and immobile, he just stared into space when he was not asleep and relied completely on Lillian to feed and clean him—a task that included changing his adult diapers, as he couldn't even make it to the bathroom. Checking on his diaper rash and bed sores, Lillian walked to his dresser to retrieve some antiseptic cream and cotton buds.

While applying the cream to his rash and wounds, she noted that he was staring directly at her. She didn't know if he was lucid or in a world of his own.

'I tried calling Grace last night, but she didn't pick up,' she told him, referring to her younger sister living in Singapore. 'I sent her a message too but there's been no reply so far.' There was no reaction that registered on her father's face, he just looked at her blankly. 'Maybe she's overseas and will call when she gets back.' Lillian had no heart to tell her father the truth. Her younger sister had blocked all communication with Lillian, and in effect with their father, and had no interest in knowing how Uncle Gan was doing.

'Richard sent me some money a few months ago but I haven't heard from him since then.' Lillian lied to appease her father, as he had asked about Richard before. In actuality, her elder brother had never sent any money. With his mouth agape, Lillian saw a a trickle of drool make its way down her father's chin. She grabbed a tissue to wipe it off. Strong emotions were stirring within Lillian and she felt a mixture of anger and sadness rise up from her solar plexus. She began to mull over the past, especially her childhood, and thought about how her father had treated her. She tried to bite her tongue but, in the end, she had to let it out.

'You remember when I was young and you used to tell me how hopeless I was?' She asked him in a controlled voice that, despite her best efforts, was rife with emotion. 'You would say to me, "Why can't you be like Richard or Grace?"' There was still no flicker of acknowledgement on Uncle Gan's face, but Lillian pressed on regardless. 'I just want you to know that despite everything you said to me that deeply hurt me, I always believed that you loved me and that is why I never stopped loving you, daddy.'

To her surprise, her father let out a slight grunt and his eyes began to well up. He had obviously heard and understood what she said and even though it was too late to do anything, she'd be able to rest easy, knowing that she spoke her mind. In her heart, Lillian forgave her father for all he did and didn't do and, in doing so, she set herself free.

She didn't know it then but that was the last time she would speak to her father or dress his bed sores or do anything for him.

The next morning, Uncle Gan breathed his last breath.

Chapter 42

It was a blistering day when Iqbal clocked in for work that morning at the Harmony Heights maintenance room. He usually started his day by sweeping the leaves from the driveway and porch, after which he did gardening work around the grounds of the condo. His new responsibility of cleaning the swimming pool was done after lunch, at around 2 p.m., before the kids and office workers came back to the condo.

Today, however, his supervisor Rajen told him to clean the pool first because he wanted Iqbal to saw off some overhanging branches on the huge rain tree by the tennis court in the afternoon. The branches belonged to *their* rain tree, the very one where he would meet Widya during their lunch breaks. The condo didn't have a saw, so his supervisor had to go to the hardware store that morning to buy one and therefore the trimming of the rain tree branches had to be done in the afternoon instead.

And there, with that simple change of schedule—a twist of fate, as some might call it—a life would be changed forever. Iqbal went into the storeroom and gathered all his pool cleaning tools. Juggling all the equipment in both hands such as the leaf rake and skimmer net, the pool vacuum and leaf gulper, Iqbal also carried the bucket of chlorine granules to sprinkle in the pool after cleaning it. This was the culprit behind Iqbal's allergy. The constant contact with this powder had caused the red and angry rash on his hand.

After changing into his trunks, Iqbal made his way to the swimming pool and, as it was just 9 a.m., there was no one there. The sun was strong, and the heat was getting unbearable. It would take him about an hour to do a thorough job of cleaning the pool and the first step was to use the leaf rake to scoop up any dead leaves which had fallen into the pool.

As he didn't have a pair of sunglasses, the glaring morning rays of the sun reflecting off the water made it difficult for him to see properly. Standing at the edge of the pool, Iqbal scooped up as many leaves as she could, his hand moving up and down the telescopic pole to reach any debris in the middle, at the sides and anywhere in between.

He thought about his life so far while cleaning the pool. How his mother had worked so hard selling *goreng pisang* by day and doing alterations and tailoring for customers by night. He didn't really want to drop out of school before his SPM, but he didn't have much of a choice, as his grades were deteriorating and he was falling by the wayside. There were no schools for special needs children in his kampong so he had to give up on school altogether. He often thought about how his mother was doing. He wanted to send her some money, but he just wasn't earning enough.

Suddenly, something in the middle of the pool caught Iqbal's eye. With the sun's reflection on the water, it was hard to make out what it was. He realized that it wasn't on the surface. It shimmered brightly at the bottom of the blue-tiled swimming pool. Blinking twice, Iqbal initially thought it was just an optical illusion, a mirage which had tricked his eye. But the sparkle from this object was different from those of the sun's rays.

Jumping into the pool, Iqbal ducked his head under the water and swam to the deep end. He propelled his head forward while the fluttering of both his feet aided his body to descend to the bottom of the pool. Opening his eyes underwater, he finally saw what it was that had caught his eye a few minutes ago. He reached forward and grabbed it with his right hand.

Making a U-turn underwater, Iqbal kicked his legs vigorously to bring himself to the surface of the pool. When he emerged, his eyes were stinging from the chlorinated water, and he was gasping for breath. Swimming to the side of the pool, he paused for a while to catch his breath before lifting his hand up from under the water and unclenched his fist to see what he had just retrieved.

He looked in disbelief at what he held in the palm of his calloused hand—an object which glittered in the morning sun with an intensity that Iqbal had never ever seen before in his life. It was the gold and diamond-encrusted Cartier watch that belonged to Candy.

* * *

Luckily, it was only a sprained ankle and a mild concussion that Shivana suffered from her tumble down Terence and

Candy's staircase. She could have easily broken her neck considering the height of her fall and had fared well all things considered, but this was no consolation to Padma, who was furious about what had happened.

Still ruminating about what Shivana had told her had happened at Terence and Candy's dinner soirée, Padma's well-thought-out plans and carefully calculated schemes were now in disarray. She had hoped that Dinesh would eventually propose to Shivana and her only daughter would marry into one of the wealthiest Sindhi clans in South East Asia. If Dinesh was unfaithful to her daughter now, what were the chances that he wouldn't stray during their marriage?

Of course, Shivana could overlook his indiscretions. Padma's generation of women often did. But times had changed, and Shivana's peer group no longer felt subservient to men. *But sex is only an aspect of a relationship*, Padma thought. *You can't have everything, and nobody is perfect.* Shivana could just pretend she didn't know what was happening. But you cannot unsee something once you witnessed it first-hand and Shivana had a mind of her own. She was not someone who was easily influenced by others, even her own mother.

With all these thoughts swirling around in her head, Padma decided that she needed to get out of her house. She needed to go somewhere that could provide solace even though it was just temporary. Grabbing her handbag and a shopping bag—that she'd recycled from the material of an old sari—she left her flat in a hurry to go to an old stomping ground.

As it was a weekday, there weren't many shoppers in the huge mall located at the outskirts of town. Feeling more anxious than usual, Padma headed to the department store she frequented often. The soft sounds of the background music and arctic air-conditioning soothed her raged nerves somewhat while she wandered around aimlessly. With hardly a soul around, she practically had the whole store to herself, and she enjoyed the solitude. From the ladies' department, she took the escalator up to the men's, children's, and finally to the home department.

Admiring the Noritake dinner service, she picked one up and traced her finger around the raised enamel dots around the circumference of the fine bone China plate, which was rimmed with a gold band. Her next stop was the crystal section, which beckoned to her with their glittering facets. Stepping in, her eyes were temporarily blinded by the strong glare from the shards of light which were dispersed all around. Caressing a tall tulip vase, she moved it slightly for it to catch the light so it would refract back at her. She had always wanted one like that but had never gotten round to buying it.

Her final stop was the homeware appliances and kitchen accessories department. She looked at the pots and pans and chopping boards and mixing bowls. But something colourful caught her eye and she walked over to the shelf at the far end of the department. A set of silicon measuring spoons took pride of place in between a rolling pin and a pepper mill. She had to have it. Glancing around furtively, she saw no one at all so she slowly opened her shopping bag and dropped the set of measuring spoons in. For good measure, she grabbed a garlic crusher and soup ladle as well and dropped it into her shopping bag.

A wave of excitement followed by a sense of relief washed over her. She took a deep breath and when she exhaled, she felt instant gratification. Closing her eyes for a few seconds to savour the moment and relish her accomplishment, she then walked towards the exit of the department store.

Unbeknownst to Padma, she was on the watch list of the store's security department. A blurred printout of her from a previous shopping expedition was pasted on the TV monitors in the security room and this time, the vigilant guard on duty spotted Padma in the store. With his walkie-talkie, he quickly alerted the guard standing at the entrance of the store and instructed him to apprehend Padma before she walked out.

As soon as the guards approached her just two steps short from the exit, Padma knew what had happened. When the guard asked her to stop, she let out a shriek of frustration followed by a few expletives. She handed her shopping bag to one guard while the other guard rummaged through her personal effects only to produce the three items she had stolen. Padma could already see the headlines screaming out from *The Star* the following day. 'Wife of Retired High Court Judge Nabbed for Shoplifting' or 'Former Judge's Spouse Caught Stealing Red-Handed'.

Of all the people in her family, Padma was the last person anyone would have thought would bring shame and disgrace to them. Her constant pontification and boasts about moral superiority coupled with her finger pointing at other people's lack of ethical values had backfired in the most catastrophic way. Padma's karma had finally caught up with her and it was a lesson that she, and everyone at Harmony Heights, would never forget.

Chapter 43

After a simple dinner—stir-fried veggies with tempeh and steamed rice for Jan and Erika and spaghetti bolognaise for Sonya—Erika proceeded to wash up while Jan prepared Sonya for bed, making sure she brushed her teeth and reading her a bedtime story.

It was the time of day (or night) that both of them looked forward to, as it was quiet and peaceful, and they could relax with a glass of wine, the perfect way to wind down the day. Curled up on the sofa with a chilled glass of Cloudy Bay Sauvignon Blanc, which they had brought from Australia, Jan reflected on the past few months since she and Erika moved into Harmony Heights. It was kismet that they had ended up living here. Never did she think she would chance upon such a diverse community who, despite their foibles and idiosyncrasies, would embrace them and their modern-style family wholeheartedly and be so welcoming and accepting of them.

Naturally, not everyone she met at Harmony Heights was friendly or took to them, but they were all polite and respectful.

'Do you like living here, Erika?' She asked her other half, who was working on a presentation on her laptop on the dining table.

'Yes, I do, very much,' Erika replied without taking her eyes off the screen.

'And to think this is the first and only condo I looked at! Usually, people view tons of places before they find a suitable place.'

'I came here with an open mind without any expectations and I'm pleasantly surprised,' Erika added.

'Surprised at what darling?' Jan enquired further.

'That Malaysians on the whole are an accommodating and easy-going lot.'

'You think?' Jan asked, curious if Erika was just being politically correct.

'Well, the ones I've met here and at work are pretty decent,' Erika replied, looking at Jan lovingly.

'That's great . . . I'm glad you like it. I wouldn't have been able to put up with a bitching and complaining partner haha!' Jan snickered before resuming, 'I'll leave you to your work now. Oh, and don't forget. We have to attend the condo's AGM tomorrow morning.'

'I remember,' Erika responded while smiling at Jan.

With that, Jan went into their bedroom, lit her purple-coloured candle to enhance her psychic abilities and took out her deck of tarot cards. She hadn't done a card reading for some time and it had just occurred to her that tonight was a good time to do one. Sitting cross legged on her bed, she closed her eyes and breathed in deeply for a few seconds. Her anxiety attacks had lessened greatly since they had moved to Harmony Heights and she felt calmer and more relaxed. Her meditation and breath work certainly helped but opting to work part-time was what greatly reduced her stress.

Shuffling the cards, she created a three-card tarot spread. There wasn't any specific question Jan wanted to know but she was just curious if there were any messages from her angels and guides. The first card she turned referred to the past and she drew a Nine of Wands, which related to the ending of a cycle. This was clear as leaving Australia with her partner and daughter and starting a new life in the country she'd been born in was definitely the end of a cycle and the beginning of a new one.

The middle card—which represented the present—was the Ten of Cups, the happiness card. Jan could not have been happier. Ever since they'd moved to Harmony Heights, she'd made new friends and had been working part-time, giving her more space to engage with herself and her loved ones. She felt so fulfilled and content in all areas of her life, she really couldn't have asked for anything else. Feeling blessed and grateful was really about aligning one's self to the abundance that the universe offered. Jan believed that the state of one's mind created the vibrational match for manifesting more of the same.

Finally, the last card, which showed what's in store in the near future, was quite a shocker. It was The Tower, which denoted danger, crisis, and destruction. Studying the card closely, Jann saw an illustration of a tall medieval tower with a bolt of lightning striking the top and flames curling out of the windows. Two figures with disconcerting facial expressions could be seen jumping down. *Goodness! What the hell does this mean?*

Was the meaning of this card literal or symbolic? Apart from the frightening and ominous connotation, it could also mean the destruction of old habits, the crumbling of one's ego or that ground-breaking change was imminent. *Hmm* . . . Not wanting to read more into this, Jan scooped up the cards and put them back in the box and blew out her candle. It was almost midnight and she wanted to have a good night's sleep so she could wake up early for Harmony Heights' AGM the next morning.

* * *

It was the Saturday when Candy was supposed to attend Harmony Heights' annual general meeting. As her father was the developer of the condo, Candy had only attended the AGMs in the past to represent him. But because of what had happened, she decided to forgo it this time.

Arranging to meet her BFFs, Renee and Pam for lunch, she also brought along Max and Melissa, as both Renee and Pam would be bringing their kids too and they could play together while the three of them would talk. Her maid Lucia came along so she could look after the twins and Candy could be free to relax with her friends.

Upon entering the Dôme Café at Suria KLCC, Candy was immediately transported back to her teenage years and carefree school days. She chose this place to meet with Renee and Pam because the three of them would hang out here often, either after school or at weekends. Warm and inviting, this café with its wood and shiny brass accents, comfy club chairs and cozy banquettes brought back memories of many weekday afternoons when Candy would meet and hang out with both Renee and Pam after school for tea as well as on the weekends when she would go with her friends for a bite to eat after a shopping expedition at the mall. Today, however, it brought comfort and solace to her bruised and broken heart.

Choosing a banquette in a corner for privacy reasons, she settled her twins and Lucia in the adjacent booth. While waiting for Renee and Pam, she couldn't help but think about the unfortunate discovery she had made on Terence's phone. How a relatively innocuous WhatsApp message had sparked off a chain of events which affected not one but several lives. Reassessing her marriage, Candy looked within herself to see if she had any part to play in what happened. She did her best to be a good wife to Terence. Often avoiding conflict with Terence, one tactic she learnt to enhance her marital relations was to stop assuming that her husband knew exactly what she felt or needed.

She never demanded anything from him that she, herself wasn't willing to offer, as she wanted her marriage to be equal. She tried her best to make him feel appreciated and didn't invalidate or criticize his feelings, no matter how insignificant she thought they were. She stopped trying to win fights with him but instead tried to find solutions that both of them were happy with, usually making compromises. Choosing peace was more important to her than proving her point, even when she knew she was right. But this discovery changed everything. She may have tried hard to make her marriage work but Candy drew the line at infidelity. That was one boundary she wasn't going to shift.

Questioning the whole idea of marriage, Candy wondered what purpose it really served. Was it just a social construct invented by people to make life more convenient? Did it mean that just because it was accepted and many people subscribed to it, it was suitable for everyone? Surely there must be some people who were not cut out for this holy union? Just as that thought entered her mind, Renee and Pam arrived with their children. Turning heads as they walked in, these three young *tai-tais*—including Candy who was already ensconced in the booth—were casually but elegantly dressed, cradling the most coveted handbags of the season—a Birkin, Bottega, and Balenciaga.

Having heard had about what happened to Candy, both Renee and Pam took turns to give her a long and warm hug each before shuffling into the banquette.

'I'm so, so sorry about what happened to you, dearie,' Pam said, breaking the ice.

'Thank you, but I don't want to talk about it anymore, I've already told you both everything,' Candy said, eager to move forward.

'Sure, we respect that,' came the chorus from both her friends.

'But tell us what the two women were fighting about at your party?' Renee asked.

'Oh gawd! I didn't even know who they were. They were the guests of some friends of Lucas. Apparently, they were fighting because one of them bad-mouthed the other about stealing someone's boyfriend,' Candy explained to her girlfriends, allaying their curiosity. 'But there was bad blood between them already. They broke two of my crystal Tiffany champagne flutes by the way . . . that's the last time I'm having people I don't know in my home.'

'Or just use some Ikea wine glasses the next time and save your Tiffany ones for more civilized guests!' Pam said and the three of them roared with laughter. It was just like old times again, except they had children in the next booth and all three were now married, save one marriage that was on the verge of a divorce.

'Oh look!' Renee exclaimed while perusing the Dôme menu. 'They still have the yummy chicken pie and curry puff!'

'We used to order them as our after-school snacks, remember?' Pam recalled.

'Yes! And the *nasi lemak* with *chicken rendang* and the club sandwiches! Oh yummy!' squealed Candy in delight, almost forgetting her heartache for a moment. 'Let's order all of it! If we can't finish it, the kids will!'

When all the food came—and there was plenty for the three of them and their children and helpers—there was a momentary silence as the three friends devoured the comfort food that evoked their teenage memories. After this lunch, none of them would mention the word diet or intermittent fast again with the same conviction, reaffirming their belief in the healing power of food.

'I'm thinking of working again,' Candy announced between mouthfuls of cheesecake, its rich and creamy texture satiating her stomach and soothing her soul.

'Working as in joining the workforce?' Pam reconfirmed.

'Yes, working as in putting to use my degree that I spent three years busting my ass for!'

'What are you planning on doing?' Renee wanted to know.

'Well, you know I have a degree in psychology and I thought that I could work in a women's aid organization or an NGO.'

'Fantastic! Go for it!' Both her friends exclaimed, happy to support her.

But, inevitably, their conversation led back to the elephant in the room, or in Candy's case, the rotten skunk.

'Are you going to mend things with Terence?' Renee asked gently, her eyes shifting away from Candy's to avoid any embarrassment.

'Can you forgive him?' Pam enquired sensitively.

'I really don't know at this point, I can't tell both of you yet,' Candy replied, her voice breaking as she held back her tears. Her heart was still broken, and it would take a long time to unbreak it and heal from the hurt.

As a coping mechanism, Candy tried to look at everything good in her life thus far. Her two children, her good health, and not worrying when the next meal, or in Candy's case, the next 'it handbag' will come from. She tried hard to appreciate where she was in her journey, even if it wasn't where she wanted to be. She didn't realize it at that moment in time, but many years down the line, she would look back and realize that she had to go through all that pain to arrive at where she was. All that heartbreak she endured served a purpose as each phase of her and everyone else's life brought its unique lessons, growth, and moments of beauty.

But in this current chapter of her life, Candy still had a long and bumpy journey ahead of her. With Max and Melissa at only five years of age, she would have to think long and hard and weigh the pros and cons before she decided on anything, as her choices would also involve her two children. Leopards don't change their spots overnight and Terence was a cheat and a scoundrel and if articulated in psychobabble, he was a narcissist of the highest order.

Chapter 44

After driving Candy and her two kids to Suria KLCC, Shamsul quickly drove back to Harmony Heights, as he had lots to do that day. He had already bought four cylinders of propane gas as instructed and had secretly brought them up to the storeroom on the thirty-sixth floor.

Locking himself in the storeroom, he knew he was safe and wouldn't be disturbed as he had secretly taken Terence's key from his boss's bunch a few weeks ago already. Now, no one had access to the storeroom except him and he could carry out Tiger's instructions in peace. Opening the boxes that he had hidden under the table, Shamsul started to unpack the bottles, containers, and the various equipment and apparatus that were neatly packed inside.

He knew Candy wouldn't be calling him just yet, as she was having lunch with friends while Terence was tied up at the AGM. This was the perfect time to start making crystal meth, ice, or *syabu* as it is commonly known. Not aware that the chemicals he had just unpacked were extremely hazardous and highly flammable, Shamsul unfolded the piece of paper which had the instructions written on it as to how to go about producing crystal methamphetamine. He put aside the rubber tubing, glass beakers, and funnels and grouped together the plastic containers containing acetone, hypophosphorous acid, and lithium.

Opening a bottle of anhydrous ammonia, Shamsul wrinkled his nose in disgust at the sharp and pungent odour it emitted and quickly closed it. A plastic gallon jug of hydriodic acid was placed next to a card box while the Freon gas canister stood near the phenylpropanolamine. They say a little knowledge is a dangerous thing, but no one had told Shamsul that no knowledge at all might be lethal. The chemicals that he'd got from Tiger plus the propane gas he had bought was akin to making a small bomb capable of blasting an entire house to smithereens.

Confused about all the different chemicals and materials, Shamsul studied the instructions again, not quite sure that the task he had agreed to undertake was so easy after all. What did Tiger think he was? A chemical engineer? He was told that it would be quick and easy, not more than a couple of hours' work but from what he gathered now, it would take more than a day and that was just to figure out what goes where and what is added to what.

A surge of panic suddenly overcame him, and he needed to take a minute to calm himself down. His go-to emotional crutch was nicotine. Shamsul moved towards the windows beside the table where the four cylinders of propane gas were placed. He opened them, breathed in the fresh air, and then lit up a ciggie, inhaling deeply to pacify his nerves. After going through two cigarettes in quick succession, Shamsul convinced himself that it was now or never, and he needed to get this done. He moved back to the large table to start making crystal meth and in doing so, sowed the seeds of his own destruction.

* * *

Preparing for Harmony Heights' annual general meeting was a mammoth task for all those involved—from Arumugam and Ms Chew who had to prepare all the requisite documentation and for the five management committee members who had to familiarize themselves with the agenda, including the audited statement of accounts as well as all the other items which were tabled for discussion. But most importantly, the responsibility of the entire meeting fell on the chairman, Terence.

Just before the AGM, the cheque of RM 800,000 which Ms Chew had given Terence on the sly, cleared after two days and he used the money to secure a contract for the construction of a warehouse his family company was bidding for. Ms Chew, of course, wasted no time in pestering him to delete the revealing video of her and Arumugam, which Terence did in front of Ms Chew. She was assured by Terence that no one apart from them had seen it and that deleting it would be the end of the matter.

But, of course, Terence being who he was—a shrewd businessman with a slight edge—didn't delete it. He made a copy of the video, not on his iPhone but in a pen drive which he kept securely. He wasn't planning on extorting anything else from Ms Chew but just for his own safety, he decided it was better to keep leverage than discard it.

Arranged to be held on a Saturday so that the working residents of Harmony Heights could attend, the venue of the AGM was the multipurpose hall that was beside the gym and in front of the swimming pool. Although attendance wasn't compulsory, the turn out rate was good, with the majority of residents attending. The requisite quorum was easily achieved, and the AGM was able to commence.

Amongst the attendees were Lillian Gan, Nisha Vaswani, Sukhminder Kaur, Tan Wing Shing, and Karim Abdullah, who were the members of Harmony Heights' management committee. Other residents, like Jan and Erika, Azizah and Zainal, and Dr Desmond Choo and his wife Hway Ping were also attending. Candy's absence was conspicuous. As the daughter of the developer of Harmony Heights as well as a resident, Candy had attended every AGM since the management corporation had been formed. But given her personal crisis and current mental state, which nobody here knew about, it was understandable that she gave it a miss this time.

Sitting on a long table at the front of the hall with a projector screen to the left side, Terence was in the centre, with the committee members to the left and right of him. Arumugam and Ms Chew stood on the right side of the room with the former observing the meeting and the latter busy taking a head count of the residents and those eligible to vote.

With a call to order, Terence welcomed all the residents who were present and introduced his committee members. With rows of chairs arranged, akin to a town hall meeting, some latecomers to the AGM quietly snuck in and sat in the back rows trying not to draw attention to themselves. Sticking to the agenda, Terence first outlined the remedial works which had been carried out in and around Harmony Heights during the past year and went through each item, skimming over the smaller ones while providing more information on the bigger items.

Some residents asked to upgrade the lifts while another about why their suggestion to the committee about retiling the corridors and common areas was ignored. With patience and tact, Terence answered each of them, giving satisfactory explanations with nary a hint of irritation or annoyance.

When it came to the part where nominations for a new chairman and committee had to be sought from those present, Terence nominated Erika and this was seconded by Azizah. Five more new members of the management committee were nominated and soon after, voting by a show of hands commenced. Erika was overwhelmed with a sense of pride and belonging when almost all of the residents present voted for her to become the next chairman of Harmony Heights' management committee, effectively taking over from Terence. She had never, in her wildest dreams, ever envisaged that this small community, which she and Jan had moved into only recently with their daughter, would embrace them and now, endorse them.

Who would have thought that one half of an interracial lesbian couple with an adopted Bangladeshi daughter would be voted in as the next chairman and win the hearts of such a diverse collection of people? No one, least of all Erika. Jan was also touched by this accepting gesture. She believed that it was no accident that the very first property she viewed turned out to be the one which now championed them.

When it came to the item on the agenda about the condo's management accounts and financial statements, Terence turned on his laptop and presented the audited statement of accounts from the previous year onto the projector screen, giving swift and adequate pointers on the fixed and current assets as well as the income and expenditure account. He quickly glossed over the maintenance account and the sinking fund, informing everyone that the audited statement of accounts for the preceding year had already been distributed to each resident.

Just as Terence was about to conclude the AGM, a solitary hand shot up at the back of the hall.

'Are you sure the sinking fund still has RM 2.6 million?' A middle-aged man stood up and asked Terence.

'Well, yes according to the latest bank records,' Terence answered confidently. 'Erm, you are mister? Could I have your unit number please?' Terence asked the man, not recognizing him at all.

'I'm a proxy for Flat 17-A, the owners are away, and I am representing them.'

'Can I have your name please?' Terence insisted curtly, his patience wearing thin.

'It's Mr Seah Kong Choon,'

'Alright, Mr Seah, you can stay back after the meeting to discuss this if you'd like but we have to conclude the meeting now.'

'No, I don't think so because I have the bank account statements right here and it shows only RM 1.8 million in the sinking fund, not RM 2.6 million as stated by you.'

Gasps of surprise and astonishment could be heard echoing around the multipurpose hall. Lillian Gan, not one to conceal any reaction whether good or bad, widened her eyes in astonishment.

'According to these statements RM 800,000 has been withdrawn recently, do you know anything about this Dato' Sri Terence?' This incalcitrant man demanded.

For someone who was quick minded and thinks on his feet, what Terence did next shocked the entire room. Putting two and two together, he knew it was either Ms Chew or Arumugam who had leaked the fact that he had withdrawn RM 800,000 from the condo's sinking fund for his own use and this called for an instant and immediate revenge. It was like a counterpunch in a boxing match.

'Just a minute Mr Seah, I have the answer for you in here,' and with that reply, Terence took out the pen drive from his trouser pocket, waved it at him, inserted it into the laptop and clicked play.

Immediately, the video of Arumugam humping Ms Chew on a desk in Harmony Heights' management office was projected onto the screen for all to see. If the gasps of surprise and astonishment were heard earlier on, shrieks of disgust and shock were now heard all round.

'Turn that bloody thing off!' Arumugam could be heard shouting from one end of the hall as he made a beeline towards Terence. But Terence had anticipated his reaction and had already gotten up and moved to stand behind the two Nepalese security guards while cradling his laptop, far from the reach of anyone, especially Arumugam who made a futile attempt to grab the laptop from Terence.

Ms Chew ran out of the hall with both her hands covering her face in shame. Dr Desmond Choo, whose hypocrisy and obvious lack of empathy was on full display, shook his head in disgust while Hway Ping covered her mouth with both hands and looked on in disbelief.

'Ya Allah!' Azizah called out loud, both her hands apart with her palms raised upwards while Zainal muttered some holy Quranic verse. Jan looked flummoxed and her mouth dropped open while Erika looked at Jan's expression and looked back at the screen, not quite sure how to react. While some residents were appalled, others were incredulous that such an explicit video was being shown in public.

And just as the video reached a climax, a loud and thunderous explosion sounded, followed by an ear-splitting boom that reverberated throughout the room. The multipurpose hall shook from the explosion and some people mistook the tremors for an earthquake. Someone shouted, 'Everyone get out!' And everyone in the room got up and started to run out in a panic. Luckily, the entrance to the hall was large enough for everyone to get out easily without any delay or obstruction.

Gathering on the lawn in the open air outside the multipurpose hall, the residents looked up at the top two floors of Harmony Heights where black smoke was billowing out from the windows. The explosion had also ripped a large, gaping hole in the wall. Flames were curling out of the opening. There was rubble on the ground and some pieces of concrete had even fallen in the swimming pool below.

For a few seconds, everyone was frozen, processing what had just happened. All eyes were transfixed on the top floors of the building. Finally, someone shouted out, 'That's the penthouse! Terence, where is your family?'

Terence who was standing the farthest from the door was the last to get out of the multipurpose hall. He regarded the scene before him with horror and quickly rang Candy. She informed him that she was out with their children having lunch. Somewhat relieved, he told her about what had happened. A resident called 999 and told him that the fire services were on their way.

Suddenly, a smaller but equally loud explosion was heard and this time three windows from the uppermost floor blew out, showering shards of glass and metal below. The residents who were standing on the lawn ran to take cover to avoid being cut or injured by the shattering glass. The second explosion destroyed Candy's much cherished wardrobe with its motorized rail and designer categorized system. Her belongings were blasted out of the windows. Her tweed Chanel jackets and pleated asymmetric Balenciaga skirt, her emerald-green draped Valentino gown, her Saint Laurent one-shoulder cocktail dress and her Dolce & Gabbana jeans, all flying out of the broken window and then floating down like autumn leaves. Some articles of clothing were ablaze as they landed, scattered all over the grounds of Harmony Heights.

Iqbal, who was trimming the hedges in another part of the condo, heard the sound of the explosions and came running to the lawn in front of the multipurpose hall. While waiting for the bomb-squad to arrive, he grabbed his pool scooper and helped fish out some of the items that had fallen into the swimming pool. He managed to retrieve one side of a suede and crystal studded Jimmy Choo stiletto and a purple Dior saddle bag. Hanging on a branch of the rain tree was a crimson jacquard weave Shiatzy Chen dress which was in shreds, while a half-burnt, heavily-embellished antique gold sequin short dress by Farah Khan and a torn Victoria Beckham ruffled silk georgette blouse were floating in the pool. But perhaps the most tragic sight was that of Candy's ivory Celest Thoi lace and embroidered wedding gown, lying lifeless and in tatters on the tennis court. Covered in soot and burnt at the hemlines and sleeves, a large rip over the heart area, could be seen across the bodice.

If Candy had been present, her heart would definitely have been broken again, but this time it would have been caused not by another human being, but by material objects. The scene resembled a stampede at a jumble sale except that these clothes weren't old and unwanted but rather the cherished and precious collection of Datin Sri Candy Fong.

Chapter 45

Wearing a wide-brimmed straw hat while tilling the soil on her father's paddy field, Widya was bent over under the blazing sun. She straightened her back momentarily to wipe the perspiration off her forehead. Looking at Mount Bromo in the distance, she wondered if she had made the right choice in leaving her employment in Malaysia.

Suddenly, her mobile phone tinkled and started to vibrate. She dug into her trouser pocket to retrieve it. The text notification was from her bank. It must be their reply on whether the student loan she had applied for had been approved or not. For a second, she closed her eyes and said a little prayer. When she had visited her village bank a few weeks ago, the manager there had told her she couldn't get a full loan so she'd only applied for a fraction of the amount she needed, which wasn't very much.

At this point in time, Widya really had no idea how she would pay for her course, accommodation, and living expenses while studying. She would have to do part-time jobs, but would that be enough to cover everything? She envisaged a difficult road ahead for the next three years. But Widya was determined to see herself through. Somehow and in some way, she would make it.

Squinting her eyes and using her other hand to shield the sunlight to make out the text message, Widya initially thought that she was looking at a mistake the bank had made or a phone scam. The amount of money that had been transferred into her account had to be in rupiah, because the amount did not make sense otherwise. However, on closer inspection, she saw the message in full.

It was not in rupiah but in ringgit. RM 100,000 had been transferred to her savings account. She couldn't believe her eyes. At the bottom of the message was a note from Iqbal. She read it aloud to herself, 'You helped me before you left so please accept this money to pay for your university course. I think it is enough for the entire duration of your course. It's also to pay you back for the money you gave me to buy a motorbike. I got a second-hand Honda and I'm never late for work now and it's all thanks to you!' A thousand questions raced through her mind after she read Iqbal's message. Where had he got such a large amount of money from? Why did he send it to her? How would she ever pay him back?

Tears welled up in her eyes and as Widya bent down to continue tilling the soil, she thought about Iqbal and how she missed him. She also thought about her past employers, Azizah and Zainal, and she wondered how they were doing. All her prayers had been answered and even though she missed the life she had left behind, a chance at a better one now awaited her. In the middle of the rice field and under the sweltering Indonesian sun, a single tear came out of Widya's left eye and rolled down her cheek then dropped onto the earth, nourishing it with all the dreams, hopes, fears, and sorrows she had experienced in her twenty-three years of life.